# DEAD WRONG

Noelle Holten is an award-winning blogger at www.crimebookjunkie.co.uk. She is the PR & Social Media Manager for Bookouture, a leading digital publisher in the UK, and a regular reviewer on the Two Crime Writers and a Microphone podcast. Noelle worked as a Senior Probation Officer for eighteen years, covering cases of domestic violence and abuse. She has three Hons BA's – Philosophy, Sociology (Crime & Deviance) and Community Justice – and a Masters in Criminology. *Dead Wrong* is the second novel in a new series featuring DC Maggie Jamieson.

@nholten40
www.crimebookjunkie.co.uk

Also by Noelle Holten

*Dead Inside*

# Dead Wrong

Noelle Holten

One More Chapter
an imprint of HarperCollins*Publishers* Ltd
1 London Bridge Street
London SE1 9GF

www.harpercollins.co.uk

This paperback edition 2020

First published in Great Britain in ebook format
by HarperCollins*Publishers* 2020



A catalogue record for this book
is available from the British Library

ISBN: 978-0-00-833226-6



Set in Birka by Palimpsest Book Production Ltd, Falkirk
Stirlingshire

Printed and bound in Great Britain by
CPI Group (UK) Ltd, Croydon CR0 4YY

*For #MyTribe. You know who you are.*
*Thank you for believing in me when I didn't believe in myself.*

# Chapter 1

## LORRAINE

'So – are you dangerous?' Lorraine danced around the hall playfully. He frowned; to her he looked unsure whether she was serious or flirting. The party had been epic, and she was still buzzing from all the cocaine in her system.

'Nice place you have here.' She ran a finger along the hall mirror and smiled at her reflection. The house had an old-fashioned feel to it – wooden floors covered with well-worn rugs, cream-coloured walls and a strange-looking bookshelf that seemed out of place in a hall.

Tilting his head, he stared directly into her eyes. 'Do I look dangerous?' He caressed her arm; the goose bumps rose on her skin and she wondered whether he was toying with her. Her body shivered with excitement.

'You seem OK to me. Can't be too safe these days though.'

''Course not, sweetheart. But I'm a pussy cat. Can't you tell?' He placed his hand on her elbow and began directing her towards the stairs. He smelled of one of those nice deodorant sprays, not as pungent as cologne.

A knock on the front door made them stop.

'Are you expecting company?' She pouted her lips, hoping that he would get rid of whoever it was quickly.

'Only you, love. Have a seat through there,' he pointed to the living room, 'and make yourself comfortable. I'll take care of this.'

She watched him as he made his way to the front door.

He looked through the peep hole, his hands clenching into fists, his body stiffening. 'What the fuck?' He muttered and stepped outside. Although she heard raised voices, she couldn't make out what was being said or whether the mystery visitor was a man or a woman.

*Wonder what that's about?* She didn't want to be caught eavesdropping, and when she entered the living room and saw the bag of white powder on the table, she knew what she would prefer to do. Lorraine walked over to the couch, sat down and made herself comfortable.

Within ten minutes, he returned to the room.

'Everything OK?' She tucked a lock of hair behind her ear.

'Yeah, fine. Shall we get this party started?' He sat down beside her and caressed her leg.

She reached across him, picked up the plastic bag of white powder and shook it. 'Can we have a bit of this first?'

'Oh babe, I have something better in mind for you. A little something special ...' He bent over, opened the small drawer at the front of the coffee table and took out a needle filled with what she assumed was heroin.

'Hmmm. Not so sure about that, hun. I prefer a bit of sniff these days if I'm honest. Gear doesn't sit well with me anymore.' She rubbed her forearms.

'C'mon babe, don't be like that. I thought you trusted me. I promise, this stuff is out of this world – it'll make you feel sooooo good.'

She thought for a moment, imagined the needle piercing her arm and a warm glow consuming her. 'Fuck it, you only live once!'

He smiled as he wrapped the tourniquet around her arm, choosing a vein, tapping the needle twice before inserting it into her arm. 'That's right, babe. You only live once ...'

The world shut down around her. She lay back on the couch and let the gear take over.

Closing her eyes, she smiled and whispered to herself. 'Sooooo good.'

When she finally came around she was tied to a bed, her eyes and mouth covered with some form of material bag. The stink of urine and sweat filled her nose and the low, gut-wrenching moan she heard echoing off the walls told her she wasn't alone.

# Chapter 2

Maggie had thought her nightmares were over when serial killer Bill Raven, 'The Chopper', had been convicted just over two years previously. Having returned to her team at Stafford Police Station following a secondment in the Domestic Abuse and Homicide team, she believed she had left that particular case well and truly closed. Although the remains of Raven's victims were never found, he confessed willingly to abducting, dismembering and then disposing of three females whom he named. Forensics at the time corroborated his account.

Then, a few weeks ago, she had received a message from DI Rutherford, her boss at the Major and Organised Crime Department in Stafford. Maggie had been attending an event where Lucy Sherwood, a Probation Officer from the Domestic Abuse and Homicide Unit, was speaking. It was a message she would never forget.

*Your secondment is over at the DAHU. Raven has appealed his sentence, claimed he's innocent. Timely I'd say as there has been another murder. Either a copycat or the real killer picking up where they left off. Get your arse in here.*

She had seen the news – body parts had been found in a bin – and sweat had begun to trickle down her spine. Forensic details had not been released to the public, but when Maggie had returned the call to her DI and learned that the body parts had belonged to Lorraine Rugman, the first victim that Raven had named in his confession, Maggie's world had begun to fall apart.

*No! No! No! This cannot be happening. This is not real …*

And then the anger had come. And the questions.

*Is the wrong person in prison? Is Raven toying with the police?*

Now three weeks had passed since Maggie had returned to her team and the nightmare had only got worse. She couldn't get him out of her mind. The greasy hair, the stubbled, ragged face. His lanky frame hollowed out by years of drug use. And the smell – the pungent smell that oozed from his pores, burning her nostrils. But the worst thing was his voice. That arrogant smooth voice that made her skin crawl.

She threw off her blankets and went to find coffee.

Ugh. It was in her head now, his voice.

It was like he was in the room with her ... no wait.

The voice was coming from downstairs.

# Chapter 3

*'You must see it now. I couldn't be guilty of the murder of Lorraine Rugman, or those other women. They may still be alive. My solicitor has launched an appeal with the Criminal Case Review Commission, so as much as I would like to tell you all the details, I can't. My thoughts are with the victims' families at this moment in time. I can't be selfish and just think about how all this has impacted me alone. Those poor women … God only knows what they went through … or are still going through. I hope they catch the real killer soon …'*

Maggie could hear his voice emanating from the living room. That slow, monotone slur creeping its way into her eardrum like an unwanted worm. It still sent shivers down her spine. She went downstairs, made herself some coffee and stood in the kitchen, listening to the TV in the other room. She couldn't believe that Raven's solicitor had launched the appeal in just three weeks, almost as if he had known the body parts were about to be found. Raven had been prepared. With his previous appeals exhausted, the discovery of Lorraine had brought new evidence to the case.

*He's dangerous.*

*More people will die if they let him out, why can't they see that?*

'Why are you just standing there? You're as white as a ghost, Maggie. Are you ill?'

Maggie snapped out of her daze. The TV had been switched off and she looked up to see her brother, Andy, standing in the kitchen staring at her.

'I'm OK,' she said. 'What were you just watching?'

'That weirdo, Bill Raven, the one who's appealing his conviction – he's speaking to some journalist. Telling his side of the story. Miscarriage of justice, he says, and an agency called the CCRC has taken his case. Who are they? There's something not right about that guy. I know he has mental health issues, but those eyes ... creepy if you ask me.'

Maggie gripped the handle of the mug in her hand. She watched as a drop of coffee tumbled through the air as if in slow motion and landed on her wood floor. She followed him into the living room. 'The CCRC is an independent body that investigates cases where people feel they have been wrongly accused or convicted. It means he may get out.'

Sitting down next to her brother, Maggie placed the mug on the table and ran her fingers through her hair. Scrappy came into the room and rubbed against her leg. She picked up her furry friend and gave him a cuddle; he had a knack for relaxing her. She'd be lost without him. Andy switched the TV on again and there he was. She glared at the face which had haunted her sleep for months, the vile descriptions he used as he confessed to chopping up his victims. An icy tremor raced down her spine. Maggie vowed she would not let Bill Raven creep into her head again.

'Seems like he's winning everyone over with his bullshit. I don't care what they think, he's got to be involved. I mean, why would you confess to something you didn't do?'

Maggie looked at her brother.

'The journalist he was talking to said that the prison psychologist diagnosed delusions of grandeur or some such crap. Apparently, that's why he confessed. How messed up do you have to be to claim to have killed three women, right? I think someone is jumping on the *Making a Murderer* bandwagon.'

'Ha! Sounds about right, but this isn't the US. I know there have been times when innocent people have been punished for crimes they didn't commit; however, my gut tells me that's not what happened here.' Her leg shook with frustration. 'I wish I could say more, Andy. Everything about this guy is not right.' Shaking her head, Maggie continued, 'Anyway, he's taken up enough of my morning.'

'Bit weird how the body parts just turned up, don't you think? What if he wasn't involved?' Andy didn't seem to take her hint.

Maggie shrugged her shoulders. 'I can't talk about an active case. All I know is that Bill Raven is hoping to use the coercion card to get out of jail free; we have another possible murderer lurking about and I'm being told to tread carefully and focus on the current investigation.' She shook her head. 'Anyway, enough. What are you doing today?'

'I'm on the afternoon shift for the next few days, so I'm just going to chill this morning. My work rota for this month is all over the place.' He scratched his head. 'You sure you're OK? Don't worry about that guy, he'll get his comeuppance.'

'Easier said than done, but thanks – I'm sorry for snapping. Look, I'll see you in the morning, OK?' Maggie grabbed what she would need for the day, put her coat on and headed to the door. 'Make sure you lock this when you leave and don't forget to let out Scrappy.' She didn't wait for an answer.

# Chapter 4

Maggie looked at her watch. She had some spare time and decided to walk the twenty minutes to the train station rather than jumping on the bus. With Andy using her car for work these days, public transport gave her the opportunity to get some exercise.

The train was packed with morning commuters, each in their own little world. She stared out the window – always amazed at the beauty of the surrounding rural landscape. Long grass filled with wildflowers and edged with brambles whooshed past as she rested her head against the glass.

When she arrived at Stafford train station, Maggie had a leisurely stroll through Victoria Park and headed over the footbridge towards the centre of town. The familiar quacks of ducks sounded like mischievous laughter. Fifteen minutes later, she walked into the police station, her mind still buzzing with news stories about Bill Raven's recent appeal.

Maggie stopped short when she nearly bumped into her colleague, PC Bethany Lambert. She apologized, walked over to her desk and dropped her bag on the floor.

'What's eating you?' Bethany raised an eyebrow.

'Haven't you seen the news? That arsehole is all over it. Since when did he get a personality transplant and elocution lessons?' Maggie rolled her eyes. 'What happened to the unshaven, gaunt, incoherent man I interviewed over two years ago? If they hadn't had his name on the screen, I would never have recognized him.'

'Look, maybe getting clean and taking the medication has worked? It's possible ...'

'What the hell? Are you on his side?' Maggie's brows snapped together.

'No. I'm just looking at everything objectively. We're trying to focus on the actual killer, and if DI Rutherford heard the way you were talking, she'd shoot you down in a nanosecond. I know how you feel about all this, we *all* know how you feel about this, but you need to let your personal views go and focus on the evidence. He couldn't have done it – he was behind bars when the murder was committed.'

'Then tell me how he knew the name of the first victim, Lorraine Rugman?'

Bethany just shook her head.

'Great ...' Maggie turned her back to Bethany and started up her computer.

'Pull your big girl pants up and stop feeling sorry for yourself.'

Maggie would let that go. She knew deep down that Bethany and the whole team had her back. Bethany was right – Maggie was feeling sorry for herself.

'Look, I'm sorry. I just would've liked a bit more support.'

'Now that's not fair. We all know why you arrested him

– no one is questioning that. But we need to lock that away for the time being and focus on who is responsible for the recent killing. Clearly Lorraine Rugman and possibly the other two missing women, Yvonne Greene and Zoe Bridle, weren't even dead at the time he confessed. They could still be alive for all we know.'

Maggie rubbed her forehead and imagined two women tied up somewhere, locked away for years, without anyone even looking for them. A chill ran down her spine.

Someone coughed and they turned to see DI Rutherford standing in the doorway. She glanced between them and swallowed. 'They're saying it was a false confession. That the police coerced it out of him, taking advantage of his mental illness and drug-induced psychosis.' Rutherford paused, perhaps thinking that Maggie might interrupt, but she held back. 'Mr Raven has agreed to speak to us in prison, to try and help us piece together what happened. To explain his reasoning and how he knew the name of the first victim. Before we start jumping to any conclusions, let's wait to hear what he has to say, OK Maggie?'

'Yes, ma'am.' Her jaw tightened. She'd almost forgotten DI Rutherford's ability to get under her skin.

Maggie needed to settle back into her team and her DI's way of working after having been seconded for nearly a year to the Domestic Abuse and Homicide Unit. She had forged some meaningful friendships at the DAHU and was really impressed with the multi-agency approach. It was her intention to use this model, as much as her DI would allow, within this team. It just took one thing to blow a case open and

Maggie didn't want to mess up just because the police were sometimes too precious to ask for assistance from other agencies.

The current detective sergeant of her team was on long-term sick leave and had yet to be replaced. DI Rutherford hinted that she was hoping Maggie would apply for the Acting Up position, but it just wasn't going to happen. She enjoyed the operational side of her job, being in the thick of things and using her brain to piece the puzzle together. Ridiculous targets, politics and a lack of resources within the force would frustrate the hell out of her. She had encouraged her partner, Nathan Wright, to go for the post, but he seemed to be of the same frame of mind as her, or so she had thought.

# Chapter 5

*Speak of the devil and he shall appear.* Maggie laughed to herself as Nathan Wright tried to sneak past DI Rutherford unsuccessfully.

'I'll see you all in fifteen minutes for today's briefing,' DI Rutherford commented before returning to her office.

Maggie couldn't be one hundred per cent sure, but a strange look seemed to pass between them.

'What was that about?' Maggie poked him on the arm. Nathan seemed unable to make eye contact with her. He wasn't the best at hiding his feelings and usually Maggie could read him like a book. She watched as he shifted nervously from foot to foot.

'What are you talking about?' He walked towards his office.

'Stop-right-there. Look at me. Can you please tell me what the hell is going on?' Maggie didn't like to be caught off-guard and paranoia coursed through her veins.

Nathan fumbled his words and started pulling at his right index finger. 'Uh. I don't think I'm allowed to say anything just yet, but the guv will tell you ... I mean all of us, in the briefing.'

Her eyes squinted, and she stared at him. 'You'd better tell me now. I don't need any more surprises today ... have they got a new DS? Is that it? Shit – not Cooper? I hate that misogynistic bastard—'

'OK. OK. Stop stressing. I'll tell you on the condition that you act surprised, and maybe a little bit pleased, when the announcement is made. We *are* getting an Acting DS but it's not Cooper ... it's ... me.' He looked down at the floor, and guilt flooded over her.

'Oh my god, Nathan, great news! Why didn't you say? I thought we were closer than that. Thank God, it's not Cooper!' Maggie felt a rush of relief, tinged with shock.

'So, you're not pissed off?' He studied her face, as if he was trying to find a smidge of anger.

'Why the hell would I be pissed off?'

'Well, even though we both took the sergeant's exam, we sort of had this unspoken pact that neither of us would go for it.'

'I was a little taken aback, but it'll be a great experience for you and I couldn't wish for a better boss – I mean, who else will let me get away with slightly longer lunch hours?' She grinned and waited for Nathan to catch on to the joke.

'Don't say that! I'll be taking this very seriously and can't afford to give people any special favours.'

She burst out laughing. 'I'd never do that; I think you'll make a great DS – but I'm curious, what made you change your mind?'

Nathan explained to Maggie about how his wife wanted to start a family. He believed that not only would the DS opportunity afford him a more comfortable lifestyle, he would also be in a more stable position that would put his wife's mind at rest. Although Maggie wasn't wholly convinced, his mouth said one thing but his eyes another, she would support his decision because that's what friends did.

'Well let me be the first to ... secretly ... congratulate you. I'm dead chuffed and will do whatever I can to back you up, OK?'

'Thanks. That means a lot. You know how much I look up to you.'

'That's only because you're a foot shorter than me ...' And with that, any tension between the pair had been broken. Maggie knew she might struggle a bit to think of Nathan, one of the few people who really understood her, as her superior.

'So, am I calling you boss now? Or would you prefer guv? Or how about your excellence?' Maggie exaggerated a curtsey before him.

'Let's just leave things as they were. Nathan is fine, you cheeky cow.'

'Oi, sir! You can get yourself in trouble for saying things like that.' She laughed as she watched her partner squirm. Nathan looked around the room to make sure no one had overheard their conversation.

'Be careful, or I'll make sure your next duty is one that will wipe that smile clean off your face ...'

'Now THAT is better. Spoken like a true DS. Right then, are you ready to head to this briefing?'

He took a deep breath. 'Ready as I'll ever be ...'

Maggie walked down the corridor to the incident room and found a seat at the back. She was curious as to how the rest of her colleagues would react to the news, but she also wanted to sit far enough away from DI Rutherford to avoid giving the game away. This was Nathan's moment and she didn't want anything to spoil it.

# Chapter 6

Maggie squeezed into the incident room and took a seat next to Bethany. With the evidence boards set up and the additional chairs, there was barely enough space to stretch your legs.

DI Rutherford walked to the board at the front of the room with a concentrated frown and began describing the most recent findings. 'Good afternoon. I appreciate it's really cramped in here, we normally don't have this many people, so I'll try not to keep you longer than necessary. I just want to recap, especially for the benefit of the field team joining us today. A little over three weeks ago, a member of the public was pulling her bin to the kerb for collection when she noticed it was particularly heavy. She thought the neighbour had dumped extra items inside. But when she tore open one of the bags, she was horrified to find dismembered body parts. These were the remains of a female, now identified as Lorraine Rugman.'

'What made her decide to actually open the bags, ma'am?' Maggie hadn't been part of the crime scene investigation and her curiosity was getting the best of her.

'The witness said there was an odd odour as soon as she lifted the bin lid. She believed she might find something inside that could help identify whoever had dumped the bag.'

'Were there any other witnesses?' One of the field officers called out.

'An older gentleman across the road claims a security light came on across the road in the early hours of the morning and he saw someone poking about the bins. He couldn't give a full description, as he wasn't wearing his glasses. It wasn't until the next morning when he heard his neighbour scream that he knew he possibly saw the killer.'

'Other than what we have already been given, has any new information come in that we can share with the field officers, ma'am?' Maggie was churning the information through her head at a mile a minute.

'We were waiting for pathology to confirm the weapon, but it looks like some sort of saw was used to dismember the body. We haven't found any other body parts relating to the victim, and at the moment, we're treating this separately from the original Chopper Investigation.'

The pathology department had been slow to deliver the information to the team due to a number of staff shortages. Dr Blake was involved in interviewing agency staff to fill the gaps while they waited for the relevant checks to be undertaken.

'How do we know for definite that Raven wasn't responsible or at least involved in this murder? Could the body parts have been frozen and then later disposed of by someone working with him?' Maggie finished speaking, and the DI sighed wearily.

'I don't have to remind you, but I think I will anyway, *DC* Jamieson. In fact – all of you listen up. Bill Raven's appeal is based on those body parts turning up and it's looking very likely that he may be released. But just in case you haven't digested everything you've already been told, here is the pathologist's report which came in this morning.' She waved a folder in the air and the crowd of officers took a collective breath. She continued speaking. 'The pathologist confirmed the limb and torso were *not* frozen. Lorraine Rugman had been missing, presumed dead, for over two years and the time of death, estimated at between two days and two weeks prior to them being found, *proves* that Raven was behind bars when the murder was committed. As for whether or not he could be involved in some way – well that's what we're here to investigate, isn't it?'

Maggie folded her arms and sank down in her chair. Her mouth felt suddenly dry. 'Is it possible that Lorraine was ... that the other women Bill Raven named ... have been kept alive for nearly three years?'

'If that's true, we don't have much time. Field officers will carry out house-to-house enquiries that focus on the recent murder of Lorraine Rugman, but I'll also need someone to go through the previous case, which had linked all three women, to see if we missed anything; specifically, I want to investigate if there's a link between the previous case and the murder of Lorraine Rugman. We need to use the media and appeal for anyone to come forward. Oh. There's one more thing I'd like to share with you all. Nathan has been appointed as Acting DS, so I'd appreciate if you all treat him as such.

Everyone know what they need to do, or do I have to hold your hands?'

The whole room nodded like a sea of bobbleheads and clapped for Nathan's promotion. A few shot curious glances Maggie's way, but she just smiled and clapped along with them.

Maggie shifted in her seat as her colleagues dispersed. Staring at the board before her, she reviewed all the information again and stored it for a time that she could sit and digest it on her own. Although she had been over the details a million times, since returning to the team, she was convinced that there was something they were failing to see. She just needed to find it first.

# Chapter 7

On leaving the incident room, Maggie stopped in the toilets to wash her face. She needed to focus on the press conference. The cool water felt invigorating. She used a paper towel to dab her face dry. *Why did I agree to this?*

Maggie's stomach fluttered with nerves. Although confident in most situations, Raven's solicitor had recently been using her as a scapegoat with the media at every opportunity presented. It made her question her decisions and wonder whether she had actually convicted the wrong person. She stared at herself in the mirror. Dark circles had found a home under her eyes, and she ran her fingers through her hair before stepping out into the corridor.

Nathan spotted her from the end of the corridor and walked over. 'You ready?' He squeezed her shoulder. 'You're as white as a ghost. Don't let nerves get to you – the COMMS Officer and I will be doing most of the talking.'

'Perfect. DI Rutherford has thrown me under the bus.' Maggie knew she was paying the price for revisiting The Chopper Investigation without permission. If she wasn't more careful, Maggie could be pulled off the case for good.

She accompanied Nathan down to the lower-level conference room. It was already filling with people and Maggie could feel their eyes on her as she followed Nathan to the front. Maggie sat down and crossed her legs. Despite the size of the room, it felt claustrophobic. She was hyperaware of her surroundings. The air hung heavy with the salty smell of sweat mixed with overpowering perfume. She loosened the collar of her blouse and tried to keep her breathing at a normal pace.

Nathan called the conference to order. 'Thank you all for coming. My name is DS Nathan Wright and to my left is my colleague, DC Maggie Jamieson and our Communications Officer. We all have busy lives, so shall we just begin? I'd like to read a brief statement and then I'll open up questions to the floor.' He waited while the last-minute stragglers sat, and a silence fell over the room.

Maggie heard the *click click click* of cameras and blinked as their lights flashed. She looked around the room and her head began to spin. Taking a big gulp of water and a few deep breaths, she waited for Nathan to begin.

'You'll all be aware that the partial remains recently found on the Blackwood Housing Estate belong to Ms Lorraine Rugman. Previously, we had reason to believe that Ms Rugman was murdered by Bill Raven. Mr Raven had confessed to the crime in late 2016. The pathologist's report now confirms …' He paused and looked around the room. 'That Mr Raven couldn't have physically been involved in this crime, as the pathologist estimates that the victim had been killed within at least a two-week time frame of the discovery of her remains.'

The journalists let out a collective gasp and glanced at each other in anticipation. Before Nathan could continue, a young journalist jumped in with a question.

'DS Wright, can you tell us if you are working with Mr Raven's solicitor to support his appeal and explain what you mean by, *he was not physically involved*? Do you believe that he has *some* involvement in the recent murder?' He looked from Maggie to Nathan with a smirk.

'I'm afraid I am not at liberty to discuss Mr Raven's appeal or answer anything relating to Mr Raven specifically.' Nathan glanced around the room and pointed at a black-haired female journalist who seemed as if she was about ready to jump out of her chair.

'Can you tell us whether you have any suspects at this time?' Her eyes were wide with excitement. Maggie guessed she must be new to the job.

'We have a few people who we are keen to speak to. We'd actually like to appeal to members of the public to come forward and think back, not only over the last few months, but to 2016. Anyone with information, please contact us, even if you think it's unimportant.' The same journalist had an evil glint in her eye as she lined up another question.

'One more from you before we move on and give someone else an opportunity.' Nathan frowned.

'This question is for DC Jamieson.' The room turned to face Maggie. 'How does it feel to put an innocent man behind bars?'

Maggie opened her mouth to answer, she had been prepared for this, but she couldn't get the words out. Nathan reached across, touched her arm and interrupted.

'Which part of we're not discussing Bill Raven's case did you not understand? I'm sure our COMMS Officer will be more than happy to shut down this press conference now. Is that what you want?' Nathan nodded at the COMMS Officer.

The female reporter was not satisfied. 'DC Jamieson, do you think you should keep your job if you let the real killer walk free while—'

'That's it. Enough.' Nathan stood as the COMMS Officer terminated the conference. 'You can all thank your colleague over there for the abrupt end to this press conference. Thank you to those who respectfully followed my instructions. Any other questions can be answered through our Communications Team.'

Maggie got up and waited for Nathan to go ahead. She maintained eye contact with the journalist who seemed hell-bent on showing her up in front of everyone. The woman eventually looked away, and Maggie left the room with her head held high. As soon as they reached the stairway, out of the sight of the journalists, Maggie leant against the wall and bent over, ashen faced.

'Are you OK? Do you want some water?' Nathan sounded concerned.

'Sorry. I just feel a bit faint. That reporter really had it in for me, didn't she? Fuck sake ...'

'Don't let her get to you. We both knew that you would be used as the fall guy ... or gal.' He winked. 'Well, I wasn't about to let that happen. You do know that this isn't your fault, right?'

She took a deep breath. 'I know. But it doesn't make it any easier.'

*Especially since I am not sure it's true. Did I put an innocent man behind bars?*

# Chapter 8

Maggie collected her thoughts before she had to re-interview some of Lorraine Rugman's associates. All three of the women had been interviewed in 2016 following Raven's confession and subsequent conviction, but the team agreed it was worth going over old ground to ensure nothing was missed the first time around.

The first two women had little to offer. Both had admitted to knowing Lorraine but hadn't seen her for a few years, even before Raven's confession. One had become stroppy during the interview saying she was 'sick of repeating' herself and 'shouldn't the police stop hassling women and start looking for the arsehole who is killing them'. She had a point.

The only new bit of information they added was the fact that Lorraine had been using just prior to her going missing, as both women often bumped into her when they were scoring heroin. She was also seen a few times on the corner of Green Avenue and Clacton Road, a known area for prostitution in Stafford. Neither could give a specific time frame, but believed it was before Raven had been convicted.

Maggie wanted to speak to the last woman on the list.

Sasha Thompson had been questioned in the original Chopper Investigation and provided Adrian Harrison, Bill Raven's associate, with his alibi. After refilling the jug of water in the interview room and making sure there were enough plastic cups, Maggie called Sasha through.

Sasha was in her early thirties. She had short, brown hair in a messy style, wasn't very tall in stature, but had a noticeable bruise on her face, something Maggie had seen on many of the victims of domestic violence she had come across. The vacant look in her eyes, sweat and sallow skin indicated that she may be clucking due to heroin withdrawal. Maggie had come across this a few times where users *dabbled* for long periods, not realizing the drug had sunk its claws in. She wore baggy clothes, probably in an attempt to hide a skeletal frame.

'I'm DC Maggie Jamieson. Do you know why we asked you to come in today, Miss Thompson?'

The woman sat, open legged, across from Maggie. 'Yep. Something about Lorraine Rugman and my previous statement? Nasty business what happened to her, wasn't it? What kind of psycho chops up a woman?' Sasha's shoulders shook and a look of disgust crossed her face.

'Yes. Nasty indeed. Thanks for coming in. We're trying to gather as much information as we can about Lorraine's last known movements. I see you were interviewed just after Bill Raven confessed, back in 2016.' Maggie looked up from her notebook. 'Can you tell me a little bit about yourself? We don't seem to have much from your original interview.'

Sasha shrugged. 'I was adopted by a pair of pricks when I was three, but I probably would have been better off with my parents. After a few years of getting kicked about, Social Services took me out of that home and I was put in care where the abuse continued. I've been in prison a few times, as I'm sure my record shows – shoplifting, drugs, but nothing in the last ten years. That's my life. Anything else?'

Maggie noted the track marks on Sasha's arms and considered asking about the bruise on her face. Perhaps Maggie should report her to someone. Sasha took a sip of water, her skin pale under the strip lighting, and Maggie felt a surge of pity for her. There were so many women like this who had been dealt a bad hand of cards in life and never stood a chance. 'If you want to talk about anything, I can put you in touch with someone.'

Sasha laughed weakly and shook her head. 'Don't you worry about me.'

They fell silent for a moment and Maggie glanced at the clock. 'We really need your help with this case. Can you recall anything significant that happened in 2016 that you may have missed?'

Sasha bit her lip. 'Not really. I spent most of that time with Adrian, off my face on drugs. In fact, I couldn't get rid of that arsehole. He was my ... business partner at the time.'

Maggie knew that Harrison dealt drugs and, given Sasha's evasive response, Maggie figured this was the *business* she was referring to. 'Care to elaborate on that, Miss Thompson? You were Mr Harrison's alibi, weren't you? What can you tell us about him?'

'Actually, no. I don't care to elaborate and yes I was, what of it? I'm not really sure what else I can add to what you lot already know. Adrian is a loser. And I mean that in the nicest way. He's a bit of an attention seeker, but most people find him annoying. Once he likes someone, he latches on to them. Bit like a pet dog.'

'Interesting way to describe your boyfriend.'

'Boyfriend? Ha! Where did you get that idea? Just because you shag a guy a few times doesn't make him your boyfriend, DC Jamieson.'

'Oh. Your previous statement said he was your boyfriend.'

'Well clearly that's a mistake. He's a friend and a boy. That's about it.'

Maggie pulled out Sasha's original statement and went through the rest of it with her.

'Can you account for your whereabouts around the time just before and on the day that Miss Rugman's remains were discovered?'

'Is this a joke?'

'I'm afraid not. Can you answer the question?'

'Do I need a lawyer?'

'I don't know, Miss Thompson. Do you think you need one?'

'I know what you coppers are like.' She shifted in the seat. 'Just covering my arse. I can tell you exactly where I was. In Manchester with some mates. I can even give you their details if you want.' Maggie watched as she rummaged through the bag she had with her. Her hand shook as she pulled out a small, red notebook. 'Do you have a piece of paper and a pen?'

Maggie tore a sheet from her pad and pushed it across to Sasha, with the pen she had been using.

'What were you doing in Manchester?'

'Catching up with friends and taking care of a little business ...' She handed Maggie the piece of paper and her pen. 'Call them. They'll tell you.'

'OK. Thanks. Is there anything else you want to add?'

'Nah.' She bit her lip.

'Do you have a contact number and address where we can reach you in case we have any further questions?'

''Fraid not. I'm sofa surfing at the moment and lost my mobile when I was in Manchester.' She pointed to a number on the paper she had just given to Maggie. 'Ring her if you need me, she'll pass on any messages.'

'Thanks for your time.' Maggie escorted Sasha back to reception and waited as the woman signed out. 'Here's my card, if you need to reach me.' Sasha pocketed the card and left the station. Maggie sighed and returned to her desk upstairs.

'Did you get anything new to add to the investigation?' Bethany turned her chair towards Maggie.

'I wish. The only connection between the women and Lorraine is drugs and sex work ... none of which brings us any closer to our killer.'

# *Chapter 9*

Bill Raven watched himself again on the television and smiled. *I'm fucking famous.* He deserved all this attention. He was dominating the television channels, and had reporters harassing the prison on a daily basis to speak with him.

*Finally.*

He looked at the cheap watch he had been sent by an admirer. People were sending him things regularly, they adored him. It was almost time for his medication, to keep the voices away.

*Ha! The voices …*

Coming off heroin in prison was hard – it wasn't the plan, but it had to be done. Heroin, pretty much any drug, was available to him, but it countered the effects of the pills and that just wouldn't do.

The prison psychologist wouldn't sign him off medication supervision until Bill could demonstrate that he would stay clean. He had to prove that he would take the prescription and, truth be told, the meds calmed him down. Complete sobriety often led to him getting aggressive, and that wouldn't do either. They couldn't see that side of him yet. Plus, he had to stem the voices, right? The ones that made him do bad things ...

*Yeah, that's what happened.* He smiled to himself.

The guard came and unlocked his door. Raven smirked as the man kept his distance. He could use their fear ... one day. But for now, he needed to collect his tablets before he could have a shower. He was excited. He had a big day ahead. The police would be visiting him to go over everything he remembered from his original confession. He had been waiting for this. He would tell them as much as he could, not everything of course. He had some business of his own to take care of first.

He imagined the day he would be released. With his old flat not available to him, his solicitor had said he would probably be placed in temporary accommodation while they sorted out his personal matters. When Raven was in his mid-twenties, his grandmother had sold the large home he had grown up in as she couldn't afford the upkeep. He had fond memories of that place. He sighed. She had bought herself a more manageable property and, before any of this *inconvenience*, she had passed away leaving him the small bungalow in Doxley, a rural village just outside of Stafford. But there was paperwork and other matters to be dealt with before he could move in. With the money she had left him, he was going to buy himself a little van and set up his own business – a gardener, maybe. He liked working with his hands. He had a lot of plans and was looking forward to getting started. He rubbed his palms together.

When he had first been arrested, Bill had felt strangely

euphoric. *Fame at last!* No more being the brunt of jokes, bossed about – he was *the man*, and everyone wanted to know his story.

Telling the police he was responsible for murdering Lorraine, Yvonne, and Zoe made him feel powerful. The look on their faces as he described what he had done. Raven licked his lips.

Being charged. *Oh, they all thought they were so clever.* Poor, poor Maggie. He wondered how she felt now as she watched her career falling down a black hole. He wished he could have seen her face when she first learned about his appeal.

And finally, being convicted. Seeing the look of distress on the jury's faces as the verdict was read out. He took a deep, satisfying breath. Closed his eyes and tried desperately to recapture that feeling again.

With his appeal in place, he had access to all the paperwork that had ultimately led to his conviction. The trial hadn't been long because he had pleaded guilty. Three women had been presumed dead and a few small bits of forensics had backed up his confession. A hair here, a droplet of blood there ...

Bill *did* know all three women. He had met them, sold drugs to them, partied with them. Witnesses had placed him with – or in the vicinity of – all three women at some point prior to their disappearance. He'd made sure of that.

Snippets of events flashed through his brain at lightning speed.

Blood. There was blood everywhere. It covered the floor like a velvety red carpet. Dripping down the walls – slowly. He had been hypnotized by it all.

Then there were the receipts that had been recovered by the police. So clever and probably the most damning of all because he had no explanation for why he had them. Well none that he was prepared to share. Bill had been seen on CCTV purchasing a hack saw, plastic sheeting, a roll of large black bin bags and a six pack of duct tape. The receipts for all items were found in a pair of jeans he had stuffed in the back of his closet. Maybe he was going to help a friend fix his roof?

The police hounded him in interview. Interrogated him until he was so exhausted, he just admitted it all – or that's what his solicitor now claimed had happened. Bill had been off his face and did struggle to really remember everything. That much was true. The police had a nice scenario: he had kidnapped the women, cut up and disposed of their bodies in unknown locations and then confessed because of his overwhelming guilt. That worked, and it saved him from getting caught out in his lies, though he was too clever for that really. He confessed to killing the women because he already knew they were missing ... and would never be found. They may as well have been dead. But were there more? *There could be more.*

Bill's psychosis was a godsend and he had his heroin and crack cocaine use to thank for that. The periodic psychotic breaks had been detailed in keywork sessions at the drug and alcohol agency he attended over the years. Not long before he confessed to the police, he had stopped taking his anti-psychotics and begun self-medicating with whatever drug he could get his hands on. He had needed to block out reality and live his fantasies. It had been too long.

The meds ruined his thoughts – he couldn't wait to be free of them, so he could see, feel and taste the fear. The thrills were what made him feel alive.

# Chapter 10

Maggie embraced the silence when she got home. She chucked her coat over the railing and removed her shoes, leaving them on the small shoe rack her brother had made. Andy wasn't due in from work for another hour and she decided to use the time to unwind. She needed to have a conversation with him and wasn't sure where to begin.

Her brother had moved in a few months earlier after coming to Maggie with his financial problems. Maggie had agreed to pay off his heavy gambling debts to avoid further strain on his relationship with their parents. In exchange, he would do any home repairs and, in the long run, she probably got the better end of the deal.

Unbeknownst to Andy, their parents had said they were hoping to visit in a few weeks. He had done a fantastic job on redecorating the spare room, but Maggie wasn't sure when or how she would explain to their parents the current living arrangements. *Why do families have to be so complicated?*

Maggie called out to Scrappy, her fiercely independent ginger cat, as she made her way into the kitchen. 'Scrappy. Come on and get your dinner!' No response. *That's odd.* She grabbed the can opener out of the top drawer, figuring if he heard her opening a tin of food, he'd show his furry face. He didn't.

Maggie opened the back door and looked into the garden. She grabbed her sweater from the hook and pulled on her rubber boots, making her way down the path and calling out to the pain-in-the-backside cat of hers. 'Scraaaaappy. Here kitty cat. I have your favourite din dins.' She tapped the tin with the opener.

When she got to the bottom of her garden, she noticed that the gate was open a crack. It was usually locked and she cursed her brother under her breath. Maggie pushed the gate closed, pulled the bolt across and made her way inside. Scooping his food into his bowl, Maggie placed it on the mat by the door and then took off her boots. There was a chill in the house, so she kept her sweater on and poured herself a glass of wine.

She ambled towards the living room and reclined in the settee, putting her feet up on the table, just as her brother came through the door.

'Hey, did you leave the back gate unlocked?' She called out to him.

'Well hello to you too!' Andy laughed.

'Sorry. How was your day, dear brother? Did you leave the back gate unlocked?' A smile tugged at her lips.

'Not me. I haven't been out there for a few days. Why? Was it open?'

'Yeah, it's unlocked. I noticed when I went to go look for Scrappy.'

'That's weird. Do you want me to check it out?'

'Erm – police officer here ... no need. I am not worried. Probably someone trying it on, or kids – you know what they can be like. You only have to reach over to unlock it. But if you have a strong padlock spare, it might be a good idea to put that on, just in case.'

'I'll sort it.' He scratched his head.

'Was Scrappy around when you left?'

'Pretty sure he was; he usually goes out his flap when I leave. But I can't say for definite.'

'OK. So, how was your day?'

'Fine. Same shit, different day. I'm thinking of maybe looking for something in the building trade. I'm getting sick of the monotony of it all in the factory and the shifts can be draining. You know how I feel about starting my own business. Any experience would be good at this stage.' He looked deflated and Maggie frowned. 'Don't worry. I won't be leaving anytime soon. Just something to think about.'

'Phew! I had a mini panic then. There's still so much to do on the house!' She grinned and then fiddled with her hair. 'Do you have a minute to chat?'

'Sounds ominous. Let me jump in the shower and put some dinner on. Have you eaten?'

'Not yet. What are you making?'

'Might use up the veggies and do a stir-fry or something.'

'Perfect! I'll start chopping.'

He paused at the doorway. 'About this little chat. Do I need to be worried?'

'Don't be silly. It's just a conversation that we probably

should have had two months ago.' His frown deepened and she tried a reassuring smile. 'Seriously,' her voice sounded forced. 'It's nothing to worry about, now go.' She imitated whipping a tea towel at his backside as he left the room.

# Chapter 11

Andy wouldn't be in the shower for long and Maggie knew she had to get her words and thoughts together before she broached the subject with him. She regularly spoke to her mother on the telephone and tried to visit her parents in Glasgow at least twice a year. They understood that her job was important, and her mother had once told her how proud her father was of her – though he never told her that himself.

When it came to her brother, however, both of her parents had reached the end of their tether. Recalling her last conversation with her mother, Maggie sighed.

*'Have you forgot what he was like growing up? Always in and out of all levels of trouble. Granted, he never brought the police to the door, but he was close enough at times.'*

Maggie had put the phone on speaker and carried on reading.

*'Always wanted to have the better things in life, and even though your dad and I tried our hardest, the ungrateful sod wanted more … are you listening?'*

*'Yes, Mum …'*

*'That brother of yours … hmph … turning to gambling and*

*each time he won a little, he wanted more. Selfish, Maggie. Not a care in the world about any of us. And no shame in taking our money, our savings.'*

Maggie could almost see her mother's head shaking.

*'Yes, I was foolish. Giving him money behind your dad's back. You wouldn't believe the rows that caused when he eventually found out. Your father can't stand the sight of him now.'*

Maggie felt bad for her parents. She had always suspected their mother gave him more money than even she or their father knew about.

She shook her head and focused back on chopping the vegetables for dinner. It was about time things changed on that front. Her plan was a welcome distraction from the crap that her work life had brought with it.

Maggie was proud of Andy and how much he had turned his life around since their initial head to head a couple of months ago. He was paying off his debt, steering clear of gambling and attending Gamblers Anonymous. All of this in such a short period of time might win their parents over. Hope fluttered inside her.

She looked up and saw his gangly legs as he stomped his way down the stairs. He popped his head in the doorway, drying his hair with a towel.

'Do I have time to make a cuppa before this lecture? Do you want one?'

She laughed. 'Behave! It's just a chat. And yes, I'd love a coffee.' The wine was making her feel a little light-headed. She returned to the living room and sat down.

When he joined her, he held her coffee out, handle towards

her, something he used to do as a kid to show how hard he was as the cup burned his hand. Rather than messing with him, she took the cup and thanked him.

'OK, so ...' she took a deep breath, 'I wanted to talk to you about Mum and Dad ...' She waited for the protestations and when none came, she went on. 'Nothing definite at the moment but they may be coming down next month to stay—'

'And you want me out? That's OK, no need for any explanations. I'll start looking in the morning.' He pressed his lips together.

'Fuck sake, Andy. Would you let me finish? I don't want you out. In fact, I'm really glad that you're here. Getting to know you after so much time apart has been nice, and the work you've done has probably saved me a small fortune, though maybe I shouldn't point that out.' She saw a smile form on his face.

'Well, that's good. I know I'll eventually have to move out, but I think this is the perfect set-up for me at the minute. Your work ethic and, frankly, your bitchy attitude, and I mean that in the nicest possible way, is what's driving me to do well for myself.'

'Aww. Now don't be getting soft on me. Look, I just wanted to give you enough notice and I guess I'm going to have to do the same with the folks. I don't want to drop a bombshell on them, but they need to know. I just think that now is the time to burn down some of the barriers that have been up for far too long. I know it's early days, but you've done incredibly well.'

'Now who is getting soft ...'

'Oi! I can still kick your arse both verbally and physically if I really wanted to, never forget that.' She raised her fist and shook it at him.

He held his hands up in surrender. 'OK, copper. Calm down. So how are you going to approach this with Mum and Dad?' He turned the mug in his hands and stared at the floor. 'I've put them through a lot. And I'll never be able to afford to pay them back, but maybe if my new venture works out, I can at least show willing and make a start.'

'I think that would be a great idea, but like you said, small steps. You still have a long way to go before you can say you've kicked your habit, you know. Relapse usually happens when a person feels they have beat the problem.'

'Trust me, I'm done with all that shit. I'm a whole new person. There's no such thing as a little bet for me these days.' He paused, caught Maggie's eye and took a deep breath. 'If it wasn't for you giving me yet another chance, I'm not sure where I would be.' His eyes glistened.

Maggie wasn't one to handle emotion easily, especially since she rarely saw her brother cry. If her memory served her correctly the only other time she witnessed any emotion from her brother was when their grandfather died and that was twenty years ago. She immediately changed the subject. 'Hey. Well will you look at us now. Two adults having an adult conversation. So, we're good then? Now all I have to do is convince Mum and Dad ...'

# Chapter 12

DI Abigail Rutherford looked around the open-plan office. 'Anyone seen Maggie?'

The small team of officers that formed Staffordshire's Major and Organised Crime Department looked at each other before DS Nathan Wright piped up. 'I think she's on lates today, ma'am.'

Abigail looked at her watch. 'Damn. OK, thanks Nathan. When she gets in, can you tell her I need to see her? It's urgent.' The CCRC were investigating Raven's appeal and needed to speak to Maggie.

She shook her head at the thought that Raven was now claiming that he was unlawfully arrested and imprisoned. The worst thing was he may have grounds for that appeal after all. She was under a lot of pressure both at work and at home. With her second divorce looming, her head was a mess. Her only saving grave was that she'd never had children with either of her husbands. She couldn't think about that now. Instead, Raven's situation and the predicament her team currently found themselves in had to take priority.

Abigail was torn between viewing Raven as a potentially

dangerous offender and needing to keep an open mind that he could be acquitted and released.

She loaded up the details on her computer and began to trawl through the original statements taken by Maggie. She had no doubt that Maggie did everything by the book, and as the Crown Prosecution Service, or CPS as they are better known to those in the criminal justice services, believed there had been enough evidence to charge and convict Bill Raven, she had no cause to be concerned. At least she hoped she didn't. But she also knew that if Maggie let her obsession with Raven continue, it could lead the whole department into a nightmare.

She was startled by a knock on her door and nearly jumped out of her seat. Seeing Nathan, she smiled.

'Sorry, ma'am. Maggie texted to say she's meeting up with some of her old colleagues from the DAHU – sorry, Domestic Abuse and Homicide Unit – and then heading to the Crown Courts to speak with someone in the CPS.'

'Did she say who? Or why?' Abigail frowned.

'Sorry, ma'am. She didn't. Do you want me to get back to her and ask?'

'No. That's fine. I'll speak to her.'

Although Maggie needed some time to readjust, Abigail wouldn't tolerate having her instructions ignored. Their DCI was already on the warpath for reasons yet unknown to her and he'd come down on her like a ton of bricks if she didn't keep her team in line. The Chopper case had almost destroyed Maggie the first time around, and Abigail wouldn't let it happen again. Reaching for her phone, she dialled the only person at the CPS she knew to have any influence and hoped that Maggie got the message.

# Chapter 13

Maggie arrived at Markston train station with plenty of time before her planned meeting with PC Mark Fielding and Probation Officer Lucy Sherwood. As annoying as it could be to take public transport, it also helped clear her head.

Mark still worked with the domestic abuse team, but Maggie knew he was spending more and more of his time at the haven Lucy had set up for victims of domestic abuse after her own personal experiences the year before. Maggie loved the name – SAFE – it stood for Strength. Acceptance. Freedom and Empowerment. Maggie still shuddered at the thought of what Lucy had endured.

She missed working with the domestic abuse team, even if it had been draining. Walking through town, Maggie headed in the direction of Costa. She ordered a cappuccino with an extra shot, grabbed a table outside and enjoyed the feel of the sun on her face. She pulled out her mobile and began scrolling through the news on the internet. When she saw the headline 'Raven's Appeal Makes a Mockery of the Police' and read the section outlining her incompetency, she wished she had not bothered. All the papers seemed to follow along the same theme. Maggie bet that Raven was feeding them information, as none of what she read had been discussed in the press conference.

Looking around, she saw two figures she instantly recognized. Maggie waved as they approached the table.

'Hello! It's so great to see you both.' Maggie stood and hugged Mark and Lucy before sitting back down.

'Are you okay for a coffee, Maggie?' Mark pointed to her half-drunk cup on the table.

'I'm good for now, thanks.'

'What are you having, Lucy? I'll get these in and you two can have a catch-up.' Mark smiled and affection glowed in Lucy's eyes.

'Cappuccino, please.' Lucy pulled up a chair, so she could face Maggie.

As Mark walked away, Maggie grinned. 'So, is there something I should know?'

Lucy waved her hand. 'Don't be silly. Mark and I are just friends.'

'You do remember I am a detective, right? I won't interrogate you, this time ...'

'I like Mark. I'm not going to lie, but I'm just not ready at the moment. Not after ... well, you know.'

Maggie placed a hand gently over Lucy's. 'I was just teasing. For what it's worth, I think you and Mark would make a great couple. Just promise you'll let me know when it does happen.' Maggie winked and saw the corners of Lucy's mouth turn up in a smile.

'Right then, here's your cappuccino.' Mark took a seat beside them. 'So, what's been happening since we last saw you, Maggie? The Chopper's appeal sounds like a nightmare.' Mark placed his coffee on the table.

Maggie didn't want word getting back to DI Rutherford that she was still following up on things outside of the current investigation. 'It looks like Lorraine might have been held captive for nearly two years. The other women could still be alive, too.' Maggie took a sip of her cappuccino. 'Raven has a clever solicitor trying to make a name for himself, and he managed to convince the CCRC that Raven was not of sound mind when he confessed. We have about six weeks until his next appeal hearing. With the latest murder, the conviction may well be overturned. There's obviously more to the story, but that's the basics.'

'Holy shit. The other women, the ones he also claimed to have murdered, might still be captive somewhere? So, Raven does have grounds for his appeal? But you're not convinced, are you?'

'The CCRC are going through everything with a fine-tooth comb. I'd rather not talk about it. What's been happening at the unit. How's everyone?'

'Well Kat is looking to become a detective. She signed up to the accelerated programme and seems to be enjoying it. She'll need to watch that mouth of hers though. Her brutal honesty will be her downfall if she's not careful.' Both Maggie and Lucy nodded agreement.

'What about DS Hooper? He must be close to retirement now.' Maggie recalled how keen the DS had been to leave the police after his years of service.

'As he reminds us every bloody day with his countdown calendar. He's saving up his annual leave and I think he only has a month or two left. Lucky bastard.'

'I thought you liked working for the police?' She looked him in the eyes, knowing she would see the truth no matter what came out of his mouth.

'I do. But sometimes I just want a change. And with Hooper leaving, God knows who'll replace him. Lucy did the right thing when she left her full-time position with Probation. At least with the agency work, she gets to pick and choose her hours.'

The quick glance over at Lucy was not lost on Maggie.

Mark continued, 'I'll carry on in the unit but keep my options open.'

'Definitely the right thing to do. How's Dr Moloney?' Maggie hoped no one would notice the heat rising in her cheeks.

'Busy but OK, I guess. A little stressed, what with all the profiles she is putting together on our nominals. Have you not seen her?' Mark caught her eye.

'Uh ... no. Why?' Maggie swallowed.

'Just thought you might have, what with all that Raven stuff going on.' Another look passed between Lucy and Mark.

'You pair want to tell me what is going on? I can see the looks, you're sitting right in front of me.' Maggie sat back in her chair and crossed her arms.

'It's nothing. We know that you and Kate worked well together when you were in the unit. We just thought you'd have kept in touch.' Lucy smiled, like butter wouldn't melt.

Maggie took a sip of her coffee. 'I've been meaning to have a proper catch-up, but if you say she's stressed, then maybe I should leave it.'

'I should be seeing her later. How about I tell her you'd like to catch-up? She has your number, right? She can call you then when she is a little less under pressure.'

'Sounds good.' Looking at her watch, Maggie knew if she didn't get the next train back to Stafford, she would miss the opportunity to talk to her contact in the CPS. 'Right. It's been lovely, but I need to get back.' After hugging them, Maggie picked up her bag and headed to the train station.

*I have a few questions and there's no way I am going to let the prosecution service wriggle out of answering them ...*

# Chapter 14

Arriving in Stafford, Maggie stopped at the Starbucks in the station and grabbed an Americano. She hadn't been sleeping well and needed more caffeine in her system to face the long shift she had ahead of her today.

The courts were busy when she arrived. Maggie made her way to the CPS offices and was greeted by one of those receptionists whose smile never reaches her eyes.

'Can I help you?' Maggie cringed at the sound of the receptionist's whiny voice. She barely glanced at Maggie before returning to her computer.

'Please could I speak to the prosecutor in Bill Raven's case?'

There was a long pause as the receptionist continued typing on her keyboard. Eventually she paused and looked up. 'Do you have an appointment?'

Maggie had to take a deep breath. 'No. I'm with the police – DC Maggie Jamieson.' She reached into her pocket and took out her card, thunked it hard on the counter.

As if it was contaminated, the woman moved the card closer with two fingers. 'I'm afraid you still need an appointment. We're very busy.'

Maggie looked around at the empty hallway. She gripped the desk and her knuckles began to whiten. 'I don't need long. Can you just call up and see if he has a few minutes ... please?' Maggie returned the fake smile she got earlier.

'Well ... I'll try. But I wouldn't hold your breath.' The woman punched three numbers onto her telephone keypad and looked at her nails while she waited. 'Good morning, sir, I have a DC Maggie Jamieson here and she said she'd like a quick word. Do you have time?' Again, she looked at her nails, and Maggie wished she could hear the other side of the conversation. 'Hmm ... uh huh ... OK. Yes, I'll tell her.'

Maggie straightened her blouse, waiting for the woman to buzz her through.

'I'm sorry. He's very busy. He can't see you today but suggested that you make an appointment and he'll talk to you then.' She looked down at an open diary. 'I have a free slot next Thursday then another—'

'Never mind. I'll catch him another time. Thank you for trying.' Maggie did her best to contain her anger. She'd never had a problem speaking to the prosecutor before; he always made time to see her. *What the hell was going on?*

The woman responded with her fake smile again. 'OK, thanks for coming by. Have a nice day.'

Maggie clenched her fists as she left the office. She wondered if DI Rutherford had warned him not to speak with her.

The ten-minute walk around to Stafford Police Station served to make a slight dent in her anger. She needed to keep it in check. Although she respected her boss, there was an air of condescension about her that ruffled more than just Maggie's feathers.

Maggie climbed the stairs to the second floor and chucked her jacket over her chair. Just as her computer booted up, DI Rutherford called her over to her office.

'Yes, ma'am. Coming.' Maggie let out a sigh and slouched over, opened the door and took a seat in front of Rutherford's desk.

'Maggie. Did you have a good morning?'

'I did. I had a few hours before my shift started and went across to Markston.'

'Yes ... I heard. Did you stop by anywhere else? And Maggie, think about your answer.' The DI glared as she tapped her desk. Maggie sat up in the chair and noticed the dark lines of exhaustion on Rutherford's face.

So, she had spoken to the prosecutor. 'Yes, ma'am. I stopped by the courts. I wanted to speak to the CPS, to see if they had anything useful for the current investigation.'

'Ah. Just for the current investigation then? You know, if I find out you're doing anything to jeopardize this case – like going on a wild goose chase against Raven, for instance – I'll have your head on a plate.'

'Yes.'

'We have a briefing in an hour and I expect you to be there, focused, having left your views on Raven outside the room. Do you understand?' DI Rutherford gave her a look that was more than a warning – it was a threat.

'I do. May I go now? I've a lot to do before the briefing.'

'Of course. And Maggie ...'

'Yes?'

'Someone from the CCRC wants to speak with you today

at 4 p.m. Don't be late.' The DI sighed as she looked towards the ceiling.

Maggie responded through gritted teeth. 'I won't, ma'am. Thank you.'

She turned abruptly on her heels and left the room. Touching the base of her neck, Maggie squeezed and felt the tension release. At her desk, Maggie took her keys out of her pocket and opened the cabinet that was tucked underneath. Fingering through the files, she went to the very back and pulled out the one labelled 'THE CHOPPER'.

*DI Rutherford had said to leave her thoughts out of the room – she didn't specify which room.*

# Chapter 15

After going through her private file on the original Chopper case, Maggie sat back to gaze out of the window. DI Rutherford had a bite that would scare off even the most hardened criminal, but she was also the loudest to cheer and give praise to those who deserved it. Maggie had heard rumours that she was in the midst of a second divorce after she found her husband cheating on her. Apparently, he couldn't cope with the long hours she put in at the office which left little time to think about starting a family. It was no wonder her boss looked tired. With everything that was going on in her personal life and now the CCRC scrutinizing the original case file ... Maggie's shoulders tightened. The MOCD's reputation – her own reputation – could be on the line.

'Penny for your thoughts.' She looked up and saw DS Nathan Wright.

'Sorry Nathan, I was miles away. Just thinking about the review commission and what they might find.' Maggie cleared her throat.

'Don't worry. You worked hard on that case and you're

meticulous. There's no way you screwed this up, trust me.' He gave her shoulder a squeeze.

'I wish I had your faith. I worked some ridiculously long hours at the time. What if I missed something?' Maggie swallowed.

'The CPS agreed that the evidence pointed at Raven. You didn't prosecute the case, the CPS did, so if there are any doubts, it should be them that needs to worry. If they had any questions about the evidence, it was down to them to get the answers.'

'When did you become so wise?' Maggie smiled.

He shrugged and gave Maggie's shoulder another reassuring squeeze, then walked back to his desk.

Maggie pulled up the details of her interview with Bill Raven on her computer and went through it thoroughly. One of Raven's points of appeal related to insisting he was pressured into answering. Maggie noted numerous breaks in the interviews where she had asked how he was doing and neither he nor his solicitor had made an objection. Maggie also came across a point where she had commented on his state of mind. Again, no objection or concern from his solicitor.

'Is that a smile I see on your face?' Nathan called out from his office.

'I've just read the statements and there's no way I was at fault here.' She bit her lip.

'Exactly. See what I mean, you're shit hot on details. Wish I could say the same about me!'

Maggie laughed. Nathan was a 'by the book' officer, but

his notes could do with some work. She frequently felt he was her moral compass. Whenever she was unsure of something, she often thought to herself *what would Nathan do?* Though she would never tell him that.

# Chapter 16

Maggie headed upstairs to meet with Donald Stanford from the CCRC. She wiped her hands on her trousers before knocking on the door. Her nerves were on the verge of exploding.

'Come in.' The deep bellowing voice did nothing to set her mind at ease.

'Hello, sir. DC Maggie Jamieson.' She held out her hand, waiting for him to shake it.

The man stood and extended his arm. 'Pleased to meet you. Can I call you Maggie? And please, call me Don. Make yourself comfortable.'

'Thank you.' She took a seat across from him.

'I take it you know why you're here? Your DI should have explained the process, that way we can just get on with things and I won't have to keep you from work.'

Maggie nodded.

'Good. I've read all the statements taken from the moment Bill Raven was arrested and subsequently charged. I have to say, you seem to be very detailed, Maggie.' He smiled smugly.

'Thank you. I try to ensure that all bases are covered.' Maggie forced herself to smile back.

'Yes, you do.'

'Is there a problem?' She was a bit surprised by the frown on his face.

'Err, well ...' He leaned forward. 'I wouldn't say a problem, but I did come across something of interest.' He cleared his throat. 'Mr Raven was questioned a few times, for long but manageable periods. You seem to take great care about his well-being, making sure he was comfortable.'

'Yes ...' Maggie felt a bead of sweat run down her spine.

'During the second interview,' he turned his laptop towards Maggie. Pointed to a paragraph. 'Could you read that section for me?'

Maggie leaned forward and scanned over the text, then nodded when she'd finished. *Damn!*

She'd wait to hear what he had to say before responding.

He spun the laptop towards himself. 'Mr Raven tells you that he stole a pig, killed it, collected its blood and brought it back to his flat. Did you investigate that claim further?'

Maggie swallowed. 'I'd have to check my notes, but as far as I can remember, we didn't. When Bill Raven was arrested, the duty GP was concerned that he may have been suffering from drug-induced psychosis. His behaviour was erratic. One moment he was lucid, the next he was rambling about nonsense. The GP gave him meds and said we could interview him. When he fed us that story about stealing a pig, we believed it was a psychotic episode. If you look at the transcript, he starts talking about blood dripping from the ceiling, the way it looked under the glare of the lights, what it felt like to walk barefooted through pools of blood. Then he gets increasingly distressed and starts making strange noises, shouting, grunting and squealing like a pig.' Maggie took a sip of water and tried not to think about those initial interviews and the long hours she spent with him, listening to his every word. 'I'm sure you've noted I stopped to ask him if he was OK. Our reason for not wasting time on pursuing that point was the fact that no one reported a missing or stolen pig. As you can see from the interview, Mr Raven mentioned the pig and then moved on to something else entirely.'

'Yes, he did. However, just prior to his appeal – around a month ago now – it seems further tests were undertaken, and that Mr Raven did indeed, at some point, have pig blood in his flat. You see, despite the initial tests finding nothing, a piece of wood was retested, and a small droplet had not been affected by the cleaning agent he had used.' He raised his eyebrows and continued. 'Not only that, but when we checked the records, a local farmer *had* reported the theft of a pig.' He stopped there and Maggie sat back in her chair.

There was a long moment of silence and Maggie felt her hand begin to tremble. 'With all due respect, sir, that offence would have been dealt with by another team. There was more than enough other circumstantial evidence that led us to believe Raven was guilty – his confession for one.'

'DC Jamieson ...' Maggie shifted uncomfortably in her seat as he leaned forward. 'Mr Raven alleges that he tried to tell you about the pig incident numerous times, to explain why there was blood in his flat, but you dismissed it. Because he was so tired, after hours of interrogation, he felt the only way that you would relent would be to admit to everything.'

Maggie let out a bitter laugh. Her hands balled into fists and she could feel the heat rise on her neck. 'The statements are all there. Are you insinuating that I doctored evidence? We wouldn't have known about the murder, or the missing women, if not for Mr Raven coming to the police station and confessing.'

'Please. Calm down.' He raised his hands in a patronizing manner. 'I'm not saying you doctored evidence at all. However, Mr Raven claims he told you things ... in private ...'

'I can assure you – if Mr Raven ever said anything to me in private, it would have been recorded in my notebook and then transferred onto the system. It just didn't happen.'

'Well, that's what we're here to—'

'I'm sorry,' Maggie cut him off. 'This is getting ridiculous. I thought this would be more objective but you're all playing into Raven's hands. He must be laughing in his cell right now. I'll admit, I underestimated him, but he *is* involved in these crimes.'

'Maggie, don't—'

'And if you don't start focusing, more people are going to die. I'm through answering your questions without my union representative.' Maggie stood and picked up her bag, then stalked from the room without another word.

# Chapter 17

Bill had heard voices for as long as he could remember. It had started with the weed, but he'd graduated to heroin and other class A drugs just before his eighteenth birthday. The whispers had only got worse. His parents were so fucked on crack that they barely noticed; his mother a schizo like him who never went to her appointments. Bill was raised off and on by his grandmother from the age of nine, and she was the only person who made him feel loved. He missed her home, his childhood home. So many happy memories, all lost when she had to sell it and move into a smaller place. She had died before any of the crimes came to light and he attended her funeral knowing that she would never learn of this period in his life. One day he would be free to leave flowers on her grave.

Whenever things had become too much, and the cravings returned, he thought about his waste-of-space mother. The beatings, the way she leaned close and screamed, spittle showering his face ...

*'So how has everything been since my last visit, Mrs Raven?'*

*The woman looked around the room and must have noticed the dirty walls and smell from the couch as she rubbed her nose.*

*'Just great. He's been a good boy, haven't you darlin'?' He flinched when she tried to ruffle his hair.*

*'Really? Only the school have been in touch …' The woman frowned as Bill crawled with embarrassment into the corner. 'One of his teachers told me that Bill smelled funny, like he never washed, and they had seen nasty bruises on his legs and arms.'*

*His mother glared at him before turning around and flashing a smile at the social worker. 'There must be some mistake.' She looked at the broken watch she wore on her wrist. 'Oh, is that the time? We'll have to reschedule as Billy has an appointment and we can't be late.' His mother pointed at the door.*

*The social worker left reluctantly, glancing back at Bill and smiling. 'I'll be back soon.'*

*All hell broke loose when his mother came back into the room.*

*'You little piece of shit. Are you trying to get me in trouble?' She poked him in his chest, but he didn't understand why. He never did.*

*'I … I didn't say anything, Mum … I swear.' He clenched his hands repeatedly.*

*'You fucking little liar. Dirty, piece of shit. I should throw you out with the rubbish. That's all you are, a piece of dirty trash. The rats can have you.' And then the blows came, raining down on him until his mother had exhausted herself and needed her drink or drugs, whatever she had in the house.*

*Dead Wrong*

*Bill dragged himself up the stairs, into his bedroom where he lay on the floor. Shivering cold. His mother never washed or changed the sheets on his bed. The smell of piss burned his nose.*

*One day she would see who the piece of trash was.*

# Chapter 18

Bill was looking forward to his meeting with the police today. He specifically requested DC Maggie Jamieson, someone he had spent a lot of time thinking about. She was a fascinating and worthy opponent and he couldn't wait to watch her squirm. He remembered their first interviews together and the way she tapped her pen when she was thinking about something. How she delicately placed her hair behind her ear. He smiled. He knew what perfume she liked to wear and what she smelt like after a day of interviews in a small prison cell. He rarely had any memorable visitors, or any real mental stimulation, so he was going to savour this.

He looked at his reflection in the stained mirror screwed to the wall. Ran his fingers through his hair with a smile. He wished he could have worn the new suit he had purchased for his court appearances. Smart, equal to his visitors. But he would have to make do with his new haircut and freshly shaven face. He wondered if Maggie would recognize him and be impressed by the effort he had made for her. Gone was the gaunt unhealthily thin heroin addict he had been. Time spent eating starchy prison food and going to the gym had soon sorted him out. He had taught himself to speak properly. Listening to his psychiatrist's posh accent. Watching television programmes and mimicking the voices. He liked the way he looked and sounded now and the way that people glanced at him. They respected him, feared him, maybe even admired him.

He gathered together his appeal paperwork, rehearsed his arguments again in his head. Imagined Maggie leaning closer across the table in the interview room. Thought about her begging him to drop his appeal, imagined reducing her to tears, ending her career. Walking to his bed, he crouched down and left the psychological reports under his pillow. If they wanted to look into the darkness of his mind, they'd have to do that homework themselves.

Bill enjoyed games, especially those that fucked with people's minds. He was smarter than them all and he'd had longer to prepare.

He sat crossed-legged on the floor, completely still, controlling his breathing as he waited for the guard to come and retrieve him. He stared up through the prison bars, biding his time until he was free again. Eventually the guard called his name and led him towards the legal visit area. As he passed the other inmates they hooted and banged against the bars of their cells. Those on the landing moved out of his way and lowered their gaze as he passed. The officer brought him to a room, and he sat at a table to wait for Maggie.

After a few moments, he saw her through the room's plexiglass windows and he took a sharp intake of breath. He hadn't realized what it would be like to see her after all this time. He felt himself stiffen.

Bill stood as the door opened. Electricity coursed through his veins. *Breathe, Billy-boy. You need to keep calm.* He took a deep breath and counted to ten as DC Jamieson entered the room.

'Where's DI Rutherford? Will she not be joining us?' He rubbed his hands together.

'The DI is on her way. Why don't you have a seat, Mr Raven.'

She seemed to be trying to hide her fear under a mask of confidence, but he could see right through it. Just like he could with the guards. He watched her closely as she pointed to the plastic water jug on the table.

'Would you like a drink?' She began to pour herself a cup and raised her eyebrows waiting for his answer. He thought he saw her lip twitch.

'Yes, please. The new medication I'm on can leave my mouth very dry.' He licked his lips slowly and she looked away. 'You're looking very thin these days, DC Jamieson. I hope this situation is not the cause.'

Maggie ignored the comment and sat down across from him. She took a pad and pen out of her pocket. She began to fidget with her notebook. Just as he was about to say something, DI Rutherford entered the room.

'Good morning, Mr Raven. Hello DC Jamieson. Shall we just get started? Where's your solicitor?' DI Rutherford walked quickly inside. Raven knew he would need to watch this one.

'As I'm helping you with your enquiries, and not being interrogated, I told him not to join us. I hope I'm not wrong.' Raven smiled. 'I'm happy to get started. I wouldn't want to keep you any longer than necessary. After all, you have a killer to catch, don't you?' He laughed.

The DI frowned.

'Something funny, Mr Raven? There are families who want answers and the public want to feel safe again. I don't think this is anything to smile about, do you?' The DI stared at him.

He folded his hands together before answering. 'Oh, it's no laughing matter. I'm so sorry if my facial expressions annoy you, but as I explained to your colleague earlier ...' He took a sip of water. 'Sometimes my medications can play havoc with my feelings. I was smiling at the fact that I'm here to help bring the real killer to justice.'

Maggie squinted and eyed him cautiously.

DI Rutherford leaned in. 'Mr Raven, you said you wanted to help us with our investigation, so do you have some information to pass on? I have to admit, I wasn't too keen on this meeting, but your solicitor convinced my DCI that this is an avenue we should explore. Please,' she stressed, 'do *not* waste our time.'

'No time will be wasted. I can assure you. I'm here to help – you know that – so should we start from the beginning?'

# Chapter 19

Maggie refused to look away from Raven; his soulless eyes would not haunt her this time. Her leg shook restlessly under the table. DI Rutherford would be pissed off if Maggie hijacked the interview.

'I've had a lot of time to clear my head in here,' Raven said, as his eyes flicked over Maggie. 'A lot of time to think. Can you imagine what it's like to be kept in a cell on your own for a crime you didn't commit? Ridiculed by the media and disowned by your friends?' He leaned back in his seat and spread his legs wide, that smile that Maggie hated creeping across his face. 'It's taken me this long to recover, for the medication to start working, for the heroin and crack cravings to die down. Only in the past month have I started to piece together what happened.'

Maggie clenched her fist under the table, but she couldn't stop herself from replying.

'Mr Raven,' Maggie spoke firmly, 'we won't ask you again. Rather than carry on with this ridiculous charade, do you have anything useful to share with us?'

'Is she always this rude, DI Rutherford?'

Maggie wanted to reach across and punch Raven in his smug face.

'DC Jamieson's question is a valid one, Mr Raven, so answer it.'

Maggie couldn't hide her pleasure at her superior's support.

He sneered. 'I do know things. Lots of things. When I was having my episodes, I believed that I was committing horrible crimes, that I was some sort of monster incapable of human empathy, that all I wanted to do was walk barefoot through pools of blood.' He caught Maggie's eye and smiled. 'But – I know now – that it wasn't me. Maybe I heard something, or witnessed something, and it traumatized me. That happens you know.'

Maggie leaned forward. She decided to take a different tack. 'Take your time. What horrible things do you remember?'

He rubbed his temples. 'It's difficult to recall. Do you think someone could have told me what they did? Confessed to me in secret. With all the drugs I was taking, maybe I just internalized their story?'

'I suppose that could be possible. Do you have any idea who might have told you such a story?'

'Wouldn't it be wonderful if I could remember, DC Jamieson? Wouldn't you just love to be able to reach back into your mind and remember everything in perfect detail? I could go back to the first time we met, that red jacket you were wearing, how you had just been for a haircut, how you had slept badly and forgotten to iron your shirt, how—'

'Enough.' DI Rutherford scowled. 'Stick to the question.'

Maggie swallowed and felt cold fear wash over her. He smiled and leaned back in his chair. 'I'm afraid I didn't commit these crimes. Surely even you can understand that Lorraine was murdered while I was in prison?'

Maggie's fear turned to anger, and she could no longer contain herself. 'Let's say I am buying this bullshit. If what you say is true – reach into those memories of yours and tell me how you knew Lorraine's name when you initially confessed.'

'Maybe I was hallucinating, or it came to me in a dream.' He smirked.

'And what makes you so sure these were hallucinations not memories? I think you're lying and you're doing a really shit job of it. I think you abducted those women, but you couldn't even finish the job. You had to get someone to take over and kill them for you.' Maggie grinned at him. 'Is that it? Is someone else pulling the strings here? Pulling *your* strings?'

Raven's hand clenched, and Rutherford kicked Maggie under the table.

'I'm sure that what DC Jamieson is trying to say,' Rutherford smiled, 'is how can we use your memories to find out the identity of the killer?'

Maggie could see a nerve twitching in Raven's neck.

'No one pulls my strings, DC Jamieson, not unless I want them to.' He smiled that sickly smile again. 'The problem is, and this must be such a drag, my solicitor has lodged a successful appeal and now the CCRC is going to be all over you. I thought I might help you find the killer, but now you've insulted me I'm not even sure I want to anymore. I think it's time you go, officers ...' He dismissed them with a flick of his hand, as if they were his servants.

Maggie laughed. 'Suit yourself, but don't get your hopes up about that appeal. I'll find out the truth.' She had made him show his true colours. The Raven she knew.

'Look, Mr Raven, I'm happy to continue this discussion one on one. DC Jamieson, can you please leave the room?'

Maggie wasn't at all surprised and knew she had crossed the line, but it was worth it. 'Yes, ma'am.' She collected her things and left the interview room. As she shut the door his cold laugh rang out and a shiver went up her spine.

Maggie headed down the corridor towards the exit, now even more determined to find the evidence she needed. She took her bag and phone from the locker and stopped in the bathroom on her way out, to scrub her hands with the cheap soap. She stared at her reflection in the mirror, rubbing her tired eyes.

Outside the prison, she paced up and down and waited for DI Rutherford to finish. She took out her phone and typed a number, stared at the screen for a few seconds before deleting it. After a moment, she sighed and rekeyed the number again, hit the call button and listened to the dial tone, waiting for the one person who may be able to help.

*'Doctor Moloney speaking.'*

'Kate!' Maggie felt something like relief. 'How are you?' She could almost hear the smile in Kate's voice.

*'Maggie! What a wonderful surprise. To what do I owe this pleasure?'*

'I need to pick your brains and I'm hoping you have some free time this week. I can even meet you after work if it's easier?'

*'Are you coming to the Domestic Abuse Forum on Friday?'*

'Yes.' Maggie had nearly forgotten. Despite no longer being a part of their team, her knowledge of the cases made her the perfect police representative at the monthly meetings.

*'Excellent. How about after that? We could grab a bite to eat?'*

'That's perfect.' Maggie ran a hand through her hair. 'And ... I'd appreciate it if you kept this between us for the time being.'

*'My lips are sealed.'*

'Looking forward to seeing you on Friday.' Maggie couldn't help but smile as she disconnected the call. Dr Moloney was not only intelligent; she was one of the few people whose company Maggie genuinely enjoyed. She texted DI Rutherford to let her know she was in the café across the street and mentally began to collate everything she would need to get from her computer for her meeting with Kate.

*We'll see who has the last laugh, Raven.*

# Chapter 20

He leaned across the table and smiled inwardly as he watched the DI slowly move back in her chair, listening to what he had to say, hanging on every word.

'OK, now let's take this back to the beginning. Where did all the blood come from in your flat when you were arrested?'

'This is all in the case records. But because you asked me so nicely, it was no secret that Lorraine would come over to my flat. Adrian and I were selling drugs to keep our own habit going. Accidents happen ... so it wouldn't be surprising to find someone else's blood in our flat. We used needles, burned shit, including ourselves. People fall over, bang their heads. Have you ever watched someone take heroin? Junkies are not the most coordinated.'

'I didn't ask about Lorraine's blood. I asked about the blood in your flat when it was searched. Let's try and keep to the current conversation or we'll end up going in circles and neither of us want to waste any more time, do we?'

He tutted. 'We both know that there was little to no evidence of human blood. I remember cleaning the flat – it was dirty, so dirty – normal bleach wasn't getting out all the stains. I used oxygen bleach, you see, because it cleans much better ...'

'Mr Raven, what could you possibly be cleaning with that much bleach?'

'The pig's blood. Have you even read the case files? Why won't you listen?'

'How did it get there?'

'When I killed the pig. I have a fascination with blood, always have. It's beautiful don't you think? It's clean, completely pure. I love the way it runs down a wall and collects in bright red pools. How thick it is sometimes, but how it can also flow like water.' He closed his eyes. 'But things got out of hand – what more can I say? Now who is going in circles? In fact, you're boring me. I'm done with this.'

Before DI Rutherford could continue, Bill stood and motioned to the guard. He laughed when he saw the expression on her face.

*If only she knew what really happened.*

# Chapter 21

## YVONNE

She trembled on the cold, thin mattress as she listened for footsteps above. She had to strain to hear anything with the cloth bag over her head and her ears covered. Yvonne had no idea now how long she had been in the cellar, but the drugs were wearing off and she was desperate for another hit. It was like she was coming up for air after swimming deep underwater, but the air was poisoned, and all she wanted to do was to take another dive. To forget how weak and starving she was. How her skin covered her bones like cling film, how every bone jutted out as she slowly wasted away.

She didn't remember much about the night this all began, but she'd spent a lot of time reliving it in technicolour detail. She had been invited to a party – a friend of a friend type of invite.

*What kind of party is this? Taxi paid for. Booze free. Gear free.*

Alarm bells should have rung there and then, but she was too set on getting off her face, so she ignored any niggles of doubt.

The rest of the night was a blur of booze, drugs, dancing and sex – in that order. Yvonne made the mistake of letting her guard down and when she woke up, she was here, head covered, ears taped over, hands and legs tied to the uncomfortable bed. What felt like days passed before anyone came down to see her. The *visits* were few and far between. She had learned to hold in her piss or risk wetting herself until the person came to change the bedpan or the rare moment she was taken to the toilet, and given the vile tasting water to drink along with a piece of bread. Sometimes she was lucky and got a slice of meat – rancid meat, but it still tasted better than nothing.

She shivered. How much time had passed since she was taken? She thought about her mum and her daughter, about whether they would remember her. Did they still live in the same house? Did they still wonder if she was alive?

Has her daughter lost her first tooth? She could remember her big smile and that curly hair. A tear trickled down her face. Maybe her own mother was relieved. She'd always told Yvonne how her child would be better off without a druggie as a mum.

*Enough.* She didn't want to think anymore.

She needed a hug. Even though she couldn't see, she still *looked* around, listening for the other women. They weren't allowed to speak, but sometimes when they were alone, they would mumble comforting noises to each other in the dark.

The women must be locked away in the bathroom. If they disobeyed their captor, one would be confined in there, chained to the radiator and gagged, forced to crouch on the tiled floor for days.

There was a loud bang from upstairs and her heart skipped a beat. *They're back.* Her body shook, not out of fear, but because she knew the person would have some gear and she could once again wrap herself up in a blanket of peace.

She heard the heavy dragging sound, the one that let her know someone would be coming down the stairs. Then the creak of the door and sweat started to run like a river on her neck in anticipation. Her eyes were covered, but she could still see shadows. She didn't speak. The last time she did, a sock or something similar had been rammed into her mouth and stuck in her throat.

With each step there was a bump on the stair, as if they were dragging something behind them. Out of the corner of her eye, Yvonne could see the figure bending over, placing things on the floor beside her cot. A shiver of fear crept along her spine.

The person never spoke, but sometimes there was that horrible smell, a strong cologne of some kind. She didn't know whether it was one person or many different people and that made her even more scared. Their captor would not connect with her on any level. Maybe that meant they would let her go. Her head told her not to get her hopes up, but her heart wanted to believe she still had a chance.

Their captor approached her, and she felt the cold, sharp edge of a knife against her throat. She knew that was the warning: *Do as you're told or you'll get hurt*. She had stopped fighting long ago.

Her hands were untied and then the figure moved to her legs. Once the restraints had been removed, the figure pulled her over to whatever had been spread across the floor. Her bones cracked. She was pushed down onto her knees and a nudge in the back told her she needed to lie forward. Her muscles spasmed as she was roughly flipped onto her back, too weak to care what would be happening next. A band was tied around her arm and, with a rush of relief, she felt the familiar prick of the needle as it pierced her skin.

*No matter what happens now, at least she would feel at peace.*

She didn't even feel the knife being driven into her chest or care when she heard the snipping sound as her arm was removed from her body.

# Chapter 22

DI Rutherford came racing out of her office like her arse was on fire. 'We have more body parts, people! Maggie, grab your coat – you're with me. The Moat Pub, in Newsoll.'

'What the hell? Is that one of those pubs by the canals?' DS Nathan Wright queried.

'Spot on. Maggie and I are heading out there now to speak with the responding officers. I'd like you and Bethany to start interviewing the witnesses.'

Maggie grabbed her coat and followed the DI to her car. 'Why now, guv?'

'What do you mean?' DI Rutherford unlocked the doors and adjusted the seat, then started the car and reversed out on to the road.

'Let's say Raven wasn't involved. Why would the killer all of a sudden start dropping body parts where they can be found?'

'That's what we're going to find out. If Raven's guilty, we need to prove it.' She overtook a car, her foot hard on the pedal. 'Even if this is all just a sick game, we need to keep talking to him, let him think we're on his side. He could slip up and we could learn something.'

Maggie frowned out of the window but stayed silent.

'I don't like it either, but he's all we've got. I need you to process whatever information he gives us. But be careful: Raven is highly manipulative and deceptive. We've been warned not to harass him, so play everything by the book.'

A knowing smile formed on Maggie's face and they lapsed into silence for the rest of the journey. When they arrived at the crime scene, they suited up. The pub backed on to the canal. The water was as black as ink. Buildings surrounded them, each one with a walkway separating them and allowing pedestrians to come through to stroll along the path that seemed to stretch for miles along the canal. She imagined this was where the killer came through to deposit the human remains. Maggie noticed the crime scene tent a few feet away from the pub's patio. She and Rutherford walked over to where the body parts were laid out, away from the eyes of nosy onlookers and the general public. The Home Office pathologist, Dr Fiona Blake, greeted them both with a smile.

'Good to have you back, Maggie.' She gestured at an open bin bag on the floor with several bloody lumps inside. A metallic smell teased its way up Maggie's nostrils. She rubbed her nose and listened as Dr Blake continued. 'Another arm and two legs; the legs have been cut into two pieces, so in total we have five separate pieces here. Look at the indentation on the wrist and ankles – look at the muscle deterioration – this person has been tied up for a significant period of time. The skin is translucent and tight. There is a combination of old and new track marks, so again, I'd say drugs were definitely a significant part of the captivity. I can't yet confirm whether the victim is male or female, or whether the different pieces come from the same body. However – speaking hypothetically and off the record – the feet do appear to have similarities and I would hazard a guess and say that at least *they* came from the same person. You'll have to wait until I get back to the lab for more details.'

'Thanks, Fiona. Do you think there is a possibility that the person or persons that these parts came from could still be alive?' DI Rutherford pointed at the bags on the ground.

The pathologist stared at them for a long moment. 'I'd say it is highly unlikely. They would need serious medical attention. If these parts came from more than one individual, there is a slight possibility, but unless the killer has medical knowledge, the victim would eventually bleed out.'

When Maggie had arrived at the scene, she had noticed a bloodstain a few feet away from the tent. There had also been a damp patch resembling a puddle of water nearby. 'Were the bags found in the canal, do we know?'

'They were found by that rubbish bin at the end of the canal. The owner of the pub spotted them this morning, as he was getting ready to open. Thought someone had tried to dump them in the canal. He picked them up and carried them to this location. When he felt their weight, he tore a small hole, looked inside and contacted the police. First responders confirmed it was an arm, cut from the elbow down. Forensics are still searching the surrounding area.'

'Right. Maggie, why don't you go and speak to the owner? I'm going to finish here and head back to base. Catch a lift with someone and we'll meet up later.'

Maggie wondered if the DI had just attended to babysit her. She looked across to the patio area and saw a man sitting engrossed in conversation with a few members of the public. He was pointing at the tent and gesticulating. Maggie took in his pale complexion, the beer belly and stained apron, the tea towel over his shoulder.

She walked towards him. 'Excuse me, sir,' Maggie called over. 'Can I have a word?'

He made his apologies and headed towards her. 'Hi, officer. I'm the owner of this pub and can't believe what I found! Is this part of that Chopper Investigation?' The landlord was animated, his eyes wide with shock.

'I'm not at liberty to confirm or deny that information, sir. I'd just like you to talk me through what happened.'

The landlord relayed a similar story to what Dr Blake had said. He confirmed that he was going to take the bags to the industrial bin at the side of the building, but when he felt how heavy they were he wanted to know what was inside.

'What time did you close last night?'

'Midnight. I didn't look around outside before I left, to be fair, I rarely do. I just did the basic clean up, locked the tills and headed home. I used the side door as it leads to the parking lot.'

'So, you didn't see or hear anything unusual?'

'Absolutely nothing.'

'Thanks for your time. Here's my card. If you do think of anything, or anyone mentions something to you, no matter how insignificant – give me a call.'

Maggie left the landlord to return to his audience.

She walked the scene and mentally took snapshots in her head of the area, looking for where the killer could have arrived, any CCTV cameras, dropped evidence or potential witnesses. To her left, she noticed a more secluded alley, a good entry point to the canal with no CCTV in the vicinity. The only camera seemed to be attached to the pub and over-looking the patio area. Maggie called Bethany over.

'Have you seen any other CCTV cameras?'

'Oddly – no. Just the one and I've asked the manager for access to it. Think someone should get on to the council. I mean, even without the body parts, this area is poorly lit and could become a crime hotspot.'

'To be honest, I'm surprised it's not already. I'm going to go back now and see if I can piece together some things.' When Raven had confessed to the crimes, he had told the police that he cut up his victims, wrapping the bodies in plastic and then disposing of their remains in various areas across Staffordshire, hence the media dubbing him The Chopper. Each crime scene so far resembled exactly how he had described it – this couldn't be a coincidence.

Maggie watched as Bethany walked over to speak with the remainder of the witnesses. She asked one of the forensics team to drop her back at the station.

*Is there a new Chopper at the cutting board?*

# Chapter 23

Dr Kate Moloney was looking forward to today's training course. She had a specific interest in geographical profiling and believed it would be beneficial to the work she did with the police. Thankfully, they agreed and funded her spot on the popular course.

Kate set off towards her kitchen for a caffeine fix. While she waited for the kettle to boil, she watched the morning news on her iPad. Bill Raven's face grinned back at her from most of the channels. It seemed to be an everyday occurrence, him complaining about being bullied or moaning about losing two years of his life. She wondered how Maggie was dealing with his appeal. The papers were taking every opportunity to slate Maggie and the police. What Raven and the news never seemed to touch upon was the fact that during those two years he addressed his alleged mental health issues and got clean from class A drugs. Kate figured he would get bail while the appeal was pending but there had been no movement on that front. Clean of substances, medicated and safe to be released into the community – all of which would surely get him released pending further enquiries.

She checked her phone. One missed call. She listened to the message and a smile crossed her face. It was looking like everything was confirmed for tomorrow. Kate texted a reply, gulped down her coffee and headed off to Stafford for her training event.

Kate arrived at Stafford Police HQ with a half hour to spare. She noticed a crowd by the Costa stand, just off to the left of the reception area. After signing herself in, she made her way over and said hello to a few familiar faces.

The conference rooms were on the upper level and overlooked the reception area. It was only one flight up, so she took the stairs. Arriving at her destination, she looked around to make sure she positioned herself close enough to hear the speaker, but not close enough to be singled out if they wanted any volunteers. She recognized a small number of people and smiled in their direction as she took her seat.

'Hi, is this seat taken?' The young man grinned as he waited for Kate to answer.

'It's all yours.' She moved her bag and coat from the chair.

'I'm Charlie. I work in forensics, the pathology department.' He held out his hand.

'Uh, nice to meet you. I'm Kate. I work in the domestic abuse unit, in Markston Police Station.'

'Oh! Are you Dr Moloney?' She nodded in reply. 'Wow. Great to meet you. I've heard all about you. I worked on the domestic abuse murders with your team awhile back.' He inched closer.

'Ah, OK! Sure, you did. Sorry for not recognizing you.' Kate shifted uncomfortably in her chair. 'Looks like we're about to get started, excuse me.' Kate turned her seat and faced the front of the room, hoping he wouldn't keep talking to her.

# Chapter 24

As Maggie headed to Markston Police Station for the Domestic Abuse Forum, she wondered when the report for the latest victim would arrive. The staff shortages in the forensics department were impacting the momentum of the case. She needed to talk to Kate and get her views on everything so far.

The meeting was being held in the large conference room on the top floor. It was a multi-agency meeting looking at victims and offenders of domestic abuse. The intention was to try and highlight the riskiest individuals and the plans that are or can be put in place to manage them. When she walked in the room, Maggie was greeted with a huge smile from Lucy and Mark. Claire Knight from Social Services, and a few other faces she didn't recognize were also present, but there was no sign of anyone from Probation. Maggie looked around the room for Kate, and noting she hadn't arrived, went and sat by Mark and Lucy.

They greeted each other and Maggie took out her notebook and pen.

Maggie couldn't believe the change in Lucy from only a

few months ago. Every time she saw her, she seemed to be growing in confidence.

'All good with me. Though I could've done without this meeting.' Mark rolled his eyes.

'Do we have an agenda for today?' Kate entered the room, and Mark waved at her. Maggie immediately felt herself blush. There were no free seats near them, so Kate sat opposite, and Maggie had to make sure she didn't stare too much.

The meeting had run over, so Maggie called Stafford Police Station and let DI Rutherford know that she would be heading straight home after her meeting with Kate.

'Thanks for letting me know. Can you ask Dr Moloney to look at the victimology of the cases, and include the other missing woman Raven confessed to killing?'

'Will do, ma'am. Anything else?'

'An updated profile of the killer would be helpful. But we don't have a budget for anything formal. I understand if Dr Moloney can't do this in her own time but would appreciate any insight she has to offer.'

'I'm pretty sure I can convince Dr Moloney to assist.' Maggie cringed at her choice of words. There was almost a flirty undertone to them, which she hoped her boss didn't catch.

'I'll leave it with you then. We'll catch up Monday, or earlier if needed. I am on call this weekend.'

Maggie ended the call and put her phone on silent, then headed down to the offices of the DAHU. Kate had informed her that she had a few things to deal with before she could head out.

*There were those butterflies again.* Maggie tapped on Kate's door. Looking up from her desk, Kate gestured her in.

'Have a seat. I won't be too long.' She pointed at the chair opposite her.

'No rush. Do you want a coffee or anything?' Maggie stood by the door while she waited for Kate to respond.

'Why don't we grab one around the corner at the café. I walk by it every morning and have yet to go in, but they have a gorgeous display of cake.'

'Perfect. Are you sure you're okay with this? I don't want to take up your personal time. I bet your partner wouldn't be too happy.' She could almost kick herself. That was not subtle at all.

'Nothing to fear there. Right, are you ready?'

Maggie paused with her hand on the door. Kate was usually a master at responding to her questions without giving a hint about whether she was in a relationship. So what had changed?

The two women left the police station and began to walk along the empty pavement. Maggie caught a flash of her reflection in the mirror of a shop and felt a sudden sense of unease, a feeling that they were no longer alone.

'Maggie, are you OK?' Kate had stopped walking.

Maggie ignored her. She was staring at the bushes further along the road, convinced she had seen a blur of movement, a glimpse of someone crouching there in the shadows. She gently grabbed Kate's arm. 'Hang on a second. Did you see someone in those bushes?'

Kate followed Maggie's pointing finger and squinted. 'Sorry, I don't see anything. What was it?'

'Probably nothing. Must be my eyes playing tricks on me. Stay here for a minute. I'm just going to have a quick look.' Maggie walked over to the row of bushes and spotted something on the ground. A cigarette butt – still burning. She stepped into the undergrowth and knelt down to check the ground. A series of muddy prints led out the back of the bushes, through a patch of scrubby woodland and into a park. There was no one in sight. Maggie fingered her belt nervously as she walked back to Kate.

'Has there been anything weird happening at the station lately?' She tried to keep her voice casual. 'I just found a half-lit cigarette butt on the ground – like someone was in those bushes and scarpered as soon as they saw us.'

Kate glanced up and down the street.

'Not that I'm aware of.' Quickly changing the subject, Kate smiled awkwardly. 'Let's go get that coffee, my mouth is so dry, I could use a drink.'

'OK.' As the pair walked away, Maggie glanced over her shoulder to take a final look at the bushes. She thought about the shadow sitting there smoking, waiting for them to leave.

# Chapter 25

Kate and Maggie walked through the damp evening air and into the coffee shop. Kate paused by the door to look back along the street, thinking about the shadow that might be following them. Relief washed over her. She was glad to not be going home just yet.

Helping Maggie and her team with building a profile of the killer and looking at the victimology was exactly what she needed, a bit of change from the same domestic-abuse-offender profiles. This was the kind of work that really interested her, and she contemplated asking Maggie whether there would be any budget for a consultant at the MOCD or even a permanent position within the team. But first ... cake.

Ordering herself a strong Americano with skimmed milk, she waited as Maggie asked for a cappuccino with an extra shot. Although Maggie turned down the offer of a dessert, Kate chose a large piece of carrot cake to go with her coffee and paid for both.

'Thanks, Kate. Next one is on me.'

'Now that's an offer I can't refuse!'

'Did you get all that information I sent?'

'I did, thanks. I don't really want to take my notes out here,' Kate looked around at the other patrons in the café, 'but I've made some points and can record on my phone so that I just need to send you the notes via email.' Kate placed her mobile on the table and set the app to record.

'Absolutely. Right then, what are your thoughts?' Maggie leaned forward.

'What do we already know about serial killers? Most are ordinary people, the typical "boy" next door, which is why I laugh when people describe them as monsters. Although their acts might be horrifying, they might not always be someone who immediately sends chills down our spine,' Kate explained.

'I get that. After interviewing so many killers over the years, even I'm still shocked at how *normal* some of them are.'

Kate watched as Maggie shifted in her seat. She saw a telling glint in her eye. Maggie's interest in her work always shone through.

Kate pulled her chair closer to Maggie and reciprocated the enthusiasm. 'Based on the information you've provided so far, I personally think killing ratifies an urge with this person, and it's not necessarily sexual but there will be some level of control present. I suspect this person comes from a broken home, probably had a dominant mother who may have had issues with substances and possibly mental health. Sadly, this appears to be the usual case. I also suspect that there was no father figure, or if there was one, he wasn't much of a role model. He may have been abusive also.'

Maggie nodded. 'Sounds so cliché, but I would have said the same thing.'

'For me, I think the dysfunctional childhood created a lack of empathy in the person you're looking for. They probably have little to no remorse, are charming and manipulative – which is how they lure their victims, and I get the feeling that there is a level of enjoyment from a need to punish. The victims would have felt at ease with their killer – perhaps he offered them something, like drugs, and invited them back to his home. We know both victims were drug addicts, and their need for heroin would outweigh any reluctance to go to a stranger's home. They may even have known him through other drug associates. Sound like any of your suspects?'

'Yeah. I can think of one in particular. Do you think we are looking for a psychopath?' Maggie frowned and stared at the floor.

'Psychopaths are rare, so I'm not saying this is definitely the case – but I am not ruling it out either. This person is luring women somehow, dismembering them and literally throwing away their limbs as if the women are rubbish themselves. Worthless.'

'I never thought of it that way.'

'You're looking at things from an evidential perspective. I'm interested in what the behaviour says about the person.'

'What else?'

'This individual doesn't fear consequences, but they do have a craving for stimulation – killing in this manner excites them on some level. Dumping the bags all across Staffordshire is risky. What if they are seen? That's the excitement – thrill-seeking at every opportunity. There might be some level of revenge being played out. Though I'm not sure about this, so let's park it for now. My concern is there was a gap from the time that Raven was convicted and sentenced to now. What was going on during those two years? Why now?'

'Could the killer have been in prison themselves? Maybe an illness, or maybe they were out of the country? Could it be more than one person? Sorry to bombard you with so many questions.' Maggie started to bite her nail.

'Those are all possibilities. We need to consider a pattern. Who are the missing women? I just did a course on geographical profiling. Maybe if we look at the victims, where they lived, worked or other common factors, we may be able to locate what is termed an *anchor point*. That's what could lead us directly to the killer or killers. I'll email these notes over to you before we head out.' Kate stopped the recording and fidgeted with her phone.

'We really need you on our team, or at the very least to some of the briefings.'

'Just say the word and I'm yours ...' Kate smiled.

# Chapter 26

Maggie and Kate had talked about the case until they both realized how late it was getting and decided to make a move. After saying their goodbyes, Maggie walked to Markston train station. Everything Kate had said made sense. DI Rutherford would certainly be pleased, and maybe Maggie could persuade Kate to join the murder team. Her profiling skills would add another level to the investigation.

It took Maggie just under an hour to get home with the train delays. The lights were out, so her brother was either asleep or working. She could never keep track of his shifts. She took care to be quiet when she opened the door, but when she saw the empty shoe rack, she knew he was at work. At least she wouldn't have to tiptoe around.

After changing into something more comfortable, Maggie made herself a cup of tea – anymore coffee would ruin her hopes of sleep. She flopped down onto the couch and thought back to her conversation with Kate. She knew it was wrong, but she fit Bill Raven into the profile Kate had made. Broken home, drug addict and abusive parents, check, check and check again.

Maybe Raven had abducted the women prior to his confession and then created some elaborate plan to get himself exonerated. His arrogance certainly would love the attention. She'd keep this thought to herself for the time being.

# Chapter 27

It had been a long and exhausting week and Kate was looking forward to a weekend of lazing about in her PJs and catching up on Netflix documentaries. It had been nice spending time with Maggie. Just before she had left the café, she had emailed Maggie the notes as promised and was not surprised to receive a text on the bus ride home.

***Thanks for the email. Do you have plans this weekend? Thought maybe we could continue what we started over some lunch – my treat? M x***

Kate didn't really want to go out and instead offered to make lunch for them both, explaining that it would be easier to talk through the complexities if they didn't have to watch their words. She was pleased to see Maggie was also keen on the idea and texted Maggie her address. Kate stopped by the late-night corner shop and picked up some bits for the lunch tomorrow. She also grabbed a few bottles of wine and some snacks – Maggie might want to stay and watch a movie.

Still feeling relatively new to the area, Kate kept to herself. She could count the number of close friends on one hand, but she liked it that way. Outside of work, Kate enjoyed Maggie's company as Maggie challenged her mentally, and also valued her contributions to cases – unlike some of her colleagues in the police force.

As she neared her building, she dug her hand into her bags to search for her keys. The weight of her shopping making the task more difficult. Unlocking and opening the entry door, she walked towards her flat. It was at times like this she was glad she lived on the ground floor.

Using her key, she opened her door and stepped over the post on the floor. She'd go through it after she set the bags in the kitchen and put away anything that needed to be refrigerated or frozen. She walked through to the dining area and dropped her bag. After putting on a T-shirt and her black stretchy jeans, she went back to the living room, collected the post, then placed it on the side table by her couch while she made herself a quick sandwich and grabbed a glass of wine.

Although Kate loved to cook, after work she generally just made something quick and easy – the weekends were when she made use of her culinary skills. Kate picked up the post and settled herself on the couch, turning on the television for a bit of background noise. She leafed through the letters, until she came to the black envelope. Handwritten in gold gel pen was her name:

*Dr Kate Moloney*

The handwriting was unusual. No stamp was on the envelope, so it must have been hand-delivered. She opened it hesitantly. There was a black card inside. A gold border edging the card and written in the same handwriting as the envelope were the words:

*You're just as beautiful in person as you are from afar. xx*

Not much creeped Kate out, but this did. Her hands shook. The paper smelt odd, and she dropped it onto the floor.

*What is that smell? An alarm rang in her mind. Was it formaldehyde? Chloroform?*

As she sat staring at the card by her foot, a shadow crossed the window. Kate rushed to the glass, pulling back the curtains, and looked up and down the street – but no one was there.

Returning to the couch, she picked up her wine and took a large gulp. Sitting back down, she flicked through the channels on her TV but couldn't focus. Her heart raced as she took another gulp of wine. Anxiety crept along her spine like a snake. Was the note from one of her colleagues, someone who had seen her do a talk or a lecture? How had they found her address? She finished her wine and gradually felt her heart rate return to normal. It was probably just a prank or some sad old loser who had read one of her papers. She checked her watch and laughed to herself. Overanalysing the situation. It had to be a joke. There was a programme on serial killers in half an hour that she had been looking forward to watching. It would take her mind off things. She opened the little drawer in the side table and pulled out her notebook and pen. She never knew what bit of information she may come across and always liked to be prepared.

Kate couldn't finish the sandwich she had made, despite her stomach growling. She left the half-eaten sandwich on the table. It was getting dark now, and she groaned because she had to move. Kate turned on the lamp on the side table and walked to the window.

As she closed her curtains, she thought she saw a flash of movement across the street, but told herself it was just a trick of her imagination.

# Chapter 28

When Maggie woke the next morning, she jumped in the shower, still feeling groggy. The water splashing against her face did the trick. After drying herself, she pulled on a pair of jeans, a white T-shirt and a green hoodie. She bounced down the stairs and hadn't expected to be greeted by her brother in the kitchen.

'You're up early, do you want a cup?' Maggie put the kettle on and grabbed the cannister filled with instant coffee.

'Haven't been to bed yet. Poured myself one, thanks.' He pointed to his mug.

'Thanks for printing off all the flyers about Scrappy. Did you get many up around the neighbourhood?'

'I put a few up – you'll see them about. You might want to pop into a few shops and see if they will put them in the windows.'

'I'll do that when I go out. I'm going over to Kate's for lunch later and then we're going to go through the cases.'

'Sounds like ... fun. Kate's that one you're always jabbering on about, isn't she?'

'Always jabbering on about? What do you mean? I've hardly

mentioned her.' Maggie tried to think back to what exactly she had told her brother.

'Calm down. I only meant that you've mentioned her a few times. Wasn't she new to the team?'

'Oh, yeah – right. She's been in Staffordshire about a year now. Kate has great insight into the criminal mind.'

'Oooh. Is there anything else I need to know about you two?'

'What do you mean? Kate and I are just friends.' Maggie glared at her brother.

Andy raised his hands and changed the subject quickly. 'That's cool. If you leave some of those flyers, I'll put some more around, but it's nearly been a week. Have you called the RSPCA or anything?'

'Not yet. Instead of doing the flyers, can you ring around the local vets and RSPCA – see if they know anything. Scrappy is chipped, so they should call me if they find him.'

'No harm in checking. I'll do that, then I am off to B&Q to get some bits – I thought I'd replace that shower of yours today and then go out with some guys from work for a few beers.'

'You're a diamond, Andy. Do you need any money?' Maggie headed into the living room for her wallet.

'Nah. I get a discount, and I still owe you, so you can knock that off my bill.'

'Deal. I'll just get these flyers up and then I'm heading over to Kate's. I'll leave the car for you and grab a taxi home.'

'Thanks, I'll see you tomorrow.' He winked at Maggie.

'I'll be home later this evening, Andy.'

'You might be, but I might get lucky.'

She laughed as she shrugged her coat on and headed out.

Maggie walked into town, putting up her flyers in shops that would let her and taping them on poles in places she thought people might stop to look. She had no idea what had happened to Scrappy, it was unusual for him to stay away this long. Taking a tissue out of her pocket, she tried not to think about anything bad happening to him and wiped her eyes.

She caught the train to Markston and walked the half hour to Kate's house. She could have caught a bus, but it was a nice day and she didn't want to be crammed in with a bunch of people for the sake of knocking ten minutes off her journey. Her stomach was doing flips the closer she got. *Get a grip, Maggie – focus on the work.*

Popping into the corner shop, she grabbed a bottle of wine, so as not to arrive empty-handed. It might also calm her rising anxiety.

*Snap out of it, Maggie. Pull up your big girl pants and quit acting like a muppet.*

The buzzer for Kate's flat was difficult to find so Maggie texted her, letting her know she was outside her building.

Kate opened the door and greeted her with a big smile 'Sorry. I should have said, mine is the top left for future reference.' She pointed at the letter K on the buzzer.

'Some detective I am.' Maggie held out the bottle of wine and Kate thanked her, gesturing to her to follow through the entry way and into her flat.

'So here we are. Make yourself comfortable. I hope you like chicken ...'

Maggie breathed in deeply. 'Wow. That smells delicious.' Taking off her shoes, Maggie sat in the large chair opposite the couch and placed her work bag down beside her.

From the kitchen, she heard Kate call, 'Would you like a coffee, or shall we be rebels and crack open the wine now – you didn't drive, did you?'

'I took the train, so let's be rebels.'

'This is why we're friends.' Kate laughed as she handed Maggie a glass of wine. 'Cheers.'

The pair chatted for a while about the domestic abuse unit, and Kate hinted that Mark and Lucy seemed to be getting close, but Lucy was reluctant to be anything more than a friend to Mark for the time being.

Maggie looked over at Kate. 'Lucy will want to get the SAFE haven up and running. She's still doing some agency work for Probation.'

Kate nodded. 'Yes. I think she still wants to keep her hand in that side of work.'

'I'm just pleased that everything is working out for her. I need to give her a call and meet up again.'

Kate stood and excused herself. Maggie took the time to look around. Like Kate herself, there was a mysterious feel to the place. Candles, dark walls and a beautiful fireplace – the mantle looked like it was hand-carved – with a gargoyle resting on a large pillar at each end. *Very Kate!* She spied a black envelope etched in gold on the side table with the words: 'You're just as beautiful' peeking from the corner. *So, she is seeing someone.*

'Do you want to make your way over to the table, I'll dish up lunch.' Kate called.

'Do you need a hand with anything? I feel bad having you do all the work.' Maggie waited at the table for Kate to answer before sitting down.

'Sure, it's not a bother. You're my guest – now have a seat. Should I just bring out the wine?'

'That sounds good.' Maggie was already feeling the soothing effects of the alcohol. She'd have to watch how much she drank as she didn't want to make an arse out of herself.

The food was delicious and Maggie quickly demolished everything in sight. 'Wow. That was impressive. I wish I'd worn my leggings now.' She laughed.

'Well if you're uncomfortable in your jeans, you can take them off—'

Maggie nearly choked on her wine.

'And borrow a pair of my leggings. Are you OK? You've gone all red in the face.' Kate's eyes widened.

'Sorry. The wine went down the wrong tube. Would you mind if I grabbed a glass of water?'

'You go into the living room and relax. I'll bring it in to you.' Kate topped up Maggie's wine then fetched the water.

Maggie returned to the big chair and opened her bag. 'Will I get the papers out and we can go through what we have so far?'

Kate placed a jug of iced water on the coffee table and two glasses. From under her arm, she pulled out another bottle of wine. 'Well, we can't just drink water, it's Saturday and you're not on call!'

'I like the way you think. Oh, I meant to say thanks for your notes. I spoke to my DI last night when I got home, and she was impressed. She wondered if you'd be interested in assisting – it would be a non-paying consultancy role, though, as we have no resources or funding at the moment.'

'I'd be more than happy to help out in my free time. Do you think there'd be any potential for a more permanent role in your department in the future?'

'I think if your contribution to this case helps us catch this bastard, my boss would be pursuing some funding from the PCC. She already hinted at it after I shared your thoughts with her.'

'Excellent. Right then, show me what you have.'

# Chapter 29

The table had been littered with notes by the time Maggie and Kate had finished last night. At eleven o'clock, Maggie had gathered her things together and called a taxi. There was something slightly off with Kate; she seemed quieter than usual. Maggie shrugged. Maybe she had something going on at work. She'd check with her the next time they spoke.

Andy wasn't home when she got in, which was just as well. After seeing the black card on Kate's side table, Maggie figured that pursuing anything with Kate would now be a lost cause. But today was not the time to dwell on those things; they had a killer to catch.

Maggie still hadn't been able to speak to Lorraine Rugman's sister. One of her neighbours had said the family were away on holiday, so she left a card asking them to get in contact on their return.

Meanwhile, Nathan had suggested they go back to the area where Lorraine's dismembered remains had been found to re-question the witnesses. Her head was banging; she popped two ibuprofen before following Nathan to the pool car.

'Do you think they'll give us anything valuable?' She raised her brows.

'Hard to tell, but we'll pursue all leads. We'll have to, with everyone looking over our shoulder.'

Maggie hoped that wasn't a dig at her. Nathan usually didn't make vague statements, but with his promotion, he would be looking at things from a different angle. She scratched her head. Their first stop was to re-interview the witness who found Lorraine's remains at the Blackwood Housing Estate.

The woman answered the door in her dressing gown, matching slippers and a big smile on her face. 'Oh hello, officers. Get yourselves in here.' She looked up and down the street then shut the door behind them and shot the bolt across. Maggie and Nathan managed to get their warrant cards out before she carried on. 'I was hoping you'd be back. I noticed a strange man hanging around not long after I found those body parts. I've called out to him a few times, but he just ran off. Do you think it was the killer? I've seen on TV that they often come back to the scene of the crime.' Looking around the room, Maggie spotted *Real Crime Magazines* on the table right next to an overflowing ashtray. The wallpaper had yellowed and was frayed in the corners.

Maggie was scribbling down the information and interrupted before the woman had a chance to carry on. 'What makes you think it was a stranger and not someone from the area?'

'Well he was just hanging about. Walking up and down the street, looking around like he was scoping out the area, his hood pulled up. Really shifty, you know. I didn't get a clear look at his face, but I'm pretty sure I would've recognized him if he lived around here.'

'Can you describe him to us. From what you saw?' Maggie leaned forward and raised her pen to her lip.

'I've only seen him around when it's dark. Sort of stocky, baseball cap, dressed in black. Quite a fast walker, like he was in a rush to get somewhere.'

'Did you notice if he came to the alley near your bin?' Nathan interjected.

'Funny you should say that, he stopped outside my alley and looked across the road at the neighbour's house, the big one over there.' She pointed out the window. 'But he rushed off when I shouted out to him. Is this some nut job? I mean, should I be worried? Do you think he'll come after me?'

'Take a deep breath. We don't think that'll happen, but we'd advise you not to approach this man and make sure your doors and windows are—'

'Then why do you think he was hanging around?'

'We understand why you are apprehensive. What you've been through recently has been quite traumatic. I'll leave you my card but if you do see this person again, call 999 or ring me.'

The woman exhaled. 'Thank you. Is that it? Or would you like a coffee?'

'No, we're fine. We'll be going now. If we do have any further questions, we'll be in touch. Thank you for your time.'

As they walked away, Nathan leaned into Maggie and whispered, 'What did you make of that?'

'I think she genuinely believes she saw something even if

her description of the guy was pretty vague. Let's talk to a few more people and see if they can corroborate what she says.'

They walked across the road to the tall house owned by the man who thought he had seen the killer. As they reached his door, Maggie noticed the curtain twitch and she tapped Nathan and pointed. 'Do you think he makes a hobby out of spying on his neighbours?'

Nathan grinned. Before Maggie had the chance to knock, the door opened.

'Oh, hello. I'm DC Jamieson and this is DS Wright.' They held out their warrant cards and the man bent over and examined them closely.

'I'm Steven.' He welcomed them in and led them through to his living room. 'Has there been a development in the case?' he asked as they took seats on the manky old sofas. The room was large but littered with old newspapers and boxes. There was a wedding photo on the wall; the man looked about thirty years younger, black hair instead of the silver top he was now sporting. Maggie guessed his wife must be deceased as the room didn't seem to have a feminine touch. The laptop on the table was open and Maggie caught a glimpse of news articles relating to The Chopper case.

Maggie looked at Nathan and grinned. *Another one who fancied themselves a detective.* 'No, sir. We just want to go over what you told our colleagues.'

'Well, I can't really tell you any more than what I've already said. Without my glasses, I didn't get a good look at him. Weeks have passed and my memory isn't what it used to be.' He tapped the side of his head.

'Has there been anything unusual in the area since then?' Maggie queried.

'Well, yes actually.' He leaned forward conspiratorially and pushed his glasses up his nose. I've been chatting to a few of the neighbours and apparently ...' the man paused and drew in a breath, 'there's been some guy hanging about.' He removed his glasses and crossed his arms.

'And have you seen this person yourself?' Maggie's eyes widened.

'Well, no. Can't say that I have, but I've been keeping a closer eye on the neighbourhood, making sure I have my glasses with me.' He tugged the chain around his neck where his glasses hung.

There was a loud thump in the other room and Nathan nearly jumped out of the chair he was in. 'What the heck was that?'

'Oh sorry. Probably just a box falling over.' The man shifted his eyes between Nathan and Maggie. 'I've been having a clear out, hence the mess in here and, knowing me, I didn't pile them up too securely.' His lip twitched.

'OK. Would you like any help with those boxes? We can give you a hand,' Nathan offered.

'No. No need for that. I wouldn't want to waste your time. You have more important things to do.'

There was a long pause as the man stared out of his window at the street. It was overcast, the threat of rain looming in the distance. Eventually he sighed. 'Well, if that's it, officers, I have an appointment I need to be getting to.' He looked at his watch.

Maggie took her card out of her pocket and handed it to the man. 'If you think of anything else, there's a number here you can call.'

He took the card out of her hand with another smile and led them both to the door. Before they could even say thank you, the door was shut, and Maggie thought she heard the chain lock being secured.

'Definitely something strange about that guy.' Nathan looked up at the house.

'I'll ask Bethany to do a check on him when we're in the office. No harm in being thorough.'

'Sounds good. Now let's finish up here and head back to the station.'

Maggie and Nathan canvassed the rest of the neighbours and only one other person had confirmed seeing the man-in-black. Looks like they may have a person of interest to pursue, but with so little information, their job wasn't going to be easy.

# Chapter 30

When they arrived at the office, Nathan went to update DI Rutherford on the latest information. A short while later, the pair returned and the DI asked Maggie about her conversation with Dr Moloney.

Maggie took a seat at her desk and turned to face Rutherford. She brought the DI up to speed on her conversation with Dr Moloney and mentioned the need to look into the victims' backgrounds, as well as geographical profiling. 'We should have Dr Moloney in for some of our briefings, too, especially now we may have a suspect. Did Nathan tell you about Steven?' DI Rutherford nodded. 'Something just didn't sit right after we spoke to him. I think we need to run some checks. He did confirm that there has been a suspicious man hanging around the area. Other than saying he was dressed in black though, we don't have much else to go on.'

DI Rutherford crossed her arms. 'I agree about Dr Moloney attending some briefings, Maggie, but you know we don't have a budget for anything more than that.'

'I mentioned that and Dr Moloney said she'd be happy to do it in her own time.'

'Sounds like we have a lot to take on board. Bethany, can you pin down exactly where the body parts were found? See if there are any common features, like the roads used and their vicinity to specific areas. Also, let's get a background check on the witness, Steven was it? Can you put that together for Nathan as soon as possible?'

'On it, guv.' Bethany turned back to her computer and focused on her tasks.

'Nathan and Maggie – go through all the persons of interest from the original case and this one. Do any of them fit the profile or match the man-in-black? Contact social care, check their backgrounds. Find out who was visiting Raven in prison and when he was at the secure hospital. Maybe they were feeding him information, though that's not a priority. Contact Dr Moloney, see how soon she can come in and go through this all in more detail, particularly the geographical profiling. Perhaps she can work with Bethany on that.'

The team dispersed and would be busy with the list of tasks. Maggie watched DI Rutherford rub her temples and could empathize. For every step forward they took, they seemed to take two steps back.

# Chapter 31

Maggie was still feeling the effects of the alcohol she had drunk over the weekend and had to drag herself back to her desk after speaking with Bethany.

Maggie contacted Lucy and asked for details on a reliable social care contact. The call was quick, and Lucy suggested she speak with Claire Knight about whether Raven's records were accessible.

'Good morning. Could I speak to Claire Knight please?' Maggie listened to some cheesy music as the administrator put her through to Claire.

*'Hello, Claire Knight speaking. How can I help you?'*

'Hi Claire. My name is DC Maggie Jamieson and—'

*'Oh hi. You were at the Domestic Abuse Forum on Friday, weren't you? Did you used to work with Lucy Sherwood?'*

'That's me. In fact, Lucy is the one who gave me your number. Sorry we didn't get to speak at the forum, but we have a difficult case going on at the minute.'

*'The one that's been all over the news, with that guy appealing his conviction?'*

'That's why I'm calling ...'

*'Ask away. I'll do what I can to help.'*

'What background knowledge of Bill Raven do you have?'

*'Gimme two secs to pull the information up on my computer. We probably have a lot more in archives though if he was in the system for some time … ah, found him. Looks like his grandmother was a registered foster carer, but only for a few years.'*

'Is that normal?'

*'It can be, but from what is noted here, there were allegations that your guy bullied some of the children in her care.'* Claire paused. *'There are not a lot of details about that here though, other than to say that the grandmother had been advised not to foster any further children and I guess she took that advice.'*

'Hmmm. Interesting. From what we know, his grandmother was very defensive when it came to Raven. Maybe she knew what he was really like and decided that it was best to let sleeping dogs lie.'

*'You could be right. Can you interview her and find out more?'*

'Unfortunately, no. She died before Raven went into prison, but we could ask her neighbours. Maybe some of them can shed more light on the happenings back then or the other kids he bullied. Can I get their names?'

*'Sorry. No can do. Data protection and all that.'*

'Even though we're in the middle of a murder investigation? Is there nothing you can do?'

*'Hands are tied here. Wish I could help but if you're talking to the neighbours …'*

Maggie would ask Nathan about seeing if Bethany could try to locate the other foster kids who Raven allegedly bullied.

'OK. Thanks for your help.'

The conversation between the two agencies lasted all of twenty minutes and, in the end, Maggie had learned that it might take some time to get the records, but from what Claire did have access to, it seemed that Raven had spent a brief spell in care before his grandmother took him in permanently; those records were archived and it would take time before Claire could access them, if she could get them at all.

Maggie was also keen to learn a bit more about Adrian Harrison, Raven's mysterious flatmate – his current location was unknown, and he had been dismissed as a person of interest in the original case. There had been no evidence to suggest he was in the flat at the time and this was corroborated by Raven himself. Adrian had been known to stay out for days, using and supplying at drug parties, and Sasha confirmed he was with her on the night in question. Bethany was still looking into him. And then of course, there was the man-in-black ... and Steven, the witness ... Could any of these be Raven's partner in crime?

# Chapter 32

Maggie sat in the office and thought about their ongoing search for Adrian Harrison. Witnesses in the original case files had also mentioned a female, presumably Sasha, who the police originally thought had been Harrison's girlfriend.

From what they knew so far, Adrian was more of a follower and also a loner; no one ever heard of him having a girlfriend, so why did she give him an alibi? The only females around him were those he was selling drugs to. When she was interviewed after Lorraine's remains were discovered, Sasha had admitted that Harrison was like a leech, stuck to her everywhere she went. Maybe she just felt sorry for him.

As she twirled a pen through her fingers, Maggie could see DI Rutherford pacing in her office. Another meeting had been arranged to speak to the press, though the team had limited information to share with the public.

Nathan approached her desk and smiled. 'Are you going to the press conference?'

'I definitely want to, but after the last one, I don't want my alleged incompetence to be questioned again. Anyway, DI Rutherford made it clear that I'm to keep in the shadows if I do attend.'

'I think we always knew that the papers would target you. I guess they still don't understand that all we do is charge and arrest, the CPS are the ones who make the decision to take a case to court ...'

'Yeah, I know. It doesn't really bother me anymore,' Maggie lied. 'I probably will go, are you going to be there?'

'Would you like me to hold your hand?'

She smacked his leg.

She was pleased that despite his promotion, they could still share a joke.

Maggie rolled her eyes. 'Are you going?'

'Yeah. Gimme a shout when you're ready.'

The press conference was on the ground floor. It was not a particularly sizable room, but it had those large, stand-up room dividers that Maggie could hide behind while still being able to hear what was happening.

Maggie looked over her notes from the last press conference and pulled up some of the articles on her computer. The various local newspapers tore her to shreds with headlines like 'Police Officer Jails Innocent Man' and her personal favourite: 'Stafford Police Officer Dismembers the Justice System'. It was no wonder that DI Rutherford had decided to take charge. Looking up from her desk, Maggie noticed the DI in a very animated phone conversation. She waved a bundle of papers in her free hand, her face strained.

DI Rutherford slammed the phone down. Maggie had to

stop herself from rushing into her office to find out what was happening.

She got up from her desk and stretched her legs. Her backside was numb from sitting in front of her computer for long periods without a break and she wanted a coffee. Grabbing the travel mug off her desk, she debated whether to ask if anyone else wanted one, then made her way to the tiny kitchenette. Her memory for drink orders was poor and she wasn't in the mood to listen to any complaints about her strong tea or mud-like coffee. Maggie never understood people who drank their tea so weak it looked like dishwater. As the kettle boiled, she stared out the window at the overcast sky and felt relieved that she had brought her umbrella that morning. The weather was a testament to her mood lately – dull and dreary. The door whooshed in the corridor and she poked her head around to see what was happening. DI Rutherford stomped her way towards the stairs, probably heading down to meet with the COMMS Officer before the press conference.

Maggie decided she would follow and rushed to make herself a strong cup of coffee, screwing the lid tight so that it didn't spill. She stopped when she heard her name being called.

'Maggie! Are you forgetting something?' Nathan jogged over and fell into step beside her.

'Bit early, aren't you?' Nathan glanced at his watch.

Maggie was silent for a moment. 'DI Rutherford just raced downstairs, so maybe some new information has come to light. I was planning on eavesdropping behind the room dividers while the guv spoke to the COMMS dept.' She laughed but it sounded forced. 'You're not going to grass on me, are you?'

'Let's go and see what's happening. We may have to wait outside though.'

Maggie smiled and hoped that wouldn't be the case. The pair made their way down the two flights of stairs. The temperature on the ground floor dropped and Maggie saw the goose bumps forming on her arms. They moved swiftly along the corridor towards the conference room, past the reception area full of journalists, a few of whom she recognized.

They stopped and Maggie peered through the small glass window on the door of the room. Her DI was deep in conversation with DCI Hastings and the COMMS Officer, no doubt planning what could and couldn't be said.

Maggie carefully pushed open the door and indicated to Nathan, who followed quietly behind. They made it to their designated spot behind the room dividers unnoticed. Maggie strained her neck to listen but couldn't make out DI Rutherford's low conversation with the DCI.

She checked the clock on the wall. As if on cue, the press shuffled into the room and began to set up. A few of them paced up and down like lions at feeding time. Maggie didn't envy her boss and only hoped that DCI Hastings would hide his real personality for the half hour conference and back up his team.

Nathan elbowed her ribs.

'Ow. What did you do that for?' she whispered.

'Isn't that Raven's solicitor?' Maggie followed Nathan's finger and sure enough, the slimy bastard who made it his business to discredit Maggie at every opportunity, was standing at the back of the room with a tape recorder.

Maggie's throat went dry. 'How the hell was he allowed in?' She watched as the DCI went over. Instead of asking him to leave, DCI Hastings shook his hand and smiled, as if the two were old friends. A large vein on Maggie's neck began to throb.

Nathan glowered at them, clearly furious for being left out of the loop.

DI Rutherford tapped the microphone and the room fell silent. She started the conference and almost immediately questions began pouring in from the journalists.

'Are the police any closer to identifying a suspect?' one reporter asked.

'We have identified a few persons of interest, but I can't say more than that at the moment.'

'So, you won't be making the same mistake as last time?' It was that arrogant female reporter from the previous press conference. Maggie tensed, but Nathan leaned closer and whispered, 'Take it easy.'

Taking deep breaths, Maggie waited for DI Rutherford to respond.

'Do I have to remind you that Mr Raven is still behind bars? I'll not repeat myself and I won't apologize for my team. There was a confession, evidence and detailed information presented to the Crown Prosecution Service. The decision was made to proceed to trial based on that. I'll not say anymore and if that is all you are here for, we'll not be liaising directly with the press in the future. Does anyone else have any questions about the current investigation?'

Maggie breathed a sigh of relief.

'DC Jamieson has been sighted on a few occasions visiting Mr Raven in custody. Isn't that inappropriate given the pending appeal? Or is there something else going on?' The reporter looked at Raven's solicitor and nodded.

Maggie's eyes widened. *What the hell?* Although there was nothing untoward happening, the meetings with Raven were confidential and weren't meant to be public knowledge. What was clear was the fact that the police were really no closer to arresting anyone and the press would soon pick that up. Now they were grasping at straws and it was at Maggie's expense.

'I'm not sure where you are getting your information from but since you've put it out there, the *police* are talking to Raven at *his* insistence, not just DC Jamieson.' DI Rutherford glared at Raven's solicitor while she continued. 'So any rumours you are about to spread can be put on hold unless it is your intention to upset the victims' families and report false information?'

The room fell silent and Maggie rubbed her neck.

'I thought so.' She gathered her notes. 'On that note, I'd like to thank *most* of you for your time and trust we've put that matter to rest. In future, you might be wise to check your sources before you ask a question.'

# Chapter 33

After the press conference, DI Rutherford called the team together in the open-plan office area. The room held four desks comfortably but had enough space for a few more should the team expand in the future. Nathan pulled up a chair next to Maggie.

DI Rutherford nodded at Maggie, returning her smile. Maggie mouthed 'thank you' and her shoulders relaxed.

'Afternoon everyone. Some of you will be aware of the press conference that was just held. I won't bore you with the details, but needless to say, once again we didn't come out in the best light.' She took a deep breath. 'Bethany can update you on the case. I need a moment to collect my thoughts.'

Maggie was a little surprised that Rutherford didn't ask her or Nathan to do that, but there was always a method to her boss's madness.

Bethany stood and faced the room. Her face paled as she started to speak. 'Well I've checked the CCTV and identified three white transit vans we might want to look at further.' She stammered on nervously. 'According to the date and time stamps on the video footage, all three were in the areas of each of the body dump sites around the time we are concerned with, but so far I've only identified two of the owners. I think the third used false plates.' She took a deep breath. 'That's all. I've emailed the details to Nathan.'

'Thanks.' Rutherford smiled at Bethany. 'Nathan, let me know when the van owners have been spoken to.' Nathan nodded. 'Right then,' Rutherford continued, 'I'll go and update DCI Hastings on this new development. Keep me posted, folks.'

There was a low murmur in the room as everyone went back to work. Maggie turned on her computer and stared at the floor while she waited for it to load up. She didn't notice Nathan standing in front of her until he cleared his throat.

'What's bugging you?' He stared at her intently.

'Nothing.'

'You were just staring at the floor like you were looking into an abyss. Either you have something churning in that head of yours and you're not sure what to make of it, or—'

'Or what?' She raised an eyebrow.

'Or something else is going on outside the office.'

Maggie laughed and shrugged her shoulders. 'Well, you can wipe that smirk off your face. I've been thinking about the white vans that Bethany mentioned. Has anyone checked out whether or not Adrian Harrison had a white van registered in his name?'

Nathan frowned at her for a moment.

'Look, I think we'd be foolish to ignore Raven's associates, just because we fear any repercussions. Like Rutherford said, Raven is still inside. You need to trust me. There are too many unanswered questions. If I can rule him out, I will. Plus who's to say that the man-in-black from the Blackwood Estate doesn't own a white van. He could have parked out of the sight of the CCTV cameras. Oh and another thing, why the hell was DCI Hastings so chummy with Raven's solicitor?'

'First, don't get yourself wound up over Hastings. I'm pretty sure Raven's solicitor is friendly with the superintendent. Hastings will just be playing the game but I'll see what I can find out from the guv. As for you, I'm just concerned. I don't want to see you going down the same slippery slope again, OK? You have to promise me that if things are becoming too much, you'll let me know. OK?'

'Why? So, you can take me off the case?'

'Not at all. But I don't want you to go off sick with stress either. And if I think things are getting on top of you, I will step in. I didn't want to mention anything earlier, but ...'

'But what?'

'Have you looked in the mirror lately? You're so pale you look like you should be in hospital and that shirt your wearing, it looks two sizes too big.'

She looked down at her top. 'I'm fine. I promise. This is a baggy top, that's all. I'm packing up, heading home and putting the case to rest for the evening.' She didn't meet his eye.

# Chapter 34

Kate had been a little surprised to receive the call from DI Rutherford. The DI had requested that Kate attend a briefing to discuss her knowledge of geographical profiling with the murder team. Apparently, Rutherford had cleared it with DI Calleja on the basis that the domestic abuse unit attended and it was used as a multi-agency training session. Whatever the reason or logic, Kate was just happy to be able to have input and hoped that it would be useful to the teams.

Stafford Police Station had a training room they could use, and Maggie had arranged to pick her up on the way to work. Kate was looking forward to seeing Kat, Mark and Pete in the same room with Maggie again. Lately Kate had been feeling on edge and nervous, particularly since the letter had arrived. Although she knew it was probably just a prank, she couldn't help thinking about it whenever she was at home alone in the evening. Being with the old gang might help her forget about it.

A car beeped outside and Kate looked out the window at Maggie waving from the vehicle. She quickly checked that the windows were locked, closed the curtains and left the house.

'Morning. Bit chilly today.' Kate zipped up her jacket when she opened the car door and jumped inside.

'I almost put my thermals on, then remembered this all-day training session – I'd probably melt.'

Kate laughed as she placed her bag on the floor in front of her. 'Are you looking forward to being reunited with the domestic abuse team?'

'Can't wait! It's just a shame that Lucy and the other agencies weren't included.'

'Agreed! But if I give you all enough information, you can pass it on. Train the trainer is what they call it. Just a cheap way to get the information out really. Perhaps you'll be doing events like this in the future.' Kate smiled to herself, and Maggie raised an eyebrow.

The rest of the scenic drive into Stafford was spent catching up on each other's lives. Kate managed to forget all about the creepy letter, and Maggie had basically been spending any free time trying to connect the dots on the recent murders.

Once at the police station, Maggie helped Kate get set up in the conference room.

'Thanks, Maggie. I thought I would email the presentation afterwards to everyone.'

'I'll let everyone know you're here.'

'Great.' Kate began to set up her PowerPoint presentation. She felt calm as the familiar faces started to shuffle their way into the room.

DI Rutherford stood at the front of the room and did the basic introductions before handing the floor over to Kate and leaving. 'Thank you, DI Rutherford and welcome all. I'm here to talk to you about geographical profiling. In the simplest of terms, this type of profiling uses the locations of connected crimes to *guess* where an offender's anchor point is. Sorry, I know I am using foreign terms, but I'll try and explain what I mean as I go.' Kate took a sip of water.

'The anchor point is either the offender's residence, place of employment or some other relevant connection to the person. Simply put, it's the place from which the offender leaves to commit a crime, returns to after committing a crime, or both. Geographical profiling is most often used for murder or rape cases, but is not exclusive to this.' The room was silent as everyone took notes.

Kate continued with her PowerPoint presentation and talked them through a few familiar patterns. PC Kat Everett raised her hand.

'I don't mean to sound thick, but don't we already *do* this stuff? We use maps, flag up significant places, try and link the patterns.'

'You're right, Kat – in a way. It's how you analyse the information. For instance, to create a profile you may need to know how far the offender is willing to travel to commit an offence and whether they had a vehicle, just walked or took a bus. They may want to separate their home life from their criminal life so use their workplace as the point from which they go out and offend.'

'So, if an offender doesn't have a vehicle, and has to rely on public transportation, the more restricted they will be in terms of where they'll offend. Is that what you mean?' Kat queried.

'That's exactly it. The person isn't going to travel miles by bus to locate their victim, and what if the body needs to be moved? A level of planning would be involved.' Kate paused. 'So, in your current case,' she looked at Nathan and Maggie, 'and the body parts.' She brought up a slide that showed a map of the area, with the dump sites flagged. 'Because the parts were found some distance apart, I think we can assume the killer has a vehicle and is familiar with many areas in Staffordshire.' Pulling out a clear acetate sheet, Kate held it up to the map on the screen. She connected the body dump sites and drew a circle in the middle of the map. Everyone leaned forward. 'This.' She tapped the screen. 'Is your anchor point. Do you have any persons of interest who reside or work in this area?'

Maggie looked at the map. *Crinlock Chase.* 'It doesn't sound familiar. But we'll have to do some digging and see.' She wrote the name on her notepad.

'Well ...' Kate noticed DI Rutherford return to the room and clapped her hands together louder than she had intended. She looked down at the last slide she had to deliver. 'I see we're nearly out of time so I'll make sure these arrive in your inboxes as soon as I can. Have a think about the anchor point I've identified and come back to me if you have any more questions.'

DI Rutherford smiled. 'I'd like to thank you, Dr Moloney, on behalf of my team and the domestic abuse unit. I'm sure you've left everyone with a lot of food for thought.'

'Thank you, DI Rutherford. It was my pleasure. Just before I go – I do have a contact within the geographical profiling team – so let me know if I can be of further assistance.'

Kate caught the glint in Maggie's eyes and knew that she would probably send her a page full of questions – they were so similar at times, it made her laugh. The more time she spent with Maggie and the murder team, the more she was interested in this aspect of police work. She was beginning to feel that she had offered all she could to the DAHU and with the secondment for her post finishing at the end of the year, a discussion with her boss and DI Rutherford might be on the cards soon.

# Chapter 35

Maggie's brain was buzzing as she walked out of the training room. The whole session was something that she planned on putting to use, especially now they had a specific area to focus on. Ahead of her, she noticed PC Kat Everett chatting with some officers.

'Kat! Sorry to just butt in. Do you have a few minutes?'

'Of course. I've been meaning to call you but with all the shit going on, I figured you'd be swamped.'

Maggie smiled. 'How's the detective training going?'

'Fuck me, it's hard – but I'm loving it. I'm on the fast track programme, so I only have a couple of weeks left.' Kat grinned.

'What happens when you finish?' Maggie moved to the side of the corridor to let people through.

'If you have a few minutes, we could grab a coffee and have a chat. My mouth is as dry as a fucking bone.'

'Sounds good. I noticed an empty office around the corner.' Calling past the kitchen to make coffee, the pair entered the room and made themselves comfortable. Maggie updated Kat on the situation at home with her brother.

'That's great to hear. It looks like you're a good influence on him.'

'I still have my moments, but I have to trust him. Otherwise I could push him into it, if you know what I mean?'

'Totally get that. Addiction is fucking so hard. How's it working with Kate again? I've been trying to pick her brains on your case, but she's shtum.' Maggie was pleased to hear that. With Kate not working officially for the murder team, any leaks to the press would first be attributed to her.

'She's a big help, but a lot of the stuff she has been doing has been effectively on her own personal time, so we don't want her to burn out either.'

'Burn out?' Kat laughed. 'She's a fucking machine. In fact, you two are like peas in a pod.'

'Well don't follow our example, or you'll burn out before you even start. Have you given any thought to where you want to be when you finish the training?'

'I'm really enjoying the domestic abuse team, but there are rumours that it might be disbanded. With all the cuts, I've heard it might merge with the Integrated Offender Management Team (IOM) – they work with the prolific burglars, robbers, and substance misusers. So, I might be placed in a field team until a DC post is available.'

Maggie looked at her watch.

'Shit. Look, I can't make any promises, but we might have a vacancy in the team. If you're up for it, I can put in a good word with my boss.'

'Fucking awesome! Thanks, it's been great to chat. I'll just go and see if Kate is ready – I told her I'd drive her back to Markston. Is it me, or does Kate seem a bit off lately?'

'Not sure what you mean. Funny how?'

Kat shook her head. 'I've probably got it totally wrong and seeing things that aren't there. I just notice her looking around all the time, and at work, she closes the door to her office now. Who knows? It's probably nothing.'

'Yeah, probably best to leave it. I'm sure Kate would say if something was bothering her.' Maggie would speak to her. 'Anyway, say hi to the rest of the team from me. And keep our conversation under wraps, OK? I don't want DI Calleja getting his shorts in a twist thinking I am trying to steal his team ... even if that's exactly what I'm doing.' Maggie winked.

They gave each other a brief hug and went their separate ways. Maggie smiled to herself. Working with Kat again would be fantastic, and if she could get Kate on board as well – they'd have one hell of a murder team in Staffordshire.

# Chapter 36

DI Abigail Rutherford looked up from her computer and noticed Maggie had returned to her desk. Rather than shouting into the office, she picked up her phone and dialled Maggie's extension, asking her to come into her office once she had a moment.

Abigail heard a tap on her door. 'Come in, have a seat. I just wanted to catch up on things. How did the training go? I only caught the end.'

'Actually, I think we've always done this sort of work but maybe not in as much detail, if you know what I mean.'

'Explain.' Abigail pushed her glasses on to the top of her head.

'Well, we already pin the locations of where the victims were discovered on the map. But we also need to include the victim's address or other details and then try and look for any patterns like a point that links everything together. When Kate did her presentation, she identified Crinlock Chase as the anchor point. She has some specific case examples she's emailing over with her presentation.'

'Hmmm. Did Kate include the details you mention to get that anchor thing, whatever you call it?'

'I can't recall. I'd have to look at it again.' Maggie looked at the ceiling.

'Do you think you'll be able to map something out with what we have so far?'

'I can do a basic outline. Given it is more analysis than just drawing a line between pins on a map, it might be worth having the profiling unit run their eyes over it.'

Rutherford nodded. 'Where are we at with the case? I'll be meeting with the COMMS Officer to share a release and keep the vultures at bay for a little while.'

DI Rutherford noticed Maggie clench her hands.

'Christ, why are we even speaking to the press so much and I don't know if Nathan spoke to you but is DCI Hastings in Raven's pocket now too?'

'What do you mean by that?'

'They just twist everything we have and I'm afraid we're still nowhere near identifying the killer, ma'am.'

'Not that, Hastings. What are you implying?'

'Oh, well he and Raven's solicitor looked like best buds. The smiles, handshakes, standing by him during the press conference. What the fu ...'

DI Rutherford held up her hand. 'Stop there. Be careful what you are saying, Maggie. Your mouth might get you in a lot of trouble. DCI Hastings was following orders. That's all. Showing that we are working together to draw a conclusion to these murders. I'll not hear anything more from you on that; instead, tell me what you have on people we should be interested in.'

Maggie cleared her throat. 'Well, the mysterious man-in-black from the Blackwood Estate and Adrian Harrison are both on our radar. Maybe we'll get lucky and one of them will have a link to Crinlock Chase. I'm also waiting to hear back from Bethany about that witness – Steven – and as for those drivers she's identified from the CCTV, they were spoken to, but each had a legitimate reason or tight alibi for being in the area.'

'So, I can tell the COMMS Officer that we have a few persons of interest and that we feel we are coming closer to an arrest?' DI Rutherford tilted her head.

'Erm. You definitely can say that, but it might be stretching the truth—'

'Let me worry about that. Where are we with the forensics?'

'We have a minute amount of trace evidence from the first crime scene. Cement and dirt collected from Lorraine Rugman's remains. Dr Blake says that a saw was used to dismember her. But with the second dump site, no trace evidence was found, and Dr Blake believes that both a garden lopper and a saw were used.'

'I've read all this in the pathologist's report, Maggie. I want to hear what you think.'

'Well, I think the victims have been held captive on minimum food and water. The women were virtually skeletons and not because they were decomposing. The recent track marks on the arms found also tells us that they were injected with something. Given all the victims were heroin users, I think that they were supplied the drugs to make them more compliant. Dr Blake is running some tests on the hair samples as it won't be in their blood system anymore. These women were probably targeted because of their lifestyle, looked on as easy prey. They were known to have previously disappeared for long periods of time, so their families were unlikely to report them missing.' Maggie took a breath and collected her thoughts. 'We need to find where they were held captive and also check the Missing Persons reports to see how many other women in the area, who were substance misusers, have gone missing. They all have some connection to Raven. He's the puppet master in all of this, but I still can't figure out how. If I could talk to him again, I might be able to trick him into giving something away. You know how arrogant he is, he's bound to want to talk to us.'

DI Rutherford stared at Maggie for a long moment, then leaned back in her chair and blew out an exasperated breath. 'All right, see if Nathan is free. Keep it professional. We've had enough complaints for one case. Got it?'

'Yes, ma'am.'

Rutherford ran her fingers through her hair and went back to her paperwork, leaving Maggie to make her own way out. Abigail knew that real life was not like books – cases weren't solved in a week or even a month sometimes – but she feared the worst. She trusted Maggie's instincts and would give her as much leeway as she possibly could – but she wouldn't let her cross the line. She could only hope that Maggie would find something before the shit hit the fan again.

# Chapter 37

The hot shower was exactly what Kate Moloney needed. She was exhausted and achy. Doing additional work for Maggie on the new case in her spare time, along with her regular workload, was really putting the pressure on her and she didn't want to let anyone down. Though she wasn't about to admit that out loud. And then there was that creepy note, the one she couldn't stop thinking about. It had lodged itself in her mind like the memory of a bad dream.

Kate turned off the shower and grabbed the towel off the heated rack. It hadn't just been the note, though. She'd been certain that someone had followed her home last night, a dark figure who kept just out of sight at the end of the road. Of course, it could all be just her overthinking things.

Instead of being pleased about a day off, Kate wished she was going in to work. Her DI insisted she use up her days or she would lose them. Her planned trip to Ireland to see her parents next month was also playing on her mind.

Towel drying her hair, Kate walked to her bedroom and then stopped dead in her tracks as she heard the postman push open the slot and slip her mail through the door. She looked down the hall at the doormat and her stomach dropped. This was the moment she had been dreading ever since that first letter appeared. Panic rose like an invisible hand gripping her throat.

Another letter. Black envelope. Gold writing. She shuddered.

She pulled on a pair of leggings and a black T-shirt and headed out of her room and into the corridor; the wood floor was cold beneath her feet. As she walked towards the front door, she saw it. The black envelope stood out like a beacon among the white envelopes on the doormat.

Her hands shook as she opened the letter.

*I miss you. I need you in my life. Forever. I'll make it happen. X*

What the hell does that mean? Kate was of two minds whether or not she needed to speak to the police. What if it was all a joke – she didn't want to expose herself to ridicule. She put the letter in her side table drawer.

She heard the familiar patter of padded feet as her overweight black cat Salem came over and squeezed his way in between her legs. 'You've decided to make an appearance then, have you? Do you want out?' As if he understood, Salem waddled over and sat in front of the big front window, looking up and waiting. 'All right then. But only for an hour.' Kate bent over and gave Salem a scratch on his head before she let him out. She took the opportunity to look up and down the street. Nothing out of place. No one lurking in the shadows. Kate closed the window and secured the latch.

She'd listen out for Salem; she wasn't going to leave her window open.

Kate headed to the kitchen to look for her mobile phone as that was the last place she remembered having it.

'There you are.' She picked up her phone and opened her contact list. Scrolling through, she found the number she was looking for and hit CONNECT. Straight to answerphone. *Damn.*

# Chapter 38

After closing the window beside her, Maggie shuffled the papers on her desk, looking for her notebook. A fly buzzed around her head and she swatted it away. Nathan had arranged another interview with Raven today, and she had prepared some questions.

She paced up and down as she waited for Nathan to finish talking with DI Rutherford. No doubt being instructed on what could or couldn't be asked. She wiped her clammy hands on her trousers and sat back down. She didn't know what to do with herself. When Nathan eventually left their boss's office, Maggie shot out of her chair.

'What's the rush? Don't you want to go through things first?'

'What do you mean? I've got some notes and questions that I'm hoping we can ask ...' She held out her notebook and watched as Nathan scanned the pages.

He nodded. 'Just make sure you don't add any additional ones, when we're in there, or DI Rutherford will eat us alive.'

'I've learned my lesson on that front.'

'Lead the way then.' He gestured towards the doorway.

Maggie walked briskly down the corridor, trying to keep her breathing in check. Bill Raven was being accompanied by a prison guard following another appearance in court. At least the courts were taking their time. Maggie was told that he had arrived with his solicitor fifteen minutes ago and had been escorted to one of the interview rooms. Her palms felt sweaty as they approached the room.

She slowed down to let Nathan catch up and barely listened to him waffle on about his wife and her desire to have kids. She knew he was trying to distract her and hoped she was smiling in all the right places. Arriving outside the interview room she stopped and took another deep breath.

'You ready?' Nathan lightly tapped on the door to let Raven and his solicitor know they were there. Someone shouted, 'Come in', and Nathan held the door open for her.

They walked inside. 'Good morning, Mr Raven, Mr Quinton. Thank you for joining us today. This is my—'

'Why do we always have to do these ridiculous introductions?' Raven interrupted. 'I think we all know each other. Before we start, I want it to be known that if this turns into a witch hunt, I'll be leaving. I'm not being put through that whole mess again.'

Maggie could feel his eyes bearing down on her.

'Mr Raven. I can assure you that we are only here to gain whatever information you have or can share with us.'

Raven coughed and cleared his throat. The sound grated on Maggie's ears.

'If at any time you feel uncomfortable or you want to stop, you just have to say the word. OK?'

Raven nodded.

'Right, I believe it was agreed that we could record this conversation?' Mr Quinton acknowledged Maggie with a curt nod, and Nathan turned on the recording device and went through the formalities.

Maggie opened her notebook and took out a pen. 'I wonder if you could share with me a bit about your background, more specifically, the time spent with your grandmother. I've had access to the old social care records, but I would prefer to hear it from you.'

'Well that is curious, DC Jamieson – why would you need to know that? Surely, I am not a suspect? I mean, how could I be?' He tugged at his standard issue prison track suit and smirked.

Maggie hoped her answer would throw him off-guard. 'Actually, it's because I would like to get to know you more. It may actually help your appeal – how you cooperated with us, were open and helped us develop a profile to show why you couldn't be the killer.' She ignored the glare from Nathan and waited for Raven's response.

Raven slid her a guarded look. 'How lovely. We'll do it your way for now. They are happy memories for me and I often think back to my time with my grandmother – God rest her soul. She took me in when no one else wanted me. Can you imagine not being loved by your parents? Beaten, yelled at, made to sleep in a pissed-soaked bed? I don't think you can, not with your upbringing. My grandmother was firm but fair. I had rules to follow, but a lot of time to myself. I didn't have many friends, you see. I remember she bought me a puppy once. *Someone else to love you*, she said. The most fragile little thing he was, so helpless. I named him Dog and spent all my time with him on the Chase. He didn't last long.'

'What do you mean he didn't last long?' Maggie swallowed.

'He just ... disappeared. My grandmother wasn't happy. Said I should have looked after him better.' Raven shrugged. 'But I did my best.' He stretched his arms and slouched in the chair.

'What can you tell us about Adrian Harrison? How did you meet him and how long did you know him?'

'I used to live with him. We shared a flat for about four years before my time in custody. I met Adrian through one of our associates.' He smiled. 'Well I guess it's no secret, both Adrian and I used drugs and occasionally sold them.'

'Did you always live at that flat?'

'I sometimes spent time at my grandmother's, when things got too much. But she got fed up of me always being off my head and told me not to visit her anymore unless I was clean. I've never lived anywhere else with Adrian. Just the address you have. He spent time with quite a few women. I mean, he was a bit of a mouse, but when he had gear, they flocked to him like flies on shit. He liked the attention, even if they were only using him.'

Maggie raised a brow. 'Do you know the names of these women or where we can find them?'

'Hmmm.' A smirk formed on his face 'Well, you know Lorraine and where you can find her. Then there is Yvonne, Sasha, Zoe and a few blokes. Adrian wasn't fussy who he hung about with. Why do you want to know so much about Adrian?'

DS Wright interjected. 'We're trying to form a bigger picture here. It may be that you have some information locked away, and we're hoping that talking about that time period may jar your memory.'

'I'm not sure there is anything more I can tell you ...' He titled his head for a moment and stared at Maggie. 'Though ... no, that's probably just a waste of time.'

'What? Anything could be helpful at this stage, Mr Raven.' Maggie cringed. She couldn't stand being so polite to this man.

'There was this guy, a real nasty piece of work. His name was ... hmm.' He tapped his finger to his lip. 'Jake or it might have been Jack; I can't recall. He was quite stocky, always wore a baseball cap, liked to dress in black. Don't they all?' He laughed at his own joke. 'This guy knew about this disused train-cargo carriage that was dumped in the middle of a field, a great rusted piece of metal full of rats and broken nails. We'd all go there and get messed up. Pissed, off our heads, whatever suited. Hundreds of people out there in the night with nothing to worry about. He lived in the same block of flats as Adrian and me. Like most of the crack heads to be fair. Not sure if the police ever spoke to him.'

Maggie swallowed and took a sip of water. 'Is there anything else you can tell us that will help us identify this man? Where in the building did he live?'

Maggie watched as Raven looked up to the ceiling, a smug little smile at the corner of his lips. The seconds passed and Maggie had to bite her lip to keep quiet.

'It's hard to remember anything from that time, like I said.

But he may have been one or two floors down from us. I'm afraid that is all I can tell you.'

'OK, that's helpful. Can we just go back to Adrian for a moment? Did you ever witness any odd behaviour from Adrian in the time you lived together?'

'Depends on what you mean by *odd*. I've seen his face blur and change into a mask, his feet melt into the floor. We took so many drugs, you see, I was never sure whether it was real.'

'What do you mean by that?'

'Well. Like the time we killed a pig. You know, when there was all that blood in our flat?'

'Yes, can you tell me a bit more about that?' Maggie tried to sound casual. Was he trying to lead the police on a wild goose chase?

'Actually, I'm sick of repeating that. It brings back bad memories.' Raven fidgeted in his seat, but it looked rehearsed to Maggie.

Maggie made note in her book to return to the subject. 'When was the last time you had any contact with Adrian or anyone from that time period?'

She watched as he scratched his head, straightened his hair. The seconds ticked by and she clenched her fists beneath the table.

'Well I'd heard that Adrian had followed some lass to Manchester or something. I don't really get any visitors, but you hear things in prison. He hasn't been in touch and I personally want nothing more to do with him.'

Maggie nodded. 'To your knowledge, does he have any connection to Manchester?'

'I don't know. I assume so, or maybe his female companion does. They probably had a massive drug debt and ran. Wouldn't surprise me.'

'Why wouldn't it surprise you? If Harrison was dealing, where was that money going?'

'Do I look like his fucking bookkeeper? How would I know – it was just a guess. You wanted an answer, I gave you one.'

Maggie paused. Raven was enjoying this. 'Can we just go back to the pig incident for a moment?' she asked, keeping her voice calm. 'I'm slightly confused. All along, you've said that *you* killed a pig and threw the blood around your flat. Today you mention Adrian. Which is it, Mr Raven?'

Raven's face went red and he tried to smile but it came out as a grimace. Nobody moved for a long moment. Raven's hands clenched. He coughed. 'I'm sorry, I think I misspoke earlier. I've been suffering from a nasty illness recently, you see, and I haven't been myself. These prisons are full of sickness. In fact,' he took a sip of water, 'I'm not feeling very well at all. I'd like to go back to the prison and lie down now.' He pushed his chair away from the table and stood.

'Well that's convenient ...' Maggie mumbled.

'Excuse me? Are you calling me a liar?' He leaned in closer and just for a moment Maggie saw a flash of genuine emotion cross his face for the first time during the interview. Anger.

'Not at all. I hope you feel better soon.' Maggie smirked as she watched him leave the room with his solicitor. The prison guard escorted them both out of the station.

'Are you trying to piss him off, Maggie? We need to keep him onside at the moment, you know that.'

'Yes, I do know that – I think we have him right where we want him ...'

# Chapter 39

'That doesn't mean a thing.' DI Rutherford paced back and forth by her desk at the station after listening to Maggie's update. 'He could easily argue he was getting confused, that he was ill or whatever he said to you. Finding inconsistencies is what we want, but pissing him off to the point that he shuts down, possibly closing all doors to solving these murders? Why do you continue to go against everything I say?' DI Rutherford raised her voice.

'But, ma'am. I'm just trying to show that something doesn't add up.'

'Tread carefully. What about this other man he mentioned? Do we have anything on him?' DI Rutherford rubbed her eyes.

'With just a first name, and he wasn't even sure of that – nothing yet but ...'

'It's late. You may as well call it a night; your shift is nearly over and there is nothing more for us to do today. You can pick this up in the morning.' Rutherford's lips pinched together.

'But—'

'Go, Maggie. I don't want to hear any more from you today.'

Maggie stomped out of DI Rutherford's office ignoring Nathan as he called to her. *He'll probably side with her anyway, now that he is a DS.* She picked up her coat and bag and headed home. *They'll see.*

An hour later and she felt calmer as she walked through her front door. She walked into her living room and slumped into the sofa.

The pressure of the case was beginning to take its toll on Maggie, and she tried hard to hide it from her colleagues. She had lost weight, had dark circles under her eyes and her hair was dry and brittle. She was run ragged on very little sleep, spending any spare moment trying to put the pieces together before they failed to save another victim.

Andy came in, stopped when he saw her. 'Are you okay? You've been so quiet lately; I was beginning to wonder if you moved out.' He frowned with concern and took a seat opposite her.

'Sorry, I've been a rubbish sister. This is what I'm like when I'm on a case.'

'You need to spend some time doing other things that don't include poring over notes and being glued to your laptop. When was the last time you went out and socialized? And before you start saying you go to the pub now and again, don't forget, I know that's with your police mates.'

Maggie laughed. 'You're right. I just don't seem to have the time. We need to solve these cases.'

'Well, taking a few hours off duty when you're actually *off* duty isn't going to make a blind bit of difference. So, get upstairs, get yourself ready and be back down here in an hour.'

'Is that an order?'

'You bet your arse it is. And I won't take no for an answer.'

Maggie dragged herself off the couch. She needed a break to clear her thoughts for a few hours. Heading upstairs, Maggie remembered the new top she still hadn't had an opportunity to wear. She wasn't much for flashy things, but when she saw the sheer black top with cut-off sleeves and glittery collar, she had to have it. She had the perfect pair of jeans and casual but classy low-heeled boots. Just getting ready to go out already had a positive effect on her mood.

An hour later, all glammed up, she came downstairs just in time to hear the taxi beep outside. Andy was already waiting in the hallway.

'What if I had taken longer than an hour?' She laughed at how presumptuous her brother had been.

'I know what you're like for one, and if you were any later, I'd make you pay the extra taxi fare.' He laughed and she playfully hit his arm.

Grabbing her red leather jacket and handbag, she was ready for the evening and even beginning to feel a bit excited. When they were finally settled in the taxi, Andy gave the driver the instruction to drop them off at an address in Birmingham.

'Birmingham? This is going to cost a fortune. Why don't we just go somewhere local? It's a school night after all.'

'Look, we never spend any real time together and you

deserve a proper night out. No offence, but the nightlight in Staffordshire can be dire at times.'

'It's not that bad. So where exactly are we going?'

'You'll see.'

When they arrived in Birmingham, Andy paid the taxi and helped Maggie out of the car. 'Right, follow me.'

It had been awhile since Maggie had been in the city and even longer since she had gone out socializing. Andy came to a standstill in front of a brightly lit building and smiled. 'OK, here we are.'

Maggie stopped dead in her tracks. 'What are we doing here?'

'I told you. You deserve a night out, have some fun, be yourself.'

'But this is a—' Maggie looked up at the sign above the door: The Rainbow Room.

'A bar, Maggie. A bar that plays music. That's all. No labels, right?' Andy winked.

It was at times like this that Maggie really loved her brother. She looped her arm in his and they walked into the bar ready to forget the case, the pressure and just escape for a few hours. And if she met someone, even better.

# Chapter 40

'Okay, people. Updates please.' DI Rutherford scowled around the room at the vacant faces. 'Bethany?'

'Well guv, I looked back over the available CCTV from the original offences when the women went missing, focusing on the last sightings. Lorraine Rugman was seen just outside the McDonald's in the town centre. Witnesses inside McDonald's said she had come in, had a coffee and talked to a man. All they could tell us was that he was quite bulky.'

Rutherford noticed Maggie was quiet, taking in the conversation between Bethany and herself.

'How do they remember her with a man?' The DI scratched her head.

'According to the notes, one of the staff was picking up rubbish, accidently brushed him with her arm, and heard him say *fuck off*. Lorraine looked embarrassed and mouthed sorry. Apparently, it stuck in her head as most people don't apologize.' Bethany stopped turning the pages in her notebook.

'Have we located the man?' Rutherford waited for a response.

'The man was found and spoken to at the time. There were

some notes that suggested he may be a person of interest, but when Bill Raven was arrested, it seemed that no one pursued it.'

'So, tell me we have arranged to speak with him.' Rutherford tapped her foot.

'Already done, ma'am. I'm afraid it's a dead end though. He admitted he used to contact Lorraine for sex. He didn't know the other missing women, and I believed him. He works as a lorry driver and his alibis check out for the dates in question.'

Maggie looked crestfallen. Abigail paced up and down at the front of the room. 'Excellent work, Bethany. Anything else?'

Bethany continued. 'There were no further sightings of Lorraine after this. She made a call from her mobile to a number which looks to be a burner phone and that was it.'

'What about the other missing women?'

'We're going through those details and should have something together by the end of the day. We're basing things at the moment on the names that Raven gave in his original interview: Yvonne Greene and Zoe Bridle.'

Maggie was fidgeting even more than usual. 'Do you have something to offer, Maggie?' Rutherford said.

'It's just so bloody frustrating.' She stomped her foot. 'It can't be a coincidence that the missing women are linked to Raven. What does the killer have to gain by this? Are they trying to mock the police or is this all just part of Raven's plans?'

'Let's look past the Raven connection for the time being. We have other persons of interest to follow up on. Soon Bethany will hopefully have some answers in relation to that man, Jack or Jake mentioned by Raven. Let's just refer to him as the J-man until we have a name. I know she's due to speak to Raven's previous landlord and also checking out that Steven fellow from the Blackwood Estate.' Rutherford raised her eyebrow and hoped that Maggie got the message.

There was a mumbling noise coming from the corner of the room which Abigail couldn't hear clearly. 'Do you have something else you want to share with the team, Maggie?'

'Nothing ma'am.' She sat back like a petulant child.

'Shall we have a word after this briefing?'

'Yes, ma'am.' Maggie blushed.

'We're waiting for forensics to come back with the confirmed ID from the latest victim. It may narrow things down significantly if we can get a connection to any of the missing women. Continue Bethany.'

'We're speaking with the missing women's families again to see if perhaps they can remember anything else of significance. Lorraine's sister is back from her holiday, and ready to speak with us. We do know that Lorraine was a class A drug user. I suspect that the other missing women are probably known to Probation or the drug and alcohol services.' Bethany closed her notebook.

'Has anyone contacted Probation yet?'

Nathan spoke from the back of the room. 'Yes, ma'am. Maggie and I are going to meet with Sarah Hardy after this and then we're going to speak with Lorraine's family.'

'Excellent. Anyone else have anything to add?' The room was silent. 'OK, you all know what you need to do, so get to it. And Maggie, can we have that word?'

# Chapter 41

'Have a seat, Maggie.' DI Rutherford was starting to feel like a broken record. 'I don't want to have to keep saying this to you, but you're on shaky ground here and if you continue to publicly pursue this line of enquiry, you'll leave me no choice but to remove you from the investigation.'

'I'm just saying what everyone is thinking.' Maggie pinched the bridge of her nose.

'No. You're not. That's the problem. What you *are* doing is muddying the waters. We have a killer out there and little to no solid leads. Bill Raven is in custody. He's no risk to the public. By continually focusing on him, you are going to confuse the team. What if we miss something important because you're inadvertently misguiding your colleagues?'

'I take on board what you're saying and although I'm not particularly happy with the threat of being removed from a case because I choose not to be blinded by Bill Raven's manipulation – I'll keep my thoughts to myself in future.'

'And watch that mouth. I'll have you for insubordination if you speak to me like that again.'

'Apologies, ma'am. It won't happen again.'

'Damn right. Now go and find out what you can from Probation. Make sure this is the last time we have this conversation. Are we clear?'

'Crystal, ma'am.'

DI Rutherford watched Maggie leave and took a large sip of water to get rid of the dryness in her mouth. The review commission were still keen to speak with Maggie and follow up with some details after their first meeting. Maggie was one of her best officers and Abigail was hoping that she would apply for the permanent sergeant's vacancy – but if she carried on like this, she would be lucky to remain a DC.

She wouldn't admit it out loud, but she also had concerns about Bill Raven and would keep a close eye on Maggie to make sure that no further mistakes were made in this case. The body parts were piling up and Abigail feared there were more to come.

# Chapter 42

She threw her pen on her desk and kicked the three-drawer cabinet which sat neatly beneath it.

'What's with the face?' Nathan walked towards her.

'It's the only one I have.' She growled back. This was a standard joke between the two of them, but Maggie was in no mood for their regular banter today.

'Okaaaay. I take it your meeting with the DI didn't go well?'

Maggie sighed. 'I don't know anymore. Maybe I just need to move on, but I have this horrible feeling. Every time I hear Raven's name or think of these cases, it boils my blood ...' She collapsed into her chair. 'He's a serial killer, Nathan. The CCRC are dead wrong if they think that Raven is innocent. And we might be the ones to hand them his ticket to freedom.'

'What happened to your *no labels* philosophy? We can't turn a blind eye to new evidence, Maggie, and what if we were the ones who got it wrong in the first place? Could you live with that?'

'Don't be that guy, Nathan.' She clenched her fists.

'What guy?'

'The prick DS who follows protocol so closely they fail to think outside the box.'

'Hey! That's uncalled for. Would you talk to any other DS like that?'

Maggie lowered her head and shook her arms. It wasn't Nathan's fault. 'You're right. I'm sorry. But I don't take back what I said.'

'Regardless of what my gut is or isn't telling me, our job right now is to follow the evidence. And it's telling me that there's a strong possibility that the J-man, or the guy from the Blackwood Estate could be responsible for the murders. What if they are one and the same?'

Maggie frowned at the wall for a moment and then shrugged. 'Who knows. So where do we go from here?'

'Well to put your mind at ease, why don't I get the prison to monitor all Raven's visitors and post? If anything flags up, at least we'll know about it. Bethany has already requested the CCTV from the prison to look at past visitors and she's located three disused freight cargo cars; I thought we could check those out after we chase up the other leads. The landlord from Raven's old address is trying to find the details of the J-man that Raven mentioned, but so far, it's a dead end.' Nathan smiled, and Maggie couldn't help but smile back.

'Sounds promising, and you're right ... monitoring Raven would ease my mind.'

'Did you just say I was right? Did anyone else hear that?' He looked around the room expectantly. Maggie burst out laughing.

'I don't know what you're talking about.' She winked. 'Probation first, then Lorraine's sister's house and the fields if there is time? Is that the plan?'

'Grab your bag and let's get a move on.'

# Chapter 43

They arrived at the Probation Office in Markston forty-five minutes later. The reception area was full for a Thursday and Maggie headed straight to the desk. 'Hi there. I'm DC Jamieson and this is my colleague, DS Wright. We're here to see Sarah Hardy.' The receptionist asked them to take a seat while she called through to Sarah. There were none free, and Maggie could almost feel the daggers being thrown their way from the offenders in the waiting room.

'Friendly crowd, eh?' Nathan whispered to Maggie. 'I can see two people who I've had previous dealings with, how about you?'

Maggie gave Nathan a look. 'Let's not give them a reason to kick off. We won't be welcome back if they do.'

The door clicked open and Sarah greeted them. 'Come through! Great to see you guys.'

Maggie and Nathan followed Sarah through the open-plan area and into the secure offices. They would be discussing Lorraine Rugman's details and didn't want anyone to overhear.

'Wow. Bit cramped in here?' Nathan laughed.

'Ha! It is, but we generally sit out in the open-plan area

where we also see the offenders. This is just the quiet space, if we need to focus on reports and stuff.'

'Well it's certainly different from how I remember Probation.' Nathan looked around and Maggie watched as he took in the white walls filled with motivational posters.

'With the separation of Probation into the public and private sectors, we got these fancy offices, more flexibility and secure laptops. Though I think most of us would rather they spent the money on staff instead of new chairs or worktops. Anyway, enough politics, would either of you like a drink before we start?' Sarah smiled.

Looking at Nathan, Maggie answered for the both of them. 'That would be great. Can we have coffee, please?'

As Sarah walked into the kitchenette behind them, Maggie and Nathan settled in the available chairs and took out their notepads. Sarah returned with the drinks and booted up her laptop.

'So, while we wait for this to wake up, what exactly are you looking for? Might save some time trawling through the records. Lorraine was well known to Probation due to her substance misuse and her past history as a sex worker.' Sarah typed in her password.

Maggie took a sip of her coffee. 'First we want to know if Lorraine mentioned any hassle or trouble from anyone?' Maggie looked at Sarah's screen.

'I've just pulled up her OASys, which is our Offender Assessment System. If she said anything that was of concern, it would have been noted there.' Sarah scrawled down to the bottom. 'Ah, here we go. She mentions being hassled for money a few times by someone named Adrian Harrison. Does that name ring a bell?'

Maggie and Nathan shared a look. 'Does she say anything else about Adrian or anyone for that matter?'

'She mentions that she thought someone was following her, but she doesn't give a name. This assessment was the last one we did before she disappeared, so I'll just check her case notes to see if she shared anything else. Given it was over two years ago, and her Probation Officer from that period has moved on, I can't ask them what they remember.' Sarah minimized the screen and opened Lorraine's case records. 'So, she told her officer that she thought Adrian Harrison might be watching her as she owed him money, but when she confronted him, he said she was being paranoid. Her officer noted in brackets *symptom of cannabis misuse* so I'm guessing that Lorraine was a poly drug user.'

Maggie tapped her pen on her notepad.

'Paranoia is common in cannabis and amphetamine users. Lorraine enjoyed both of those things, along with heroin and crack.' Sarah continued to scroll through the records. 'Here she mentions getting into an altercation with someone named Imran Patel. Doesn't look like the officer pushed her for any more information on this. Maybe you can see if the police were called?'

Maggie noted the second name and highlighted a PNC check for the relevant dates. 'Anything else you think might help?'

'Nothing more jumps out at me, but she was on a DRR – oh sorry that's a Community order for Drug Rehabilitation

Requirement – so you might want to see if her keyworker can add anything. They're based around the corner from Markston Police Station.' Sarah wrote down the keyworker's name and number, passing the information to Maggie. She radioed Bethany and asked her to follow up.

'You've been really helpful. Do you think you can just do a quick check for any relationships that we should know about?' Nathan interrupted.

'Sure thing.' Sarah paused as she searched the computer for the details requested. 'Looks like she was previously married, but the marriage was riddled with violence. It broke down ten years ago, so we won't have any information on that. Also notes she had a child but he was adopted out and she never maintained any contact with him. She was single at the time she was on probation. Ex-sex worker – she seemed to have stopped about five years before, though she might have still done it occasionally for drugs and not been caught.'

'Perfect. We'll head off now and leave you to get on. Would it be OK to call you if we have any further questions?' Maggie pocketed her notebook.

'Of course. Always happy to help when I can.'

# Chapter 44

The car ride to Lorraine's sister's house on the outskirts of Stafford was silent as they both gathered their thoughts. Bethany had come back to her and advised that after speaking to the keyworker over the phone, he had nothing of interest to share. Maggie sighed.

'What's the sister's name?' Nathan broke the silence as he stared ahead.

'Rachel Nichols. Early forties. No previous convictions.'

'Wonder how close they were? Do you remember anything about their relationship?'

'From what I can recall, she was trying to keep Lorraine on the straight and narrow. The rest of Lorraine's family had disowned her years before and had nothing to say. She stole from her family to fund her drug use.'

'Fucking hell. I bet they went through a lot.'

Maggie could see the hurt on Nathan's face. His younger sister had died of a drug overdose when he had first started in the police, so he knew first-hand what drugs could do to a family.

'You OK?' She reached across and squeezed his arm.

'Yeah, sorry.'

'We're almost there. That went quick!' The squeak in her voice was noticeable, though it made Nathan smile.

'Not as much traffic going this way. I can drop you back at the station after this, if you need to get your car and we'll call it a day.'

'I'm on the train these days.'

'Oh yeah, I forgot. I'll drop you home then.'

'It's well out of your way.'

'Not taking no for an answer. We're here.' Nathan indicated and pulled over beside the kerb outside Rachel's house.

They got out and walked up to the door in unison, the gravel path crunching beneath their feet. Maggie looked around as Nathan knocked. It was clear from the area that Rachel and her sister lived totally different lives.

Maggie wondered what had taken Lorraine down the path of drugs and sex work.

A teenaged girl opened the door and looked at them cautiously. 'Yes?'

'Hi. I'm DC Jamieson and this is my colleague, DS Wright. Is your mother in?'

In typical teenage fashion, the girl didn't respond and instead turned around and shouted down the hall. 'Mum. It's the police.' They watched her walk away, and Maggie looked at Nathan with a shrug. Within minutes, a woman appeared.

Rachel Nichols looked younger than her forty-some years. 'Sorry about my daughter. Come in, please. But take your shoes off – I've just had the carpets cleaned.'

Maggie gently shoved Nathan through the door and

followed. 'Of course, thank you for seeing us.' She slid her feet out of her shoes, grateful that there were no holes in her socks today and followed Rachel into the living room.

'Tea, coffee or water?'

'I'm actually OK.' Maggie looked at Nathan.

He held his hands up. 'Nothing for me either. Wouldn't want to keep you any later than necessary.'

'Shall we make a start then, Mrs Nichols?' Maggie sat down in a comfortable leather chair.

'Rachel. Please call me Rachel.'

'Thank you, Rachel. As you know, we've reopened the investigation into the murder of your sister, following a recent discovery.'

'Body parts … yes, I know. No need to sugar coat it. Lorraine was virtually dead before she was murdered. The drugs made sure of that.' Maggie could see a glisten in Rachel's eyes.

'We're so sorry for your loss, but yes, following the discovery of Lorraine's arm and torso we now want to speak to anyone who knew her. I'm sure this was all explained to you by the FLO, but we also believe she'd been held captive somewhere for a significant period of time before she was murdered.'

'Christ.' Rachel held her head in her hands. 'I really thought she had just buggered off somewhere before that guy confessed. And now … why didn't I try and find her? Report her missing …'

'You can't blame yourself. You did all you could.' Maggie tried to comfort her.

'I was in denial at the time. I've always felt guilty when it came to Lorraine. I owed her. It's because of me that she ended up the way she did.' The tears began to flow.

'What do you mean by that?' Maggie leaned forward.

'It's all my fault. She was just protecting me, because of what *he* did to her. She started using drugs and then selling her body to pay for them. I'd never give her money, and she never stole from me. I think she'd come to me when she just had enough. She would go cold turkey and I'd watch her suffer the withdrawal – sweats, shivering, throwing abuse at anyone who came near. Whenever she couldn't take it or the memories became too much, she left. Presumably to get drugs. And I would just wait until the next time she came. But one day, there was no next time.'

'Who hurt her? And how long were the gaps normally, between you seeing her?' Maggie had always suspected some form of abuse. Many of the women she came across, sex workers and drug users – or both – had been abused when they were young. It was their way of dealing with the pain. She waited for Rachel to respond.

'Our dad.' The words were spat out of Rachel's mouth and she went silent.

'What did your dad do?' Maggie handed Rachel a tissue.

'I'd rather not talk about it.'

'We understand, but it may give us more insight into Lorraine and who she may have ended up with.'

'I'm sorry, but I'm not going into details on what that pig of a man did.' Rachel started rocking and Maggie stayed quiet.

'OK. Did Lorraine tell anyone about the abuse?'

Rachel sniffed. 'When Lorraine told our mother what

happened, our dad left, and our mum moved on. No police involvement – everything was brushed under the carpet like it never happened. I've no idea where he is and I don't want to know. Lorraine usually contacted me every few months. When she didn't, I just buried my head in the sand. I was waiting for the police to come by and say she was found dead somewhere. Overdosed. Then I saw the news, when that guy had confessed to killing her and not knowing where the body was because he had dumped the bags all over Staffordshire. How the hell is he allowed to appeal? How could someone be so cruel and make something like that up? He *must* know something. You need to be speaking to him again, make sure he never gets released.'

Maggie looked at Nathan. 'We're looking into it. Was that your stepfather who attended court with you and your mum?'

'Yes. And before you ask, he never hurt us. He's a good man.'

'Did Lorraine ever tell you she was afraid of anyone? Or did she owe any money to anyone?'

'Ha! Lorraine owed money to loads of people. She was always in arguments with one person or another. Thankfully, she never brought any of that to my doorstep. My husband would be furious, and we tried to keep our daughter out of it, but she knew more than she let on. She was very close with Lorraine. She's still in counselling for her grief.'

'Did Lorraine mention any specific names?' Maggie coaxed.

'I'm sorry. I'm not trying to be difficult, but I can't remember yesterday let alone over two years ago. I gave all her stuff – mobile phones, a notebook with mainly gibberish and sketches in – to the police at the time.' She shook her head.

'OK. Nathan, do you have anything further to ask?' Maggie turned and faced him.

'Just one thing, did Lorraine ever mention an Adrian Harrison or Imran Patel to you?'

'Oh. Imran, she called him, Immie. Said he was her boyfriend, but I think he was her pimp. I remember him because she had known him for years, mentioned him a lot and her words were not always complimentary, if you know what I mean. But she always went back to him.' She shook her head. 'Wasn't the other guy something to do with Bill Raven? I thought they shared a flat. I remember him leering at us in court, always sat as close to Raven as he could get. Still gives me shivers. Why are you asking about him?' She wrung her hands together.

'We're trying to put together a more accurate picture of her last movements.'

'I see.' Rachel looked at the floor.

There was a long pause. 'I'll leave you my card.' Maggie placed it down on the coffee table in front of her. 'And if we need to clarify anything else or we have any new information, we'll be in contact.'

'Thank you.'

Maggie and Nathan followed Rachel out and shook her hand as they were leaving.

Back at the car, Maggie slumped back in her seat and stared at the house.

'We're going to have some late nights, Nathan.'

'Yeah. My feelings exactly.'

# Chapter 45

After Nathan dropped her home, Maggie poured herself a glass of white wine and set it on the coffee table. The house was quiet, the silence almost overwhelming. Maggie sat down and opened her laptop to find out more about Adrian Harrison.

Loads of newspaper articles appeared and she clicked in and out of each one, examining the content in the hopes that it might trigger something she could work with. Adrian Harrison was known to the police for drug use and dealing – cannabis mainly, although he was also convicted for small amounts of class A drugs. Interestingly, he had been found with quite a large stash of drugs and served a short prison sentence, eight months in total, immediately after Raven was sentenced. Maggie noted down some questions:

*Where did he serve his time?*

*When was he released?*

*Was or is he currently known to Probation?*

She was curious whether Kate's profile could add anything to the mix. Opening her email she scanned the document. Adrian was quite scrawny in stature. Looking at the picture included in the notes, he had a faraway look in his eyes, unkempt hair and a large gap in his front teeth. Kate surmised that Harrison formed attachments with people easily in the hopes of gaining approval. She based this on his risk-taking behaviour – trying to prove himself to those he looked up too. *Shame his choice in role models was less than desirable.* He was a heavy drug user, in and out of care from a young age and no siblings. Although he had spent short periods of time in custody, he didn't have any convictions for violence. Maggie closed the profile.

Putting the laptop aside, she eased back onto the couch and tucked up her feet under her. She raised the glass to her lips and took a sip of the wine, closing her eyes and thinking about all the information they had so far. Flashes of the locations where the body parts were found flickered behind her eyes. What tied those two areas together? A witness seeing a man dumping something in a neighbour's wheelie bin. Raven's face on-screen appealing his innocence. Raven in his cell while the murder was being committed.

She took another sip of wine and tried to stay focused. Too many questions. What she needed now was answers. Everything seemed to lead back to Raven, one way or another. But if that was where the evidence took her, she would have to follow it up – even if it meant going behind DI Rutherford's back and doing a little digging in her own time.

Kate might also be able to help, to come around on the weekend and go through her profile of Adrian Harrison and see if there were any other links that Maggie may have missed. She could include the J-man, and the Blackwood Estate man but with little more than a vague description for both, it was unlikely Kate would be able to add anything new on that front.

She heard the key in the lock and looked at the clock on the wall. Nearly 12.30 a.m. Where had the time gone? Her brother popped his head through the doorway.

'Hey, didn't think you'd still be up.'

'Yep.' She drained the last of her wine. 'Thinking about this case. You know what I'm like.'

He laughed. 'Only too well. Everything OK?'

It was her turn to laugh then. 'I need to learn how to shut off when I'm home.'

'You do. But I get it. In your job, there is no such thing as nine to five is there?'

'Do you want a beer? I'm going to have one more glass of wine before I hit my bed.' She got up and went to the kitchen.

'Sounds good. Has Scrappy been back?' He called in to her.

Back in the living room, she handed her brother a can of Carling and shook her head. 'I'm still hoping some lonely old woman has been feeding him. The house is so quiet and I miss his morning wake up meows. I think I better put up some more posters on the weekend.'

'I can help, I'm not back at work until Monday.'

'That would be a big help. I'll dig out another picture. Do you think you can print some more flyers tomorrow?'

'Of course. I know how much you miss him. I hear you in the mornings sometimes, tapping his can and calling out to him.'

Maggie's face flushed. She didn't like to admit to anyone

how much Scrappy had meant to her, especially after the Raven case, when the nightmares had her waking up in a cold sweat and Scrappy would come into her room and snuggle close.

She hated the memories that invaded her head when she closed her eyes. Raven's descriptions of being covered head to toe in blood. His voice, chronicling in gory detail how he chopped up the bodies, how the heads were the hardest to remove. How he had to place a foot on Lorraine's shoulder as he tugged her hair to pull the last remaining flesh that attached her neck to her shoulders. Cold, dead eyes glaring at her as he shared the thrill he got from dumping the bodies. Maggie cringed and returned to the conversation with her brother.

Shaking the impressions out of her head, she thought of Scrappy. 'He's a pain in the arse most of the time, but he has been great company over the years.'

'A partner would also do that, you know.' He raised his eyebrows.

She sighed. 'Not yet. Anyway, I'm far too busy ...'

He held his hands up in defeat. 'Message received.'

She changed the subject. 'So how's work been? Are you still thinking of leaving and starting up your own business?'

'Yes. But not until I've paid you back and have a little something saved up. Don't worry, I won't be doing anything on a whim. I feel like everything is beginning to turn around and I don't need to get involved in any of that shit I was doing before. You're a good influence, sis.'

Maggie smiled. 'Well I'm really proud of you. You've actually done a fantastic job around here, so I have no doubt that you could start up your own company.'

'Let's not get too ahead of ourselves just yet.' Andy smiled back.

Maggie yawned. 'Right. This wine has gone to my head and I am shattered. I'll try not to wake you in the morning. I want to get an early start.'

'Night then. I'll keep the noise to a minimum – I'm not really tired yet.'

'Night.' Maggie still needed to speak to their parents, but that could wait. She hoped they wouldn't accuse her of meddling.

# Chapter 46

The alarm clock blared as Maggie fumbled to hit snooze. *Just five more minutes …*

On the second round of annoying noises emanating from her alarm, Maggie stretched, dragging herself out of bed and into the shower. She wanted to be in early and check over some details before she and Nathan visited the fields later today.

The crisp morning air and the strong coffee that she held in her hands to keep warm helped keep her awake as she made the short train journey to Stafford. When she arrived at the office, she wasn't surprised to see that besides some maintenance people and the cleaners, she was the only person in. While she waited for her computer to wake itself up, Maggie sat back and reflected on the information that Rachel Nichols had shared with her and Nathan the previous afternoon. More specifically, the mention of Adrian Harrison. But he had a rock-solid alibi and absolutely no solid leads – what the hell are we missing?

She typed in her password and began her search. Records indicated that not only had Bill claimed he was alone in the flat at the time of the alleged killings, but he corroborated Adrian's alibi by providing the details to the police of a woman Adrian was with on the night. Maggie had spoken to the woman already but wondered if it might be worth another chat.

Adrian had told police that he spent a vast majority of his time at various people's homes. On the night in question, the woman he had been with had verified his account. She was also a drug user and they had no reason to doubt her. Everything checked out. According to the records, she had become verbally aggressive with the police for even insinuating that Adrian may have been with other women, but never claimed to be his girlfriend. She admitted to having casual sex with Adrian; however this wouldn't explain her anger at being called his girlfriend. She confirmed that Harrison was more of a sheep than a wolf; his other associates may hold the key.

Looking at PNC, Maggie saw that Adrian had been convicted of drug offences and imprisoned for nearly twelve months. He hadn't been in the same prison as Raven, but they had been locked away at the same time. *Damn.* But could this be the reason why no body parts turned up for nearly two years? And if this theory pans out – who else was involved, as the women would not have survived with no food or water for nearly twelve months?

With the length of sentence handed down, it was likely that Adrian would have been on some form of Probation supervision following release. The lights flickered above her and she looked up from the computer screen.

'Morning. You're in early.' DI Rutherford removed her coat.

Maggie smiled and gave a quick wave before returning to her work.

'Hmmmph. Be like that then.' Her boss smiled and went into her office.

Maggie took down the details of Adrian's last known address and telephone contact. Even though they couldn't locate him, someone in the area might be able to help. Looking at her list she marked the tasks for the day in the priority they would need to be undertaken. It was only 8.30 a.m. and would be too early to start contacting Probation. Other than the police, most agencies usually started work at 9 a.m. She noticed Nathan coming down the hall towards the office.

'Do you want a brew?' she said, noticing the dark circles under his eyes.

'Yes please. Make it strong, I spent half the night up with my missus.'

'Uh – too much information there. Spare me the details.'

He laughed. 'No, she has some sort of bug and I was up all night getting her water, a cool towel or holding her hair back while she puked her guts out.'

'I hope you haven't caught the bug and are now spreading it around the office like wildfire.' She covered her mouth and nose as she passed by him. In the kitchenette, she made two strong mugs of coffee and walked to Nathan's office.

'Why are you here so early?'

Placing the mug of coffee down on his desk, Maggie sat across from Nathan as she shared the information she had learned.

He took a sip of his coffee. 'It looks like Raven will have to be spoken to again.'

'Yeah. I'm not sure what the guv'll do. I hope I'm not frozen out of it though – I know people think I am obsessing about all this, but you have to admit that all roads keep pointing back to Raven.'

'But there is a gaping hole in your theory.'

Maggie smiled. 'Who was looking after the women when Harrison was imprisoned?' She tapped her pen on the desk.

'It would mean three people were involved in this and serial killers tend to work on their own.'

'But there are some exceptions. I was talking to Kate recently.' Nathan raised an eyebrow, but Maggie carried on. 'She mentioned a few cases where two or more people were involved. I'm hoping to convince DI Rutherford to let Kate come here again and talk a few things through with us. Share her thoughts and get her take on our persons of interest.'

'Another visit from the fabulous Dr Moloney.' Nathan made smooching noises and swivelled around in his chair.

Maggie slapped his knee. 'Kate and I are just friends. Strictly professional. For all I know, she could be married.'

'Haven't you asked her?'

'She never really speaks about anything in her personal life. She doesn't wear a wedding or engagement ring, and I don't even know if she would be interested in me.'

Nathan was one of the few people in Maggie's life who knew she was bisexual. He understood her internal struggle and never pushed her on the matter. It wasn't that Maggie was ashamed of her feelings; she just hated being labelled and the way some of her colleagues, whose sexuality was known, were treated. Despite publicly claiming to be a diverse police force, there were some very old school ideologies still floating about and Maggie had no interest in having to explain herself to anyone, especially those whose ignorance was embedded. She liked both men and women and it wasn't their sex that attracted them to her; it was their personality. She shouldn't have to justify those feelings to anyone.

'Why don't you just bite the bullet and ask her?'

'Because I'm afraid that if she is not interested or has a boyfriend, then not only will she feel uncomfortable around me, but it might ruin everything.'

'So what if she is straight and married? Big deal. She might be flattered for all you know. She might just not give a shit that you're bisexual, chalk it up to crossed wires and continue as normal. Not everything has to end in disaster.'

'Can we get back to focusing on work, please?' People were arriving into the office and Maggie wanted to end the conversation before rumours started flying around.

'There's the boss. Looks like she is heading to the briefing room. Shall I make us another cuppa, you gather your notes and I'll meet you in there? Just make sure you save me a seat. We'll head and check out the fields after that.'

# Chapter 47

Maggie and Nathan pulled up beside a rusting metal fence and killed the engine. The only sound was Nathan chewing gum and the engine cooling down. No new information had come to light during the latest briefing, so Maggie and Nathan had made a quick exit. They had driven to the locations of the empty freight cars. The first two had turned up nothing and Maggie couldn't hide her growing frustration. Now they were looking out at the final field and their last chance of catching a break.

'Fingers crossed.' Nathan opened the car door and stepped out.

Maggie rolled her eyes.

'You know what I mean.' Nathan tugged on the sleeves of his coat. 'Obviously not finding anything would be great but ...'

'No need to explain.' Maggie joined him outside the car.

He made his way to the boot and took out the bolt cutter. Maggie looked around the area. It was remote enough, swamped by long grass and tall trees and to the left, she saw a bus stop in the distance. 'Right, let's get this over with.'

They pushed their way through the tall grass towards the abandoned freight car. A crow circled above them, and Nathan kept stopping to listen for any sounds of someone in the area with them. As they drew closer, Maggie pulled out her baton and felt a prickle of fear run up her spine. The container was covered in brown rust, weeds grew around its base.

Nathan coughed and put a hand to his mouth. 'What's that smell?'

'I don't know.' Maggie stepped closer to examine the large padlock on the door of the car. She tried not to breathe through her nose. 'Think we should call this in. Your bolt cutter won't get through this. Something doesn't feel right.' Suddenly she felt very exposed out here in the field, as if someone was watching her from the nearby woodland.

'Call it in,' Nathan said. 'Get some backup and I'll go and check out the back on the container.' Nathan put down the bolt cutters and walked out of sight, as Maggie radioed the DI.

Finishing the call, Maggie walked around the container and found Nathan peering under the metal base. 'Spoke to the guv,' Maggie said. 'The field team should be here in twenty minutes. Have you found anything?'

'Nothing.' He stood up and ran a hand through his hair. 'This place gives me the creeps. There's no trodden-down grass, other than what we did today, so I assume this place hasn't been used for some time. That lock hasn't been touched either.'

As they waited for backup, Maggie kept staring across the long grass to the line of trees at the edge of the field, wondering if the killer was out there now watching them.

After about half an hour, the field team arrived with a bigger bolt cutter. Maggie held her breath as Nathan broke the lock. The door creaked open and a gut-wrenching stench washed out into the crowd of officers. Everyone gagged and retched. Maggie covered her mouth. The beam of her torch illuminated rows of rotten food. Shelving units lined the wall of the freight car.

'No one goes in or touches anything until CSI arrive.' Nathan called out.

'Why do we need CSI?' Maggie turned to face Nathan.

'Look over there'. He pointed his flashlight at a towel hanging off one of the shelving units.

It was covered in blood.

After about half an hour, the tech team arrived with a large bolt cutter. Maggie held her breath as Nathan broke the lock. The door creaked open and a gut-wrenching stench wafted out into the crowd of officers. Everyone gasped and retched. Maggie covered her mouth. The beam of her torch illuminated rows of rotten food. Shelving units lined the wall of the freight car.

"No one goes in or touches anything until CSI arrive," Nathan called out.

"Why do we need CSI?" Maggie turned to face Nathan.

"Look over there." He pointed his flashlight at a towel hanging off one of the shelving units.

It was covered in blood.

# Chapter 48

Dr Fiona Blake and her team arrived at the abandoned freight car within the hour. Maggie and her colleagues suited up and stepped inside. Lights had been rigged across the space and the smell was still unbearable.

'Well the good news is, there doesn't seem to be any body parts in here. Lesson being, tip-off from prisoners might not pan out.' Fiona winked.

Maggie felt a wave of relief tinged with regret that they were no closer to catching their man. 'What's the bad news?'

'Along with that bloody towel, there are some droplets of blood at the back. We'll get it checked, but in the meantime, I don't think there's anything left for you to do here. I'll send you my report when the team have processed everything.'

Maggie was shattered by the time they had arrived back at the office. She slumped at her desk and wrote out her report. The day had dragged, probably because of her early start. She had been hoping to catch a break in the investigation, but every time she had thought she had found something new, it always led to a dead end. She shouldn't have expected anything less from Raven; he was probably laughing at her from his cells as he gave them the run-around. She kicked the side of her desk. And of course, they played right into his hands.

'It's in!' Rutherford shouted from her office.

Maggie looked up and saw her DI waving a forensic report above her head. At this morning's briefing, DI Rutherford had advised the team that she was expecting the results from the second crime scene in soon.

'I'll email it across,' Rutherford said, then went back to her computer.

Maggie waited patiently for the details to arrive in her inbox. If the name matched another of Raven's victims, then Maggie would have a stronger argument for stopping his chance of bail.

The investigation would be much more difficult if Raven was released. Maggie was aware that a suspect can be tried again for the same offence only if there is 'new, compelling, reliable and substantial evidence' which had not been previously available.

When Maggie had discussed his appeal with the prosecution, they advised that there was every possibility that Raven could be let out on bail while his appeal was being heard. Time was not on their side.

Maggie's computer pinged, and she opened the email from DI Rutherford with the subject heading: 'Pathology Report 2'.

*Yes!* She smacked her desk and smiled to herself.

The second victim had been identified as Yvonne Green, a sex worker with class A dependency. Raven had named her as one of his victims. She scrolled through the documents on

Raven's conviction to try and get to the bottom of his relationship with Ms Greene.

'What are you looking at now?' Nathan tapped her shoulder and Maggie jumped.

'Shit!' She noticed the grin on his face.

'You've been awfully jumpy lately. I'll try to behave in future. Anyway, what's that you're looking at?'

'Haven't you checked your emails?'

'Nope. Just been speaking to the COMMS team. What's got you all excited?'

'Forensics are finally back. The second victim has been named as Yvonne Greene.'

'What? Isn't that the second person Raven named?'

'There's no way this is a coincidence. No friggin' way.'

What was left of the day was spent cross-referencing the details. When she looked up and noticed how dark it had got outside, she shut down her computer and called it a day.

# Chapter 49

Back at home, Maggie looked at the cat flap and willed Scrappy to burst through and curb the worry that had been shrouding her since he went missing. She still held out hope that he would soon get bored and decide to return. As she looked out into the garden, she noticed the open back gate.

*What the hell? Not again.*

She pulled on a pair of boots, grabbed her flashlight and headed down the makeshift pathway. The latch was up but not broken. She pushed the gate, looking left and right. She thought about Raven and how he had seemed to know so much about her. She made a note to buy a padlock when she was next in town.

'What are you doing down there?' Her brother called out from the back door.

'The gate was open again; did you forget to close it?'

'I haven't been out that way in ages.' He raised his palms. 'It wasn't me.'

Maggie's forehead creased.

'Sorry, I meant to put a padlock on it but completely forgot.

I'll make sure to do it this time.' He looked around and noticed one of the neighbours walking out into their garden. ''Scuse me,' he called. 'Don't s'pose you've seen anyone in our garden? The gate's open.'

The neighbour popped her head up over the fence. 'Did they leave the gate open? I told them to make sure they closed it once they were done.'

Maggie tilted her head, confused.

'Oh sorry, I thought you knew, they usually leave a card through the letterbox. Some fella came round to read the gas meter.' The lady pointed at the white box fixed to the house.

'What did he look like?' Maggie tried to keep her voice even.

'Had one of those caps on. Couldn't really see the face. He was quite stocky. Has something happened?'

Maggie laughed but it sounded forced. 'No. Everything's fine, thanks so much for letting me know.' The head dipped down and disappeared behind the fence as quickly as it had appeared. Maggie could hear her neighbour muttering to herself as she pottered about.

Andy went back inside now that the mystery of the open gate had been solved. But Maggie stayed outside and took a few deep breaths, the uneasy feeling in her stomach lingering. She made her way to the gas box and had a look around. The cobwebs on the box remain untouched – so no one had been to check the meter after all.

# Chapter 50

Maggie had spent her weekend engrossed in the case and getting very little sleep. With little overtime on offer, she had popped into the office to check details but mainly worked from her couch.

She hated Mondays and had just about made it into the office on time, but her colleagues didn't comment as she raced to her desk and set about organizing her tasks for the day.

'Hey Nathan, have the most recent crime scene photos come through? And have there been any updates from the freight cars?' Maggie sat down and looked over at the DS.

Nathan nodded. 'Emailing the photos to you now, but nothing back from the cars yet. Might be a few more days.' He walked over to her desk. Maggie opened her email and tapped her pen on her desk. When she heard the ping, she opened up the email. The first picture was a shot of the area where the various body parts had been located. Next, a severed arm. Yvonne Greene was just dumped like rubbish in the streets.

Nathan was standing beside her now, and looking over her shoulder he pointed at the screen. 'OK, Yvonne, another known drug user/sex worker, disappeared just shortly after Lorraine Rugman. Raven confessed to killing them both.'

'Fuck sake, Nathan. This can't be a coincidence.' She had wanted to say more but bit her lip. Everything was pointing to Raven but they didn't have one solid piece of forensic data to corroborate a link to him.

'For the time being, I'm just following the evidence and leaving my thoughts open.'

Maggie glared at him. She wanted to scream. 'What the hell, Nathan? Are you seriously on the fence here? Do you think I pushed Raven into confessing?'

'When did I say that? Don't put words into my mouth. Can we just focus on the crime scenes? Tell me what you see.'

Maggie shook her fists in frustration at how quickly Nathan had dismissed her just then, but she would choose her battles and, for now, Nathan was right – they needed to focus on the current victim.

'We have fresh track marks on the arms again, which means she was probably held somewhere before she was murdered. There are no defence wounds on the hand and pathology confirms there wasn't any grit under her nails, so little trace evidence to tell us anything. The report also highlights some sores on the back of the arm, just below the elbow and suggests these are from long periods of lying on her back. And look at those marks on the wrist. According to this, they match the ones that were found on Lorraine.' Maggie moved on to the next photo.

She stared at the screen and could feel Nathan's breath on her neck. She pushed him back with her hand. 'I can't think with you literally breathing down my neck.'

He pulled up a chair and sat down beside her. 'Better?'

She gave him a smug smile and nodded. 'Why would they be drugged? So they didn't fight back? I mean, being tied down would stop them from escaping, so why the drugs? Or could it be because the person who took them is afraid they might overpower him? I presume that there would be bedsores all over the body, like the one found on Yvonne's arm, but without the torso, this would only be conjecture.'

Nathan nodded. 'Makes sense. The lack of defence wounds would definitely suggest something along those lines. Like you say, without the rest of the body, anything else is just supposition. Do you think the killer might have taken out his anger on her torso or head? Maybe that's why those haven't been found.' Nathan flicked his eyes from Maggie to the screen.

'Hmmm. My gut tells me that the killer is just giving us enough to identify the victim but not enough to let the families get any peace. These women mean nothing to the killer.' Maggie scrolled through the next few pictures. There was little more than random body parts and the area where they had been left. Just as she was wishing for a different perspective, an email from Kate arrived in her inbox.

'What do we have here?' Maggie opened the email as Nathan moved closer to see. 'Shall I fill you in on a few things that Kate and I have been mulling over?' She laughed as Nathan's eyebrows lifted in a *what-do-you-think?* look.

'OK, well you need to keep an open mind. I talked to Kate about what the review commission were insinuating ...'

'Is this about the false confession or is there something you've been keeping from me?' Nathan's eyes widened.

'I wouldn't keep anything from you. It is about the possibility that I may have elicited what they are calling an internalized false confession.' Maggie crossed her arms waiting for Nathan to answer.

Nathan pushed his chair back. 'Internalized? What are you talking about? I don't think anyone has ever said you forced anything ...'

'Thanks. They think that because of how I interrogated him, he may actually have believed that what he was telling me is true. After my initial fury, I thought it was important for me to reflect back on the possibility. It would kill me, Nathan, if I believed for one second that I put an innocent individual behind bars.'

He touched her shoulder and gave her a reassuring squeeze. 'Why don't we get everyone together? That will save you repeating yourself. I'll gather the troops and meet you in the briefing room in fifteen minutes.'

'Sounds good.' Maggie tapped her desk with the pen. She stared at the computer screen and scrolled through the information that Kate had emailed over ... and there it was.

*Bingo! Dr Moloney, you are a genius.*

# Chapter 51

Maggie was tired but dragged herself to the office printer. She hoped to shake the feeling of defeat that had been hanging over her like a cloud. Her interviews with Bill Raven so far made her even more convinced that he had been playing a deadly game of cat and mouse. What he failed to consider was that Maggie hated to lose, and Dr Moloney had just provided her with some hope.

The corridor was busy, and Maggie squeezed her way through the collection of bodies, down the hall to the briefing room. Nathan called her over and pointed to a chair at the front of the room. Maggie hated having all eyes on her, but she sat and hooked her feet around the chair legs as she waited for the remainder of her colleagues to take a seat.

Nathan did a brief run-down on everything they had so far in relation to the two victims, though Maggie could tell from the look on her colleagues' faces that they had all this memorized. 'Can we just take a bit of time now to listen to what Maggie is going to share with you all. Over to you.' Nathan took his seat.

'Thanks, boss.' Maggie stood up and went to the front of

the room. 'I've been speaking with Dr Kate Moloney about this case after DI Rutherford and myself felt we needed a stronger profile on the killer. With Raven's bail hearing now imminent, we're running out of time.' Everyone in the room was nodding, while DI Rutherford stood in the back, staring out the door with a look of embarrassment.

'The review commission insinuated that I had elicited a false confession from Raven.' Maggie hoped she had hidden her feelings of disgust at the allegation. 'Kate and I watched the video interview repeatedly and took notes at the various points where the review commission has suggested that Raven's responses to my questions shows his incapacity.'

You could have heard a pin drop. 'Kate looked up some case examples of false confessions that showed how the interviewer repeatedly questioned people to try and draw out their true behaviour. The findings indicated that a person would not be able to keep track of all their *symptoms* and maybe even grow a bit weary of the whole thing, thereby letting their guard down.' As she was speaking, Maggie was visualizing her interview with Raven in her head, trying to pinpoint places where this could be put to the test.

'What the offender does after an interview should also be considered. Fakers might pretend to be confused throughout an interview, like Raven, but then have normal conversations with cell mates.'

Bethany jumped in with a question 'How would we know how Raven behaved after your interviews with him a few years ago?'

'Well, we wouldn't – because it wasn't something we had

even considered back then. But as we interview him now, we need to catch him out on things from the past interviews. For instance, he has already changed his pig story on two or more occasions.'

'Have we asked the prison officers to monitor his behaviour?' Bethany leaned forward.

'Yes. Interestingly, from what I've been told, and what I've seen when visiting Raven myself, the prison guards are very wary of him. They seem to do the bare minimum to ensure he gets from point A to point B, for instance. But there was also something else Kate said that piqued my interest. The crime itself.' Maggie paused. 'You see, no matter how delusional a person pretends to be, the crime scene must fit the hallucination they describe. Conveniently mixing delusions with reality is another red flag. As you will see, most of the behaviours described are so obvious in hindsight.'

Maggie took out a DVD and popped it into the combi-television. 'What we were looking for when we reviewed the interviews was inconsistencies in the symptoms and a tell-tale signal of sorts. Were there specific things that Raven did when we suspected he was lying?' She hit play on the tape and pointed out how Raven's behaviour changed as he moved from delusion to reality; how one minute he was fine but the next his eyes were rolling as he muttered about blood and animals.

As his delusion intensified, he rocked back and forth, shouted and screamed. Until eventually the guard stood up to let a nurse into the room to help calm Raven down. 'Here, look at this.' Maggie paused the shot and zoomed in on Raven's face. He had turned away from Maggie and the guard and was looking at the wall, an unmistakeable smirk of triumph across his face. It was the look of a man who knew exactly what he was doing – a man who knew that he had won.

There was a sharp intake of breath around the room. Maggie knew this had lit a fire under her colleagues and she was excited to carry on. That is, until she saw the DI's face.

'How can a psychologist tell whether someone is genuinely mentally unstable or faking it then?' DI Rutherford made her way to the front of the room and pointed at the frozen image. 'We all understand why you would want to pursue this line of enquiry, but how does that fit into the evidence we have here? And the J-man, the man *from the Blackwood Estate* or even Harrison, if we indulge you on that one?'

Maggie stiffened. 'Kate said that most techniques rely on experience and observation. This is why we felt it was important to review the video interviews.' She pressed a button on her laptop, brought up Raven's case file on the projector and began to share the findings.

'First, we reviewed Raven's history. Had he been previously hospitalized or treated before for similar symptoms? We know he was a prolific substance misuser. But as you see here,' she pointed to a section of the report, 'prior to the recent diagnosis of schizophrenia, there's no evidence to say he has *any* untreated mental health issues. Although it has been suggested that he probably has a personality disorder.'

Maggie noticed the look of confusion on her colleagues' faces and realized she would have to expand on her last point. 'I'm not saying it's not a recognized mental illness, but there are plenty of people with personality disorders who live *normal*, law-abiding lives.

'We then reviewed the original crime scene, and this is key ...' Maggie reopened the video again and pressed play. She waited as her colleagues watched Raven's responses to her questions about the crime scene and what he did to get rid of the evidence. She paused the video to point out Raven's mannerisms. Every time he mentioned the way he got rid of evidence, his eyes would move a fraction to the left. Maggie killed the tape. 'We all know the basic interview tests and we all know that eye movement to the left is a clear sign that he is lying.'

'Finally, Kate has confirmed that if an individual has hidden the weapon, washed/cleaned up the crime scene or taken any other steps to elude the police and avoid capture, this is a clear sign of *thinking* about what needs to be done, not something that someone with a genuine mental illness would do at the time.' More murmurs around the room could be heard. Maggie was enjoying this. 'Raven's flat was cleaned, using an oxidised bleaching agent, so the Luminol would be affected, a clear sign of taking steps to clean up and to avoid capture.'

The muttering got louder until Rutherford stepped forward and raised her hand. 'Enough with the dramatics. Are you saying that Raven faked his mental illness and is working with someone else? An accomplice who then carried out the killings in an effort to free Bill, so he could live out some sick fantasy? Seems a bit extreme, doesn't it?' DI Rutherford placed her hands on her hips and glared at Maggie.

'That's pretty much what I'm saying in a nutshell. What

I've been saying since this ridiculous appeal was lodged. I'm not saying that Raven doesn't have mental health issues; they could have been drug induced and now he's suffering the aftermath. Kate and I would like to speak to the psychiatrist at the secure unit where Raven was hospitalized. This is where he was diagnosed with schizophrenia after his conviction and conveniently just before his appeal, but there's nothing in the paperwork to say what work was done to treat this or what medication Raven is currently on. Seems a bit odd.'

Bethany grimaced. 'I thought we weren't investigating Raven? Isn't this a waste of our time?'

'We're looking at everything ...' Rutherford took a deep breath and turned to Maggie. 'You've raised a few good points and at this stage, if ... and I use the term sparingly ... *if* we get it wrong, and Raven is somehow involved in these murders, we need to make sure he doesn't get out of prison.'

Maggie mouthed a grateful *thanks*. 'Does that mean Dr Moloney and I can make arrangements to meet with the psychiatrist?'

Raising her hands, DI Rutherford nodded. 'Yes, but you'll only have one opportunity, so make sure you get all the information you need.'

Maggie did a little fist bump in the air.

'Let me know what I need to do, and let's make this happen.' DI Rutherford headed out of the conference room.

# Chapter 52

Maggie had arranged to pick up Kate just before nine that morning. The journey itself would take just over an hour and a half and they were booked to speak with Dr Vraines at 11 a.m. That should give them enough time to discuss things in the car and make sure they had everything covered.

Dr Vraines had a long career as a psychiatrist, and according to Google, he had won awards for some of his work within the psychiatric community. From interviews Maggie had watched, it was clear that the doctor was a bit of a know-it-all and would probably not be pleased with them questioning his diagnosis.

Andy was asleep, and Maggie did her best not to wake him, though an earthquake could occur, and Andy would just roll over and fall right back into a deep slumber. She had a quick shower, put on a navy pair of trousers, cream blouse and tied her hair in a loose bun.

Heading downstairs, she filled up a travel mug with coffee, grabbed an apple, and left a note for Andy to explain where she was going. She headed out the door and got into her car.

Maggie pulled up outside Kate's house. Kate opened the car door, her demeanour strange and anxious. Kate was a private person, so she wouldn't push it despite how much she wanted to ask.

Kate sat down and turned to her. 'Morning! Today should be interesting!'

Maggie started the engine and drove down the road. 'Did you have any problems clearing today with DI Calleja?'

'Actually, your DI had contacted him first and he was fine with it. I agreed to use some of my time off in lieu and told him this would actually be a great case study for profiling in terms of mental health, offenders and violence – all of which we deal with in the DAHU.'

'I should have known.' Maggie smiled. 'So, how should we take things forward?'

'How much of Raven's history are you aware of?' Kate rummaged around in her bag before pulling out a leather-bound notebook.

'Well, I guess I know the basics, everything we have already been through. He was known to social care as a child, lived with his grandmother because his mother had her own issues with substances, poor choice in men and mental health. Why?'

'OK, so you do have the outer shell of things, shall we say, but here is a bit more that I found out speaking to some of our Probation colleagues and social care. I hope I haven't overstepped the mark. He was a bedwetter until the age of twelve. There had been complaints from neighbours that he was torturing pets in the area, but his grandmother vehemently denied it. She was strict but genuinely appeared to care for him, so probably was a big stabilizing factor in his life. There was some suggestion that Raven enjoyed having power over people, took pleasure from negative attention; there were comments from his teachers to social care along the lines of him using things against people to get his own way. Social care brushed the information off as hearsay because he never displayed any of this behaviour around them.'

'Well that certainly does paint a different picture, and Raven said his best memories come from living with his grandmother. Along with animal cruelty and bedwetting, if we just add arson, we'd have our toxic trio.' Maggie paused. 'But doesn't that go against our theory then? He clearly had issues growing up, maybe he did have an undiagnosed mental illness.' Maggie felt somewhat deflated.

'Or ... it fits our theory perfectly.' There was a glint in Kate's eyes.

'How so?'

'Someone with untreated schizophrenia would not have known the difference between right and wrong at the time of the killings. Raven *did* as he handed himself in and confessed. My question is, how did he get Dr Vraines to diagnose him with schizophrenia, as this effectively is the main catalyst in lodging the appeal once Lorraine's remains were found.'

Maggie signalled left and drove up the secluded lane. 'Well you can ask him that yourself, we're here now.'

# Chapter 53

Stepping out from the car, Maggie took in her surroundings as she stretched her legs. She was always in awe of the landscape around some prisons and secure units. Beautiful on the outside, but housing evil behind the walls.

This building was fairly unremarkable, unlike some secure units which are often listed or old mansions. The unit was surrounded by acres of land, sculptured gardens and a massive forest in the distance. No one would ever know that such a place as Ashford Hall housed some of the UK's most dangerous offenders.

The grass was soggy and squidgy beneath Maggie's shoes as she and Kate made their way towards the large wooden door. A raspy chatter from a magpie on the roof made Kate jump.

'Are you OK? You seem a little on edge?' Maggie noticed Kate flinch as she touched her arm.

'I'm fine,' she snapped. 'Sorry, this place is a little creepy, that's all.'

Maggie didn't force the issue. Wet leaves lined the grassy path and there was a chill in the air. She pulled her scarf tighter around her neck. She didn't know whether it was the breeze or the forthcoming task – but something sent a shiver down her spine. Kate was right, this place was a little on the disturbing side.

Making their way into the building, they were immediately met with a sterile and eerie environment. Despite its modernity, everything was pure white and cold. The clinical smell assaulted her nostrils and she wiped her nose. The atmosphere surprised Maggie but only because it was unlike any of the secure units or therapeutic prisons she had visited previously.

Two people were sitting behind a plexiglass partition that had a small, circular hole for visitors to speak into.

'Right on time, are you ready?' Maggie looked at Kate.

'Absolutely.'

'Excuse me? We have an appointment with Dr Vraines at 11 a.m. My name is DC Jamieson, and this is my colleague, Dr Moloney.' Maggie and Kate held up their IDs, and a woman with a tightly wound bun, round glasses and petite frame glanced up and briefly acknowledged their presence.

'Sign in and then have a seat over there.' She pointed at the seating area to the right of the reception desk. 'Dr Vraines will be with you momentarily.'

Just as Kate and Maggie were about to sit down, they heard a buzz and a click and the door directly opposite them opened. Dr Vraines beckoned them to follow. No greeting or acknowledgement, just a long, skeletal finger indicating to the women to come forward. Dr Vraines was tall and clean shaven, dressed in a dark navy suit. His eyes raked up and down Maggie and Kate, leaving Maggie on edge.

When they finally arrived at his office, he walked behind a large oak desk and pointed at the chairs across from him. Expensive-looking leather chairs. Clearly this facility either made a lot of money, or if Dr Vraines decorated it himself, he had a lot of spare money to spend.

'Good morning. I hear you both have some questions for me about Bill Raven. Before we start, I just want to make it absolutely clear that I will not break patient-client confidentiality.'

Maggie took the lead. 'We'd never ask you to do that. Dr Moloney and I are here to find out more about his diagnosis and your assessment in terms of his appeal. We've both had access and read the paperwork; therefore, no confidentiality will be broken.'

'Well it's no secret that my assessment was key to getting this poor individual's appeal heard for crimes he didn't commit.'

Maggie shifted in her seat. After only five minutes with the doctor, she knew he would be hard work. 'Interesting that you are so sure about his innocence, given his extensive knowledge of the crimes and crime scenes. Did he tell you who he believed to be guilty?'

'I'm afraid he didn't.' The doctor looked at his watch. 'Unless I'm wrong, I believe it's *your* job to solve crimes? I merely assessed Mr Raven and treated him for his mental illness.'

Kate intervened. 'On that note, could you tell us how you concluded that Mr Raven is schizophrenic when he has never previously been treated for or diagnosed with that illness? Could you also update us on his current treatment, something that seems to be mysteriously absent from his recent reports?'

The doctor turned to face her with a grim little smile. 'Dr Moloney. Surely you know what assessments are involved in making such a diagnosis as well as the treatment?'

Maggie squeezed the arm of the chair until her knuckles turned white. Raising an eyebrow, Maggie looked at Kate.

'I think Dr Moloney is asking more for my benefit than hers. I'm sure you can appreciate that my knowledge of the subject is not as vast or experienced as yours. How do you know that Mr Raven wasn't faking the symptoms?'

'Faking? I have over thirty years' experience in the field of psychiatry and mental health, DC Jamieson. How dare you insinuate that I would not be able to spot real mental illness. Do I have to spell things out for you? Let's start with the symptoms, shall we?' He opened and read out from the file in front of him. '"Hallucinations" – do I really need to explain this to you both? I think the fact that he believed he dismembered three females is a biggie, don't you?' He shuffled the papers around. '"Delusions" – he had many, and it falls in line with the hallucinations. He actually believed he murdered three women. Plus there are his claims to have been dancing in a room filled with the victims' blood – yet there was no evidence to substantiate this claim, was there?' He smirked before continuing.

'You were part of the interrogation, DC Jamieson. I'm sure even you would concur that he displayed disorganized thinking – jumping from topic to topic, not making any sense. Mr Raven also had poor hygiene, a reduced range of emotions, poor memory and decision-making.' He closed the file.

'Instead of wasting my time with your foolish questions, what you should be asking yourself is, how do you feel about leading a vulnerable individual into making a false confession that could have him spending the rest of his life in prison!' The doctor leaned back in his chair and looked down his nose at Maggie.

She wouldn't rise to the bait. Instead, she turned the question around on him. 'Hmm. Interesting assessment and thank you for raising that last point, actually. Mr Raven was assessed for his mental health just prior to being interviewed by the police. Why were his symptoms not present at that time? Especially as he was not under any treatment but had admittedly experienced psychotic episodes, which were all recorded as being drug induced.'

Dr Vraines stood up. 'Ladies. You're clearly here on some kind of mission and I'll no longer be a party to this. I explained my findings and agreed to see and hear you out, but really, what do you hope to achieve with all this nonsense? All the evidence that was collected and used against poor Mr Raven was circumstantial at best. He was clearly unwell and had he not been coerced into confessing to these crimes, the case would have been thrown out of court.'

'Mr Raven came to the police station of his own free will. He confessed to the murder of Lorraine—'

Dr Vraines interrupted. 'I am referring to the other victims he claimed to have killed, not the Rugman woman. There was a list of them, wasn't there? Keep up, DC Jamieson.'

Maggie moved forward in her seat and Kate put her arm across her. 'Dr Vraines I think we're all going a little off topic now. Are you saying you're not willing to help us any further?'

'That's correct, Dr Moloney. I have more important things to do with my time than listen to this drivel. Are you even a qualified psychologist? Really, you should know better than this. Everything is in the reports that I provided to the courts.' He sighed, and Maggie tapped her fingers on the chair. She needed a distraction, or it would only be a matter of time before she jumped across the desk and showed Dr Smart-Arse how serious they were.

Pulling herself together, Maggie rubbed her chin. 'Well then, as you seem to have no interest in helping us piece things together, Dr Moloney and I will just go and draw our own conclusions based on the facts.'

'Do as you please. I have no doubt my assessment is correct and that you'll only be wasting your time.'

Kate and Maggie stood up and followed the doctor back out to the reception area. Before the door could close, Maggie looked into the doctor's eyes. 'Let's hope there are no skeletons in your closet either, Doctor.'

# Chapter 54

Kate pulled her jacket tighter around her body as she and Maggie made their way back to the car. She opened the door, sat down, buckled up and sighed. 'Well, he was definitely hiding something.' Kate sank back in the seat.

'You mean Dr Smart-Arse?'

Kate giggled. 'He deflected every question. The icing on the cake being his condescending tone and attempt to belittle our credentials. I wonder if we had been men, would he have treated us the same way?'

'I think he would and I really wanted to punch him in his face. Do we know much about his background? I saw all the diplomas and crap littering his walls, but maybe we need to probe deeper?' Maggie started the car and put her foot down.

'Are you heading back to Stafford Police Station?'

'I was, but I can drop you off at Markston first, if you need to get back to work immediately?'

'I promised DI Calleja that I'd be working in the afternoon, but my computer at Markston is being looked at, some sort of technical issue. I can work out of Stafford if there'll be a spare desk?'

'There's always a spare desk. That makes things easier. I can drop you home on my way this evening.'

Kate inwardly felt relief. She didn't want to have to travel home on her own with everything that had been happening. 'Thanks so much, but only if you're sure. I'll catch up on my work first when we get into the station and then do some digging on the good doctor.'

Kate stared out the window and collected her thoughts as the cars whizzed by in the opposite direction. The pair sat in silence for the rest of the journey.

Kate noticed the police station coming into view and lifted her bag into her lap. She looked at her watch as Maggie pulled into the driveway, punched in the code, and they waited for the electric gates to open. Once parked, they entered the station through the back and Maggie showed her to a free desk. Nathan offered them both coffee and went to the kitchen.

Kate logged in remotely, ready to catch up on things she had missed in the domestic abuse unit that morning. She emailed DI Calleja to let him know she was back and working out of Stafford station if he needed her.

The station set-up was very similar to Markston, although it could use a lick of paint. She smiled as Nathan placed a coffee on the desk and she immediately raised it to her lips, inhaling the addictive aroma and taking a large gulp.

Nothing important from her team to deal with right away, so Kate began searching for more information on Dr Vraines. Google threw up a whole load of links to accolades and achievements. She scrolled through them, clicking in and out and scanning the articles. When she reached the second page of her Google search, she came across an interesting headline.

Kate clicked into the article and read it twice before calling Maggie over.

Maggie leaned in to read and started laughing. 'Now I wasn't expecting that!' She smacked the desk.

'Nor was I, but it might explain his caginess. Do you think it is worth exploring?' Kate looked up at Maggie.

'Let me clear it with DI Rutherford first.' Maggie called Nathan over to look at what they found.

He read the page in silence. 'If you think there's something there, clear it with DI Rutherford and you have my backing.'

Kate felt the excited electricity in the room.

'Is there a printer I can connect to? I'll print off some copies.'

Maggie went to the printers.

Kate smiled. 'Is there someone I can speak to about seeing Raven's original psych reports, so I can compare them?'

'I'll see ...'

# Chapter 55

Back at her desk, Maggie looked up the number for HMP Featherbrook. She wanted to see who had been visiting Bill Raven. With other aspects of the case being given priority, she now had the time and opportunity to look further into this line of enquiry. The woman who answered the phone was not very helpful but eventually Maggie was put through to the prison governor. Her boss would have to write a formal request before that information could be shared. She thanked him and hung up the phone.

'For fuck sake ...'

'What's the matter?' Nathan looked up from his computer. Maggie could just about see him through his office door.

'I tried charming some information out of the prison governor so that we wouldn't have to go through the official channels – just to save some time – but he wasn't having any of it.'

Nathan laughed. 'I'm sure the guv would be happy to push the matter, after all – she had suggested it. I'd say the sooner you ask, the sooner you'll get. I'd do it, but I think they are looking for a higher rank.'

'Thanks for the offer. I know I need to ask DI Rutherford, but I'm always cautious as it's about Raven. You know what she's like ...' Maggie heard a cough in the room and looked up to see the DI standing in the doorway. Nathan sank in his chair and grinned. Maggie looked at him and mouthed *thanks a lot, arsehole*. He was lucky, he could hide in the safety of his own office.

'What do you need, Maggie?'

'The names of the people who have been visiting Raven in prison.' Maggie waited for the lecture.

'OK. I'll get on that. Anything else?'

Maggie just shook her head. She watched open-mouthed as Rutherford returned to her office. 'Did that just happen?'

'Uh, yes. And I am just as surprised as you.' Nathan popped his head out of his office. Maggie's desk faced Nathan's office door. A few more feet and she would actually be in Nathan's office. Due to the close proximity, they often could have conversations without anyone else in the office overhearing them.

'I'm not holding my breath. I think she's just placating me.' Maggie shrugged.

'To be fair, if nothing comes of it you really won't have any choice, will you.'

'And if I'm right?' Maggie stood with her hands on her hips.

'We'll have to cross that bridge when we come to that.' Nathan walked towards Maggie.

'Right, what else do we have?'

'At the moment, it remains the J-man from Raven's building, the Blackwood Estate mystery man and Adrian Harrison.

Without having the opportunity to re-interview him, Harrison's alibi still stands, as we can't really disprove what he said. We're waiting for information on the J-man, from Bethany. When I last checked, the landlord wasn't being very forthcoming.'

'OK, putting both the nameless men aside for one moment, what more do we have in relation to the possibility of Raven and Harrison working together?'

Nathan stood in the doorway of his office as Maggie pulled her chair closer.

'As much as it pisses me off to admit this, not much. I mean *why* would Raven take the fall for Harrison? And why didn't he point the finger at Harrison during his appeal?'

Nathan also didn't look convinced.

'That's what we need to figure out. I think it's worth talking to Raven again without directly asking him. We wouldn't want him warning Harrison.' Nathan's finger tapped on the door frame. 'I'm still not sure I buy it, but I'll go along for now.'

'Thanks.' Maggie bit her lip. 'At the moment, I think we need to lay this to rest while still developing other lines of enquiry. We don't want to keep finding body parts strewn across Staffordshire.'

'Agreed. OK. I'll contact the prison and see when we can book a visit with Raven.'

'Great. I'd like us to also revisit the original crime scene. Maybe find out about his grandmother's address – didn't I see somewhere that she died before all this happened and she left him her house and a significant amount of money in her will?'

'You know you'll have to clear that with the boss.' Nathan frowned.

'Of course.' Maggie smiled. Taking a deep breath, she stood and made her way to DI Rutherford's office. The DI was on the phone but waved Maggie in. She sat down and waited for her boss to finish the phone conversation.

'Right. What can I do for you now? Oh, and before I forget, you'll have that list of Raven's visitors in the morning.'

'Seriously? Wow. How did you manage that?'

'I have a few contacts who owe me a favour.' DI Rutherford tilted her head and made strong eye contact.

'OK.' Maggie took a deep breath. 'I think we need to speak to Raven again and I'd like to find out more about his grandmother. Visit the house she left him in her will. And before you shoot me down, let me explain why ...' Maggie was surprised to see DI Rutherford raise her hand.

'I don't doubt your skills, Maggie. So long as it's relevant to the current case and doesn't take up too much time, do what you need to.'

'I promise. Completely professional and key to the investigation. It seems it may have been overlooked during the original case notes as Raven had not been forthcoming about that bit of information. I want to catch this killer, boss. If I am wrong about Raven, I'll hold my hands up.'

'Then why are you still here? Just get on with it.'

Maggie strode to Nathan's office and tapped him on the shoulder. 'Make that call. We can interview Raven.'

'How did you manage that?' Nathan did a double take.

'To be honest, I haven't a clue. The boss is no idiot, she knows that despite everything, Raven is still the common denominator connected to these killings.'

'What's the plan then? I think we need to prepare ourselves so that we're not caught off-guard. Regardless of anything, Raven is a pathological liar, a master manipulator and he likes to mess the authorities about – particularly you. I read the statements from the original case. He took pleasure in winding you up, and you bit back.'

'I know what I'm doing.' Maggie held her tongue. 'I think you're right though, we need a clear plan. I'd like to find out more about how he knew the victims. Also, DI Rutherford said I'll have the list of prison visitors tomorrow. Before we go out to Raven, it would be a good idea to go through that list and ask *him* who visited. Test his honesty.'

'I'll call the prison now and book a visit.'

Maggie wasn't sure if it would accomplish anything, but she wanted Raven to know that the police were in control. He wouldn't like that power taken away and it just might give them something they could use to nail him.

# Chapter 56

The following day started with a bang.

'Hey Maggie! Leave your coat on. The female witness who discovered Lorraine has just called. She said that the suspicious male is back on the estate and has just gone into the old man's house across the road. Steven I think his name was.'

Maggie had just walked into the office. She was out of breath after foolishly running up the stairs. 'Can we do the prison visit after that?' Maggie didn't want to lose the opportunity to speak with Raven, but knew this could be an important break in the case.

'Let's just see how we get on. We may be too busy interviewing a suspect.'

They raced to the Blackwood Estate and parked outside the neighbour's house. She looked down the alley where Lorraine had been discovered. A stack of water-stained crates balanced precariously along the wall. They could see a woman in the window waving down at them with a mobile phone. She was probably filming the whole thing on Facebook. Maggie rolled her eyes. Social media can be both a help and a hindrance in police investigations. Maggie hoped it would be the former in this instance.

They got out of the car and approached the door cautiously. The ground was damp from the earlier storm and a dog barked in the distance. Nathan whispered, 'I'll have a look around back and make sure no one leaves the property. He may be more receptive to you.'

'DS Wright. That's a bit of a sexist comment.' She flashed him a wry smile.

Maggie knocked on the door, but there was no answer. She walked over to the window and peeked inside, catching a glimpse of a shadow out of the corner of her eye. It looked like someone was trying to hide behind the couch. She tapped gently on the glass. 'Sir. Can you come to the door, please? I see you there. I'd just like to have a chat. Follow up on our last visit.' Maggie watched the shadow move and she made her way to the door.

The man opened it a crack. It still had the chain on. Showing her warrant card, she introduced herself again. 'Do you mind if I come inside?'

He looked over his shoulder and, with some reluctance, removed the chain and opened the door. 'How can I help, officer?' His voice shook. Maggie walked inside and noted the way his hands were clenched by his sides. She took in the strange atmosphere and felt herself tense. All the doors to the other rooms were closed this time. She thought she heard scratching from the room directly behind where Steven stood.

'Is there anyone else here with you, sir?' Her hand went to her baton.

'No. Why do you ask that?' There was a strange look in his eyes.

Something crashed from the back room and Maggie rushed forward. She brushed by Steven and ran towards the sound. 'Police! Stop!'

The old man came up behind her. 'Leave him alone. He's my son!'

Nathan had tackled whom they believed to be the Blackwood Estates mystery man in the back garden and was cautioning him when Maggie caught up.

Maggie turned to Steven. 'Why didn't you tell me he was here?'

'Look, I was scared. I haven't seen my son for years, and all of a sudden, he turns up on my doorstep. I just wanted to talk to him. What do you think he's done?' The man's eyes shifted between Nathan and Maggie.

'I ain't done shit. Why are you arresting me?' The man was lying on his front, his hands cuffed behind him.

'There was a suspicious male reported in the area over the last few weeks. You fit that description. The fact that you ran off and Steven here lied about you makes everything more suspicious.' Maggie clasped her hands behind her back and took in the surroundings. The grass was overgrown as were the bushes that separated the neighbouring garden. She spotted something on the ground.

'Can we just go inside. I can explain everything.'

'Hang on.' Maggie walked towards the bushes and picked up a plastic bag. 'Is this what I think it is?' Maggie shook the baggy and pointed to the back door.

They followed close behind as they returned indoors.

'Explain yourself then.' Nathan took charge.

'OK. It's a bit of weed. I panicked and threw it in the bushes.' He looked sheepish. 'I haven't seen my father for about fifteen years; he just upped and left. A relative recently passed on his address details and I've been coming to the neighbourhood for about four or five weeks, trying to catch a glimpse of him and working up the courage to knock on his door. I finally did the other day when you both came over asking questions. I just got nervous. The weed relaxes me. I have a previous caution and figured if you caught me with it again, I may end up in court. That's it, I swear.'

Maggie looked at Nathan and raised a brow.

'Well your father should have been more forthcoming when I knocked.' Turning to Steven, she sighed. 'Why were you so cagey?'

The old man shrugged. 'It was a big shock to me. I wasn't the best dad and I guess I just got worried that I wouldn't get time to spend with him. I didn't know about the drugs, OK. I'm not well. I may not have long left. I just wanted to talk to him myself.'

Maggie relented slightly. 'I'm sorry to hear that.' She turned to the other man. 'You're still going to have to come down to the station and provide some details. You'll be searched at the station. If this is all the cannabis you have, you're likely to get another caution. I do believe what you're saying for what it's worth, but you may be asked to provide fingerprints for elimination purposes. Are you OK with that?'

'Yes. Anything. Can you remove these cuffs now? I'm staying

with my dad for a few days at least. I'll do whatever I need to.' He put his head in his hands.

She cleared her throat as she removed the cuffs.

Maggie handed him a card and told him to report to Stafford Police Station at 10 a.m. the following day. Someone would be there to interview him and take his prints. They left the property and returned to their car.

# Chapter 57

HMP Featherbrook was located in the middle of a giant field. The nearest village was ten miles away and Maggie stared up at the walls and shivered. Imagine living a stone's throw away from some of Staffordshire's most notorious dangerous offenders.

Nathan and Maggie waited as they were checked by the prison guards for contraband and weapons before being signed in and taken to the legal visit room where Raven would be waiting. Maggie took a deep breath as they approached the door and prepared herself for what was to come.

'Whatever he says,' Nathan looked her in the eye, 'don't let it get to you.'

They opened the door and went inside.

'Well good morning, officers. Nice to see you both.' Raven smiled up at them from his seat in front of the bolted-down table. The smile didn't reach his eyes. 'As you'll see, my solicitor isn't present. Despite his reservations and wanting to be here, I explained I'm just helping you with your enquiries. Don't make me regret that decision, officers.'

'Mr Raven. Thank you for agreeing to meet with us at such

short notice. I'm sure there'll be no regrets from either party.' They took seats opposite him. 'We won't take up too much of your time,' Nathan confirmed.

'It's my pleasure. Anything I can do to help you catch this killer.'

Maggie looked around. The room was like a giant fish bowl. No privacy, which didn't bother her and probably fed into Raven's ego and need for the spotlight.

'Is the décor not to your taste, DC Jamieson?' A sly smile crept across his face.

'I've been to prisons before, Mr Raven. Shall we just get on with things?'

'Of course, here, have a glass of water. I made sure we had some; I wouldn't want to have to cut the meeting short because my mouth got dry ...'

'None for me, thanks.' Maggie looked at Nathan.

Maggie didn't want to drink anything put out by Raven, but noticed Nathan accepted the water without thought. Maybe she was just overanalysing things.

Raven poured a glass of water for himself and Nathan. His mannerism seemed out of character. He was pouring the water slowly into each glass. Looking at the officers as he did so. Once he had finished, he eased back in the chair and took a sip. 'Oh, bit too cold for me at the moment. I think I'll let mine reach room temperature first.' Maggie watched him as he placed his cup of water on the table and stared intently at Nathan gulping from his cup. Nathan sputtered, and Maggie jumped out of her chair.

'Are you OK, Nathan? What did you put in the water?' She slapped Nathan's back repeatedly.

'Put in the water? My, *my* aren't we paranoid, DC Jamieson?'

'Maggie, I'm OK.' He shrugged her hands away. 'Just went down the wrong tube.'

'Sorry.' Maggie sat back down. 'Let's just get to the questions.'

'I'm an open book, Detective. Ask away.'

'I know it's a sore subject, but I wondered if we could start with Lorraine ...'

# Chapter 58

He admired her tenacity. DC Jamieson was relentless in her pursuit of him – he felt famous all over again. They needed him. 'What is it you want to know about my confession?'

He watched her closely. Her eyes challenged him, dared him to make a mistake, as if she thought she could catch him out. Maybe it would be fun to tease the detective a bit.

'We'd like to know a few things actually. Firstly, how did you know Lorraine?'

'Hasn't this all been covered?' He ran a hand through his hair. The brainless policeman next to Maggie hadn't even spoken yet.

'I always find that if I can hear the information first-hand, it really helps form that picture in my mind.' Maggie lifted her pen and held it to her open notebook.

'I'm thrilled you're interested in finally hearing the truth and maybe then you can stop hassling me, wasting valuable time, and catch the person who is dismembering those poor women.'

Maggie's strained smile sent a prickle of excitement down his spine.

He paused. 'Poor Lorraine, she was messed up but good as gold, you know. Always helped me when things were ... ahem ... hard. Thankfully, I have meds that keep my head clear now. But what does poor Lorraine have?' He gave a dismissive wave of his hand.

'Yes. We're all grateful for that, Mr Raven.' The sarcasm dripped from her lips. He imagined that she wanted to reach across the table and grab him by his collar. He imagined letting her do it and smiled.

'Call me Bill. We're all friends now, aren't we? Almost family?' He caught Maggie's eye. 'We would do anything for each other – house-hold chores, paying debts, fixing things – that's what families are for.' Maggie squirmed in her seat.

Through gritted teeth, she replied. 'Please stick to the question: how did you know Lorraine was going to be murdered?'

He rubbed his chin like a schoolmaster with a particularly promising student. 'Good question. Clever girl. Well I knew she was missing; you hear things in the drug community. She had debts. I thought she was in hiding, maybe even in a different country, so I just chose her name ... randomly. I was using daily back then and not right in here.' He tapped his head. 'When she didn't appear after the news stories broke, I thought she had taken the opportunity to start new in some other country. I had no idea there was a real killer. I mean, she must have been held for some time, right? Maggie, do you ever wonder how long you could survive as a captive? How long you could hold out in a dark room before you lost your mind? How long before your body gave up? I imagine if you were fed and watered, it could be years ...'

Maggie swallowed and Raven felt another flash of pleasure.

'Where do you think someone might have held her for all that time?' Maggie said. 'And why do you think they waited so long to kill her?'

'Now, now, how in the world can I answer that? I'm no killer. I don't think like one.'

The male detective jumped in. 'It's a valid question. You knew the name of the second victim and provided a name for a further missing woman.'

'Maybe you're not a very open-minded kind of person, Detective. Maybe you don't believe in coincidences. But as far-fetched as it seems, it was the same thing all over again. These women were drug addicts, prostitutes and criminals in your eyes. You and I both know that people like that disappear all the time. I just picked names out of a metaphorical hat – people I knew, people who wouldn't be missed – and like the best kind of story it came true. You don't think the killer chose his victims based on the names of the missing women I gave, do you? Now *that* would be something, wouldn't it? I was just so—'

'Yes, we know.' Maggie leaned forward. 'You were ill, off your face, in the middle of a psychotic episode. What about that associate of yours, the one who held the drug parties in abandoned freight cars? Jake was it? Or is it Jack? And your flatmate? Adrian Harrison. What can you tell us about them?'

'Did you find that guy? I think it's Jack actually. No wait, it's definitely Jake.' He winked at DC Jamieson, and she moved back in her chair. 'But Adrian? He's your focus now? How unimaginative.' Raven sighed. 'He supplied me with drugs. A small-time dealer really. He could be odd at times, and aggressive, especially if someone ripped him off, but more of a mouse than a lion.'

'Have you seen him since you were incarcerated?' Maggie looked him in the eye.

'No. In fact, he's been very quiet, if I'm honest, a little too quiet. I tried ringing his mobile, but he must have got rid of it.'

'So, Adrian hasn't visited you?' Maggie leaned forward.

'No. I was surprised. I thought he might, but I guess he didn't want to associate with someone who was convicted of murder.' Raven smiled.

'We have reason to believe your brother has visited you a few times. I thought you were estranged from your brother?' Maggie persisted.

'After he went into care and I moved in with my grandmother, I didn't see him at all. Well ... that is until recently. He did visit me here a few times. I think he had hoped that he would find something out and be able to sell his story. We were never close growing up, and he left disappointed.' He watched DC Jamieson write his response down. 'Do you want me to go slower? Or maybe you want to record this conversation? It would save those delicate hands of yours.'

'Please don't patronize me, Mr Raven.'

'Of course. Please accept my apologies, DC Jamieson. Where was I? Oh yes, I was talking about my brother.' He scratched his head. 'At first I have to admit, I did find it confusing that he'd decided to visit me, considering we had not spoken more than two words after he went in to care.'

'Why did he go into care when you went to your grandmother's?'

'He chose to. My grandmother couldn't look after two boys; I suspect he just wanted to separate himself from all of us. A new beginning, perhaps? I never thought to ask him, and he never offered an explanation.'

'Do you know where Adrian Harrison is now?'

'He gave up the flat we shared not long after I went into the secure hospital apparently. I have no idea where he went or where any of my personal items are. He got rid of everything, I guess.' He threw his hands in the air. 'But I'll be OK. My grandmother left me everything she had. It will be waiting for me when I'm released.'

'Do you know why body parts of people you claimed to have killed would be showing up now?'

He tapped the table. 'Changing the wording of your questions, won't change my answer. I wish I knew that myself, DC Jamieson. The prison psychiatrist thinks that whoever is behind the killings now must feel some connection with me. Wants my approval or praise. But how could I be pleased? Such horrendous crimes.' He smirked.

DS Wright joined in the conversation, 'That, or you took pleasure at all the attention and notoriety.'

'DS Wright, as insightful as ever. We were doing so well, but now I'm tired and think I am through with answering all your questions.'

'So soon?' Maggie grinned at him. 'I thought you would last a bit longer than that. Our time isn't up yet. Can't you just spare us another five or ten minutes? I apologize for my colleague if he offended you.' Her eyes were suddenly pleading.

'No more questions.' He stood. 'Guards. I'm ready to go back to my cell now.' He tapped on the plexiglass window. 'You can direct any further questions to my solicitor.'

A dark smile crossed his face as the officers gathered their belongings and they were escorted from the room. He shouted to them before the door clicked closed. 'Thank you both for stopping by and send my love to your brother, Maggie. It's a pity the way this ended. I'm sure there would have been so much more to discuss ...'

DC Jamieson put her foot in the door and looked him straight in the eyes. 'I have no doubt we'll be speaking again. We're definitely not through with you.' There was venom in her voice.

*Nor I with you, DC Jamieson ...*

# Chapter 59

'Fuck, fuck, fuck!' Dirt swirled around her feet as she stomped her way back to the car. The door slammed behind her as she pulled it shut, sat down and buckled her seat belt. 'I think we blew it.'

'You mean *I* blew it.' Nathan looked at her.

'I think it's fair to say it was a joint fuck-up this time. He was playing us anyway. The way he was talking. What the hell. Arrggghhhh.' She smacked her leg.

'Look it wasn't ideal. I shouldn't have insulted him. We had him right where we wanted him and I had to open my big mouth. But I guess we now know that finding this associate, Adrian Harrison, and Raven's brother has to be our top priority.'

'If his brother wanted to sell the story, why haven't we seen a story in the papers? It was a while ago. Is it worth speaking to some of our press contacts, see if they have heard anything?'

Nathan started the car and began to reverse back onto the lane leading out from the prison. 'Let's speak to DI Rutherford. If something gets leaked, she'll kill us.'

Maggie stared out the window for a long moment. 'Most

prisons have CCTV when you go visit someone. Might be worth getting Bethany to check that out. We need to check PNC for any recent addresses for all three of them. Do you think it's weird that Adrian never even wrote to Raven in custody?'

'Maybe it wasn't a wasted trip after all. Perhaps we played the right cards, even if he did cut us off before we could get anymore.' Nathan stared ahead.

They arrived back at the office in record time.

Maggie headed to DI Rutherford's office but stopped short when she saw Mr Stanford from the review commission talking to her boss. DI Rutherford's face was creased. She didn't look happy at all. Maggie loitered around the office for a few more minutes, biting her nails. DI Rutherford caught her eye and waved her in. *Shit.*

'DC Jamieson. Good timing. You remember Mr Stanford?'

'Erm, yes, ma'am. Nice to see you again.' Maggie glanced in his direction.

'He would like to speak with you once more about your interviews with Raven. A few points of clarification ... that's right, isn't it, Mr Stanford?'

He cleared his throat. 'Yes. We just wanted to go over a few things that were raised after interviewing your colleagues. What time would be most convenient for you both?'

She looked at DI Rutherford.

'Your boss has pointed out that you're currently following a few potential leads in the investigation, so right now might not be the best time.' He waited for her response.

'Now is not ideal. Maybe sometime next week?'

He pulled out his diary. 'Wednesday at 2 p.m.?'

Maggie agreed and he passed her his card holding her hand just a little bit longer than necessary. His palms were sweaty and Maggie snatched her hand back, nearly dropping the card to the floor.

'See you then. Thank you for your time. DI Rutherford. I'll be in touch.'

Maggie leaned away from him and let him pass. He seemed to falter and looked like he was going to say something further before changing his mind and heading back to the makeshift office that had been set up on the third floor.

'What a wanker ...'

Maggie gave the DI an incredulous look.

'What was that all about then?' She wasn't expecting the DI to answer.

'There's some question of your ability to remain objective in the current case and he wants my opinion on how you handled the original investigation.'

'Can you tell me what you said or is that confidential?'

DI Rutherford sighed and rubbed her face. She had bloodshot eyes. The whole team was looking worse for wear.

'Is there anything I can do?' Maggie felt a pang of worry for her boss.

'Catch this killer so we can put the case to rest and get the review commission off our backs.'

'Doing my best, ma'am. Do you want to hear about our meeting with Raven?'

'May as well.'

Maggie proceeded to update her boss on the J-man, and the chat they had with Bill Raven. She informed her boss that they were continuing to focus their resources on locating Adrian Harrison and Raven's brother, who had reappeared after being estranged for years.

'Shit. I hope he doesn't go to the media with this story. Surely if his plans were to sell his story, he would have done so already.' The DI stroked her eyebrow. 'This whole thing just doesn't add up, Maggie. What the hell are we not seeing?'

'Raven wasn't too happy with me and Nathan; he terminated the interview early. I'd like your permission to try and placate him, maybe interview him on my own?'

'Out of the question. Especially not while everything else is happening. You'll have to think of another way.'

Maggie held her hands up. 'I just think I would have a better chance one on one with Raven. He's definitely getting some sort of satisfaction out of taunting me. He knows something that will blow this case wide open.'

'That may well be true, but you need to tread carefully. Think *outside* the box.' DI Rutherford tapped her nose and gave Maggie a meaningful look.

# Chapter 60

Kate was shattered and looking forward to the end of the day. She rubbed the back of her neck. The domestic abuse unit was challenging with little reward, given the nature of their offenders.

Lately, however, even going home had its own stresses. Kate was not easily spooked but she was beginning to sense that perhaps something more sinister than a hopeless crush was going on with the letters and she didn't need the added pressure. She was still thinking about whether she should bring the notes in to work to see if her police colleagues could do anything about it. She was torn. Kate valued her privacy and didn't want to make a fuss if it all turned out to be nothing.

Kate had been thinking a lot about the type of person who would do this. Stalkers always wanted to induce fear and level some form of control over their victim. Is this what was happening here? She couldn't put her finger on it, but something felt off – the notes were not overtly threatening but did have a creepy undertone.

Kate braced herself as she walked towards the main doorway of her building. When she had moved here, she'd been glad to be on the ground floor. Looking out her window and people watching was a favourite past time. But now, it just made her feel vulnerable. A new feeling for her and one she didn't like. Thankfully, there didn't seem to be anything waiting on the front doorstep. She opened it and stopped dead in her tracks when she saw the large black box sitting outside her flat.

Kate swallowed and pushed the box aside with her foot. She grabbed her gloves off the side table by the door and put them on. Just as she was about to pick up the box, she noticed a man standing by the stairs watching her.

'Fuck!' Kate jumped.

'Oh sorry. Did I frighten you? I just wanted to make sure you got the package.' He pointed at the box. It was her neighbour, a man who lived across the hall.

'Did you let someone into the building to deliver this?' Her voice shook.

'Yes. They kept ringing the buzzer. Said it was urgent. So I let them leave it outside your door.'

'Did you get a look at who dropped off the package? Could you describe them?'

The man frowned. He looked surprised by the question. 'The voice was all muffled. They were wearing a motorbike helmet. I only caught a brief look as they walked past.'

Kate tried to smile. 'Well thanks anyway. Could I ask a favour though? Please don't let any visitors in for me if I'm not home? If the person calls again when I am out, can you give me a call?' Kate dug around in her handbag for her business card. 'I'd really appreciate it.'

'Of course, I didn't mean to upset you.' He glanced down

at the business card and raised an eyebrow. 'You're a psychologist?'

Kate said nothing.

After a moment, he pocketed the card. 'Do you want me to get rid of the box then?' he said.

'I'll take it in.' She waited for the man to leave, but he kept standing by the stairs, as if expecting her to invite him inside.

'I'll leave you to it then. If anyone ever bothers you, I'm right across the hall.'

'That's very kind of you.' The pair shook hands. She could just imagine the rumours that this conversation would generate with the other residents in the building. 'I'd better get this in. Have a great evening.' Kate picked up the box.

She waved her neighbour goodbye and closed the door, placing the box gently on the floor. She bent down, holding her hair back with one hand. She wondered if she should just call the police.

Kate took out her mobile phone. She called her parents and asked whether they had sent a package, trying to sound calm and casual about the reasons for her asking. Kate hung up the phone. It had not been her parents.

Her curiosity was getting the better of her. She took a deep breath and crouched down by the box, reached out with a shaking hand for the lid. Closing her eyes for a moment, she told herself it would be nothing, just a gift from someone – a forgotten birthday present, a box of chocolates from someone at work – but deep down she knew what it would be. She took another breath and carefully lifted the lid. The lid fell shut, and she started to scream.

# Chapter 61

Kate raced to the bathroom as the contents of her lunch climbed its way up her throat. After spitting out bile and taking a few deep breaths, she rinsed her mouth out with water and gargled a swill of mouthwash to get rid of the awful taste in the back of her throat. Closing her eyes she thought about the smell of the box as she opened it. The tang of rotting meat. Inside she had found a small wreath wrapped with a ribbon saying *Together Forever* written across it. Two vials of what looked like blood were also in the box, held together with gold ribbon. Finally two rings that looked to be made out of dried-out human skin. Her stomach turned again.

Taking a deep breath, Kate walked back towards the front door and without looking at the box dug out her mobile and dialled 101. Kate made the call to the police and after relaying her concerns, her details were taken down. She informed the call handler that she worked at Markston Police Station and would bring in the items tomorrow. Thanking the woman at the end of the phone, she plonked down on her comfy chair.

Kate turned her phone around in her hand, considering

her options. Someone was targeting her. They knew where she lived. She scrolled through her contacts until she found the number she was looking for and hit 'call'. After three rings the phone was answered.

'Hi Maggie, how are you?'

*'Hi Kate! What a nice surprise. How's things?'*

'Sorry to bother you after hours but I guess I am just looking for some advice and reassurance.'

*'Sounds ominous. What's up?'*

Kate breathed out a sigh. 'For the last few weeks, I have been receiving odd cards, notes and gifts. Usually left on the outside doorstep or posted through the letterbox. Except this evening, when one of the other residents let the person in and they left a box right outside my front door.'

*'Were the letters and stuff threatening?'*

'To be honest, at first I didn't even pay much attention. But then they started getting weirder and I began logging things down and keeping everything. Today I received something that I think could be viewed as pretty threatening: a wreath, some vials of what looks like blood and two rings, made out of what I suspect to be rotting human skin.' The bile rose in her throat.

*'Shit! Have you contacted the police? Do you want me to come around?'*

Kate's shoulders dropped. 'Thanks. That's exactly what I needed to hear. I don't know many people in Staffordshire and ... Would you mind staying over? I feel silly asking.'

*'Of course, don't worry about it. Try to wear gloves in case there's any forensic evidence. I've a late start tomorrow, so can swing by Markston with you in the morning.'*

'I've been using gloves. Guess it's all that time I spend in the police station.' Kate laughed weakly. 'Thanks again. I have wine and munchies, so we can chat or watch a film on TV if you like? Maybe even catch up on where you're at with the case? Anything to take my mind off this.'

*'I'd love to catch up on the case. I had an interesting meeting with Raven and it'd be great to hear your thoughts on that. I'll get my brother to drop me over before he heads into work. In the meantime, make sure your windows and doors are locked.'*

'That's fab. See you soon.' Kate hung up the phone and felt relieved. Although she'd had bouts of anxiety in the past, she was not normally the type to get herself in a state, but then again, this had never happened before. At work, she was used to being called names and threatened in anger, but for someone to invade her personal space and come to her home – that was a line well and truly crossed.

She gathered all the items together in a bag and placed it by the box near her front door. She wanted it out of her flat. As she waited, she went back over the past few weeks and tried to recall anything that might point to the person responsible.

It could just be some random who had targeted her. A shiver went down her spine. She hoped this was not related to the case. Everything seemed to have escalated around the time that she had started speaking to Maggie about it. *Or was it before that?* She took a deep breath and tried to calm down. She needed to use her fear to focus – who knows, it may lead them one step closer to answers.

# Chapter 62

Half an hour later, Andy and Maggie walked to the car, as a few raindrops began to fall. 'More rain.' She rolled her eyes and her brother paid no attention. He was probably wishing he was in his bed for those last few minutes of sleep. Maggie opened the car door and put her things on the back seat. They got inside and Andy started the engine.

'So, what's the rush?' He pulled away from the kerb.

Maggie fiddled with her seatbelt for a moment longer than was necessary. 'Kate ... she's been receiving some threatening messages.' The rain beat against the glass and the only sound was the windscreen wipers washing back and forth. Maggie told him about the parcel on the doorstep. 'I offered to stay on her couch for the night and help her sort it out in the morning.'

'No ulterior motive then?' His lip curved into a smile.

Maggie stared out the window at the rain-beaten streets.

'So, you and Kate ... there is something there then?'

Maggie blushed and wiped a bead of sweat from her forehead. She had been caught out by her brother, and perhaps she *should* just stop trying to hide it. Andy had always known about her sexuality, but as they had never really been close due to his gambling, it wasn't something she openly talked about with him.

She sighed. 'OK. I do like her and if circumstances were different, maybe it would work out. But they're not. And that's all there is to it.'

'Wow. In all sincerity, I'm really pleased you have finally felt comfortable enough to open up to me. You do know that I don't care about all that stuff – lesbian, bisexual, whatever. I just want you to be happy.'

Maggie reached over and squeezed her brother's hand. 'Thanks, Andy. It does feel better to be able to be more open about it with you. You know what I'm like. I just don't feel like I should have to explain myself to anyone. There are so many different views on being bisexual. It really does my head in. What's so difficult to understand? I'm attracted to a person – not their gender – but *who* they are. Do you know what I mean?'

'I hear you. Some people can be very black and white. You don't have to worry about me though, ever, OK?' He caught her eye for a second.

'Thanks. I think I've always known that about you. If only Mum and Dad were as understanding ...'

Maggie noticed her brother's shoulders tighten. 'Well I'm not sure if that will happen anytime soon, but miracles are a thing, right?' He tried to laugh it off. 'Have you spoken to them again? Any idea about when they are coming?'

'The one time I did bring it up in casual conversation, Dad's face got so red, I thought I could actually see the smoke coming out of his ears. He ranted on about how it's just not right and all the other homophobic comments you could think of … I've told them to hold off on their trip for the time being. With this case hanging over me, I really don't want any more pressure.'

'You know Dad doesn't mean it; it's just how he was brought up. Probably for the best to delay the visit – they won't want to spend all their time with me.' There was a sadness in his voice.

The conversation had turned a bit morose. She wanted to lighten the mood. 'Turn left here by the way.'

He indicated left.

'Fourth building on the right. I can just jump out here though, might be easier for you to turn around then.' Maggie turned to her brother and looked him in the eye. 'Thanks. Don't worry either …'

'Don't worry?'

'Yeah, I'll keep my hands off your girlfriends, even if they realize I'm the better looking one.' She grinned.

'Out you get.' He smiled. 'I guess I'll see you tomorrow?'

'I should be home normal time unless something major happens in the case. Have a good night.'

'You too.'

Maggie walked over to Kate's building and pushed the buzzer. She tipped her head back and smiled. Speaking with Andy about her feelings for Kate lifted a huge weight off her shoulder.

She let out a deep, satisfying sigh.

Kate let her in and was waiting by her front door.

Her hair was in disarray, her eyes ringed by dark shadows.

'I thought I was okay after we hung up the phone,' Kate said. 'But I've been jumping at every little sound.'

Maggie stepped into the room and laughed. 'You have to admit, with the lights out and just the candles on, it's a little eerie in here, don't you think?'

She was pleased to see the hint of a smile on Kate's face. 'I guess you're right. I just felt so exposed with the bright lights on and was worried I might get a migraine. The candles are easier on the eyes.'

'So, has anything else happened other than the letters and packages? Can I have a look in the box?' Maggie pushed the curtain aside and looked out the front window.

'No. Thank God! I don't scare easy, but this has really set me off. The box is over by the door. I'll get us a glass of wine and you can fill me in on your chat with Mr Raven.'

'Thanks.' Maggie walked over and, using a pen, she lifted the lid. She put a hand to her mouth and forced herself not to retch. 'What the hell is wrong with people?' She examined the two rings and took out her phone to take some photos. Something about the carefully laid out array of objects made her stomach crawl. Once she was done, she closed the lid and went into the kitchen. 'Can I give you a hand with anything?' She didn't want to alarm Kate, but the box had made her feel uneasy. All Maggie could hope for was that the culprit had made a mistake and left some forensic evidence.

'Don't worry about it, you're my guest. Though if you're up before me in the morning you'll have to make your own cuppa.'

'I'm good with that. I'm a bit of a night owl, so I hope I don't keep you awake.'

'I sleep like a log. I'll be fine.' Kate turned away and Maggie caught a flicker of worry on her face.

Kate passed Maggie a large glass of wine. 'I definitely needed this. Cheers.'

'So, what happened with Raven?' Kate sat down on the couch and crossed her legs. Maggie joined her.

'Well surprise, surprise! Raven was going out of his way to get under my skin. He was as arrogant as ever.' Maggie talked her through the interview and outlined Raven's responses to her questions. She described the way he had mentioned her brother, talked her through his mannerisms and body language.

'Interesting.' Kate stared out the window for a long moment.

'Why do you say that?' Maggie leaned closer.

'He's taunting you, getting a thrill out of your reactions. He must have found out about your brother and he knows it's your weak point. He can sense it like a shark senses blood. He knows how badly you wanted him convicted and how unhappy you are at his appeal. Has there been a press conference yet about the latest developments?'

'Our DI is doing one soon. Making another appeal for those from two years ago to come forward again. We've had a load of hoax calls, but the guv still hopes we'll get something useful. There was even some talk about Crimestoppers.'

Kate tugged her ear and the only sound was the rain beating against the glass.

'I do think there would be some value in Crimestoppers, as it might draw the killer out in the open. This killer is taunting the police, almost challenging them at every opportunity. It fits the profile we were talking about. Have you managed to get hold of Raven's full psych reports, rather than the bits of information we've already looked at?'

'Not yet. It's going to be difficult, especially while the court case is going on. Maybe Probation has that information. They'd need it as part of their risk assessment of him, I'd imagine. I'll contact the local office and see if they can share it. If that fails, I can see if Sarah or even Lucy can help.'

'OK, what else was said?' Kate shifted in her seat.

'He confirmed that his brother had visited a few times, which is odd considering they hadn't seen each other since childhood. As far as we were aware, there was no love lost in that relationship.'

'Why do you think his brother visited? Other than his word, what makes you so sure it *was* his brother?'

Maggie paused and took a sip of her wine. She hadn't thought of that. 'Raven said he was probably hoping for some form of monetary compensation. Maybe sell the story to the papers. We're asking for the CCTV and checking PNC.'

'Let's come back to the brother another time. I'm guessing you asked about how he knew the victims' names?'

'Apparently they were just random people he met through the drug scene. People who often went missing for periods of time. He thought they'd appreciate him claiming they were dead, because it would give them a "free ticket" to a new life. If that's true, why would the killer go out of their way to find these women and target them?' They fell silent for a moment. 'He's pure evil, Kate.' Maggie caught her eye. 'I know it's a cliché, but you can see it in his eyes.' Maggie's hands shook as she finished her wine.

'You may have to let that go at some point. Let's say that the killer chose their victims *after* Raven was convicted. We'd also have to presume that the killer knew the victims in some way – wouldn't we? It's possible that the reason the bodies are only showing up now is because it had taken that long to track down the three women, as they had actually gone underground to avoid debts, start over, whatever the reason. Hang on a sec.' Kate got up. She stretched and left the room. When she returned she had a large, white sheet of glossy paper and some markers. She stuck the paper on the wall.

'So, everything you have racing around in that head of yours, spit it out and I'll write it down here.' Kate tapped the paper.

Maggie smiled. Had she been at home, it would have been exactly what she would have done. 'And this is why we're friends. After this, you'll have to tell me where you got that as I usually use notebooks, but I need that in my life.'

The women worked until 2 a.m. and probably had one too many glasses of wine. When everything had been listed, both stared at the sheet on the wall and Maggie was exasperated as none of it seemed to make any sense. Hopefully once the wine wore off and she looked at it with a fresh pair of eyes it would.

# Chapter 63

## VERONICA

She felt so weak. Her face was sore. She didn't want to live anymore. Today she wouldn't fight or struggle. The tape over her ears and eyes made her blind and deaf to her surroundings. Soon someone would be down to change it. She shivered. She lived in constant fear for the moment when her captor would suddenly grab her arms. Listening to the silence her thoughts drifted.

*A noise?* Rough hands took her and she gasped. The person squeezed her arm tightly and the cot shook as something heavy hit the floor.

Her muffled screams always seemed to excite her captor and they would laugh manically, so she kept silent now, hoping for the drugs she knew would take her to a better place. She had accepted her fate long ago.

The hands released her and she thought for a moment that they might have left her again. Might have forgotten to give her a hit. She didn't want to move, in case this was all part of their sick game. Then she felt a sticky hand on her arm again and she shuddered with fear but also with relief. She might still be given what she needed. When she felt a sharp prick in her arm she gasped her thanks and heaven soon hugged her.

Her captor was undoing the restraints on her arms and legs, but she no longer cared. She just lay there like a dead weight as she was dragged off the bed and dropped on the floor. A sheet of something crinkly and cold underneath her. It reminded her of wet days wrapped in her waterproof jacket. Her mind drifted as she felt cold steel against her skin.

And then she heard the voice.

*First four.*

*Then three.*

*And now there would be one …*

# Chapter 64

Maggie woke with a pain in her back and a sore head. One from the couch she had slept on, the other from the copious amounts of wine she had drunk. She decided that after dropping by Markston Police Station with Kate, she would head home for a quick nap before starting her shift. She stared at the paper on the wall, willing a pattern to emerge that would lead them to their killer. Her head swam and she closed her eyes. It might be a good idea to bring that into work and see if her colleagues had anything to add.

She tiptoed into the kitchen and flicked the kettle on, expecting the smell of coffee to lure Kate out from her room. Maggie found two cups and waited. She didn't want to snoop but desperately needed ibuprofen. She usually had some in her bag but failing that she would have a quick look in Kate's bathroom. Running her fingers through her hair like a comb, she pulled it back into a loose ponytail and cheered quietly to herself as she found some tablets in her bag to ease both the back and head pains that were consuming her. Kate shuffled into the room.

'Morning. I've made some coffee, if you'd like a cup?' Maggie held up a mug.

'You've read my mind. I'll need two strong cups before I go, it's the only way I can function.'

'Sleep well?' Maggie blushed and hoped Kate hadn't noticed as she averted her eyes away from the T-shirt that Kate wore for PJs.

'I did, thanks. My big furball cat, Salem, kept me company.' Kate stretched her arms.

Maggie forced a smile. She hadn't told Kate that Scrappy was missing and didn't really want to get into a conversation about it.

'I hope the couch was OK? And by the way, I'm not much of a morning person so don't take offence if I just get on with things before we go.'

Maggie breathed a sigh of relief. 'I'm good with you doing your own thing. How about we say an hour and then we set off?'

After showering, Maggie took the notes off the wall. 'Do you mind if I take these into work with me? See if a fresh pair of eyes can pick up something we didn't?'

'Not a problem. Thanks for staying last night. I'm feeling a little foolish but also much better about things today. Once I get rid of that lot, that is.' Kate pointed at the box and bag by the door.

'I'm sure it's nothing, but it's worth reporting.' In reality, Maggie *was* concerned and promised herself to keep closer tabs on Kate from now on.

Her mobile phone rang, and she noticed Kate jump.

'Hello?' Maggie ran a hand through her hair. 'Nathan? What is it?' Her face went pale and she swallowed.

'Maggie?' Kate stepped forward to take her arm.

Maggie's knees buckled, and Kate caught her as she fell. The phone dropped to the floor and they could hear Nathan's tinny voice shouting up to them:

*'Maggie, did you hear me? There's been another murder.'*

# Chapter 65

After leaving Kate at Markston and making sure that the details were logged, Maggie didn't have time to go back to her flat. The crime scene was already being attended to, so Nathan arranged to pick her up from Markston Police Station. They'd head to the scene together.

If this victim was Zoe Bridle, then Maggie still might be able to link Bill Raven to these current murders. However, the more she thought about it, the more she felt as if she was in a never-ending cycle of the same evidence. The evidence that had already been used to strengthen Raven's appeal.

'How much longer before we get there?' Maggie looked at her watch. She didn't tell Nathan about her light-headedness as he'd put her on desk duties.

'According to the GPS, another twenty minutes. There doesn't seem to be much out here, so our killer definitely has a vehicle.' He pointed at the rolling hills and forest outside the window. 'This place is miles from anywhere.'

'Unless the killer just jumped on a bus or train carrying a bag of body parts.'

Maggie took in her surroundings. The gravel road could

use some maintenance; every pothole jarred her. If she squinted her eyes, houses could be seen in the far distance so they weren't as isolated as Nathan thought. She noticed a pile of rubbish in the ditch. Fly-tipping was not uncommon on these country lanes.

'No need for the sarcasm.' They fell silent for a moment, before Nathan continued. 'Why haven't we more on ANPR then? Have we become too focused on Raven again that we're ignoring other pieces of evidence?'

Maggie rubbed her temples. She could feel a headache coming on and tried to keep her frustration in check. It wasn't her colleague she was annoyed with; it was everything about this case. 'We haven't got a vehicle to mark yet, as far as I am aware. Though if we get Bethany to go through the list again, we can put markers on anyone acting suspiciously and track them.'

'Aren't we already doing that?' Nathan focused on driving, but she noticed his knuckles turn white on the wheel.

'I'd assume so.'

'Hang on to that thought. We're here.'

'Bet you thought you'd be sitting behind a desk while us lowly officers did all the hard work,' Maggie said as they left the car. The shortage of staff and lack of resources meant that although Nathan now had the DS title, he'd still be working in a DC capacity.

'Yeah. That's about right.' He strolled off ahead.

Maggie looked around the area. It was a woodland on the outskirts of Stafford known as Burley Woods. The path at her feet was littered with leaves and weeds as it led her into the darkness of the forest. The earth and the decomposing leaves smelt like the bottom of a cave. Maggie shivered.

Similar to the previous crime scene, it was remote enough for the killer not to be disturbed, but not so remote that the dismembered body parts wouldn't be found. Maggie could see her breath as she walked quickly to keep the chill off.

Maggie looked around for the first response officers and for a moment she felt suddenly alone. No one was in sight. She turned around and peered through the undergrowth, trying to spot any movement. Her shoulders tensed as she caught a flash of colour off to the left. She tried to control her breathing and resisted the urge to shout for Nathan, who was still nowhere to be seen. It was probably nothing, just a bird or a fox. Walking fast and trying not to look behind her, she continued in the direction she thought Nathan had gone.

After a few minutes, she emerged into a clearing and spotted the comforting high-viz of a police uniform up ahead. She smoothed her hair down and told herself to stay calm, then headed towards the officer.

She signed in as if nothing had happened. 'Can you tell me what you have so far?' She handed his pen back.

The young officer was tall and pale. He looked nervous, as if this was one of his first assignments and he was trying to make a good impression. 'One arm and a leg, that's all.'

'How much of the area has been searched?'

'Um.' He looked around. 'Everywhere that's been cordoned off, I think. There are people still out there though, so there may well be more to find.' He looked at the floor.

'You're right. We can't take anything for granted. Maybe the killer has done this deliberately or ...' she pointed around the area, 'an animal could have moved the body parts somewhere else. There won't be anyone arriving for about half an hour, so why don't you join the search?'

'Yes, ma'am.' He swallowed.

Maggie remembered how it felt to be a new officer suddenly thrown into the deep end. But she also knew that sometimes facing your fears was the only way to defeat them. She gave him a nod then walked towards the forensic tent that had been set up over the body parts.

She ducked inside and found Nathan speaking with the duty SIO. 'What have you got?' Maggie asked, as she peered down at the plastic bags on the floor.

'Not much at the moment.' Nathan crouched down and pointed at the two blood-spattered limbs lying in plastic bags on the floor. 'A local walker and his dog nearly tripped over these this morning. The witness didn't see anything here when they went out yesterday morning, so these were dumped within the last twenty-four hours. It might be an idea to put out an appeal for any walkers who were in the area. Where is the rest of the victim? That's what I'd like to know.' Nathan blew on his hands and rubbed them together.

'You and me both. Probably strewn across the area; we just haven't found them yet. Might be worth contacting local officers in the surrounding area, see if they've found anything.'

'We're going to have to wait until we have more information on the victim. The witness gave a statement to the first responder but will be coming into the station tomorrow. Other than that, not much else we can do here except freeze.'

'Any trace evidence?' Maggie was stalling, she wasn't ready to leave.

His brows drew together. 'It's all being collected. I'll just check in with the guv and see if there is anything more she wants from us here.' He pulled out his phone. 'It looks like Dr Blake is heading out too.'

'OK. I'd like to speak to Fiona before we go if I can?'

He saluted and then laughed. 'Yes, ma'am. I thought I was the DS here.'

Maggie punched him on the arm and ducked out of the tent. She headed towards Dr Blake, her eyes scanning the area as she went. Taking a mental picture of the landscape. With what was found so far, she hoped that the latest victim was still alive. There was always a chance, and Maggie wouldn't rest until they knew for sure.

She stopped in her tracks when she saw a white shape running through the woods. Dr Blake, her eyes wide, her coat flapping in the wind. Maggie pulled out her baton. A crow took off from a branch high above and flew up into the sky, while a gust of wind shifted a pile of fallen leaves. Maggie started running after the doctor. That's when she heard the scream.

# Chapter 66

Her heart raced as she made her way through the long grass towards the sound. Nathan burst out of the tent and sprinted after her.

Maggie caught her breath and carried on running, her baton out and ready in her hand. The long grass made it heavy going.

'We're almost there.' Nathan reached her side and pointed ahead to two figures crouched down beneath a tree; it was Dr Fiona Blake and the young officer who had signed Maggie in when she arrived.

They slowed to a jog and approached them.

Dr Fiona Blake looked up at them with a frown. The young PC was visibly shaken, his breathing heavy and his eyes wide.

'More black bags?' Maggie stepped closer.

Fiona was still catching her breath. 'Another arm and a head to be exact.'

'I ... just stumbled on them.' The young PC stammered. He stood up and started pacing back and forth. 'Thought I smelt something and then just walked right over them.' He shuddered.

'All right, son.' Nathan stepped forward and put an arm on his shoulder. The PC stopped walking. 'Why don't you get a cup of tea from the tent and have a sit down?' Nathan nodded back the way they had come.

The PC nodded, took one final glance at the bags, then hurried off towards the tent. Once he had gone, Maggie and Nathan crouched down beside Fiona. 'What can you tell us?' Maggie leaned forward to get a closer look.

'I *can't* tell you the gender, but if I had to take an educated guess, I'd say female. If I compare this arm to the one over there,' she gestured across the field, 'I'd say they were from the same person. The hands are quite delicate and the nail polish would seem to match.' Reaching down she pointed at the arm. 'See here, two broken nails. I'm hoping that there may be some DNA.' She carefully moved the arm in the bin bag to seal the hand inside a clear plastic bag. 'And look at this.' She pointed at the second bag, which had been ripped open to reveal a bloody head, the face mauled by animals. 'ID will be difficult as the foxes beat us to it.'

'Anything else?' Maggie put a hand over her mouth to cover the smell.

'The bags were wrapped tightly with silver gaffer tape, like parcel packages. Except this one, of course, which had been torn open. The officer walked right over them.'

'Thanks.' Maggie stood up and her knees cracked. She blew out a sigh. 'Going to be difficult to establish which direction the offender came from.' Maggie looked around. The body parts were dumped in two separate areas both with various entry points; the team would be busy.

'Let's grab a coffee soon. It's been too long.' Maggie nodded to Fiona and began to walk back towards the tent. Nathan stayed with Fiona to help photograph the scene.

As Maggie walked, she spotted that same flicker of colour off to the left, but this time she knew it wasn't a fox. She walked carefully towards it, treading quietly through the long grass.

A figure was standing in the shadows, watching the forensic tent from a distance, chewing his finger and shifting from foot to foot. She noticed it was a stocky male, with a black hat covering what looked to be short brown hair.

'Stop! Don't move,' Maggie shouted. The man froze as she walked up to him. 'My name is DC Jamieson. Can you come out from behind that tree, so I can have a word?'

The man's eyes darted around, but he wouldn't look at Maggie directly. 'Erm ... OK, but I didn't see nothin'.' He stepped out and began rubbing the back of his neck, looking past Maggie at the crime scene.

'Are you OK? There's nothing to be worried about. I just want to ask you a few questions.'

'I told you. I didn't see nothing, all right? Just minding my own business. Nothing wrong with that, is there?' His pupils appeared dilated.

Taking her notepad out, she raised a placatory hand. 'Calm down, sir. There's no need to be defensive. Can I get your details? You may not think you saw anything, but you could be in shock.'

'I don't have anything to say ...'

Before Maggie had a chance to react, the man shot off running through the trees towards the road.

'Stop!' Maggie shouted and gave chase, but he was too quick. When she reached the top of the road, she couldn't see him anymore. Looking left and right, she hoped to see a door close or a gate swinging open, but there was no sign of movement.

'Fuck.' She muttered as she tried to catch her breath. She leaned into her shoulder, clicked the button and radioed Nathan. 'Can you come around to Knowle Hill and pick me up?'

'What's up?'

'Long story.'

'Gimme five.'

As she stood waiting for Nathan, Maggie recorded a description of the male in her notepad. He must live in the area to have disappeared so quickly. The house-to-house enquiry might find him. Maggie would be sure to include him as a person of interest at this stage and make sure the computer was updated for the field officers. Something about his defensiveness didn't sit well. There was also something odd about him and the way he made her feel, the way he shifted from foot to foot and couldn't meet her eye.

# Chapter 67

Nathan arrived five minutes later and pulled up in front of Maggie.

As she sat down in the car he let out a sigh. 'What happened?'

'I saw a man hiding at the edge of the forest, watching the crime scene techs. When I started questioning him, he started acting strangely.' Maggie tried to sound positive, but she knew that she had messed up again. 'He wouldn't look me in the eye and the next minute he ran off. I lost him up here somewhere.' She stared out the window and they sat in silence for a moment.

'Did he go left or right at the top of the road?'

'Left.' She pointed. 'Down that way.'

'Maybe he's still hiding behind some of these bushes.'

'No, I checked it out. But we might as well do a slow drive by to make sure. If he's there and tries to run off again, we've a better chance of keeping up in the car.'

Nathan put the car into gear and made his way up Knowle Hill at a snail's pace. As they rounded a corner, Maggie noted the road branched off and told Nathan to stop. He pulled over.

'See anything?'

'Not even a curtain twitching,' Maggie said.

'Where the hell could he have gone?'

'Let's head back to the station. I'll ask the field officers to keep an eye out and contact us if they come across him.'

Maggie wished she had been in better shape, but she was grateful that Nathan hadn't had a go at her for messing up the chase. As they drove back along the windy country lanes, Maggie couldn't help but wonder whether the man in the woods was their killer. Whether she had just let him get away.

# Chapter 68

Kate hated how jumpy she was feeling lately. She had worked very hard on identifying and managing this aspect of herself and she didn't want all that work to become undone because of some sick creep.

After delivering the items to the police station in Markston earlier that day, and saying goodbye to Maggie, Kate noted the crime number but understood that unless the person sending the things left a fingerprint or some other evidence, it was unlikely to lead anywhere. She was advised to keep a log of anything out of the ordinary and told not to touch any suspicious post. She was determined to continue as normal, to not let this consume her. When she had shown Maggie the letters and the box, she hadn't seemed overly concerned, at least not to her face. Kate would take that as a good sign. For all she knew, the items could be nothing more than coloured water and pork scratchings.

The last time Kate had been overcome with anxiety, she had locked herself away. Lost a considerable amount of weight and basically stopped associating with people. That had been a time when she felt lonely and isolated in London, far away from everyone she knew. She couldn't even pinpoint the trigger, but it had felt like the weight of the world was on her shoulders. Getting the job in Markston helped, or rather forced her out of the shell.

Her focus this time would be the case. Kate found it helped to target her energy on the most gruesome and gory aspects of life. It was probably the knowledge that she was helping to put one more evil individual away. And if saving someone else helped her save herself, then that was something she could believe in.

She stood at the bottom of the path that led to the entrance of her flat. The postie had a key to deliver inside the property and there was no box outside the security door. Once inside the main entrance, she took a deep breath and walked towards her front door. Her hands shook as she placed her key in the lock and twisted it. She closed her eyes as she pushed open the door.

'I hope you open your eyes soon, or you'll miss your post,' her neighbour said. She opened her eyes and saw that he was standing in his corridor, pointing at the post just inside her door.

'Thanks.' Her breathing quickened. 'You scared the hell out of me.' The neighbour took a step forward and Kate shuffled back into her flat.

'Oh, I'm so sorry. I seem to be making a habit out of scaring you. I just thought I would say hello, make sure you're all right.' He took another step closer. 'Is your lady friend around if you need someone to come over?'

'Pardon?' Kate stared at him. 'Have you been watching me?

Are you the one sending me the cards and the gifts?' She backed away holding her keys tightly in front of her.

'What? No. No. I think you have the wrong end of the stick. I just want to make sure you're all right. Oh jeez. I'm really sorry. I just happened to see you and your friend together.' His faced turned red and he raised his hands. 'Look, if you really want to know, I thought I might ask you out for a drink sometime and I was trying to sort of – you know – make conversation.' He let out a nervy laugh. Instantly Kate felt awful for being so accusatory.

'Sorry. I'm just a little on edge. Can we just start again?' Kate sighed. 'I'm too busy to go for a drink at the moment, sorry.' She tried to smile reassuringly but he went an even darker shade.

He nodded. 'Have a good evening. I'll keep an eye out for anyone hanging around. We do look out for each other in this building.'

'That's very kind of you. Goodnight, then.'

She entered her flat and shut the door behind her. Turning the key in the lock she let out another long sigh. Her foot kicked the letter on the floor. Another black envelope. No postage mark. Same gold writing. Kate stepped over the note, and got out the plastic gloves. She didn't even bother to open or read what was inside. She would leave that to the police now.

She dashed over to the windows and checked the locks, then closed the curtains. She wouldn't leave them open anymore when she went out to work.

Kate placed her laptop bag on the coffee table, went to the

kitchen and poured herself a glass of wine. Returning to the living room, she relaxed into the comfy chair. Opening her laptop, she decided to check her emails before she started working on the profile she promised Maggie. Her eyes paused on the email at the top of her inbox. She didn't recognize the sender, nor did she realize that the glass of wine had slipped from her hand. Glass shattered across the floor and she felt the cold splash of the wine on her leg. A red stain spread out in front of her across the carpet. It looked like blood ...

The email wasn't long, but it had been sent to her office email – something which very few people outside of the police and other agencies knew. She read the message again.

*Why did you have to involve the police?*

# Chapter 69

DI Rutherford stood in her doorway and looked out at the open-plan office. She watched as Bethany went through the CCTV evidence, hoping to find that one clue that could identify their killer. With each passing day and no new leads to follow, the strain on her team was evident. The latest body parts from the woods had caused DCI Hastings to add his own pressure, threatening to give the case to a more experienced DI. She couldn't let that happen. This job had already cost her enough.

She smiled when Bethany looked up and caught her gaze. She didn't want to disturb her, so she turned and headed back to her desk. Once the door was shut behind her, she opened the police records and read each new statement carefully, searching for any inconsistencies. If Hastings knew she was doing this, he would remind her that this wasn't her job – but Abigail always felt the best way to understand her team was to keep a hand in the operational side. After all, how could she question or challenge her officers if she didn't understand their job?

'Do you have a minute, guv?' Bethany stood at the door waiting to be asked in.

'Of course, have a seat. What's up?'

'Well I've been looking into Dr Vraines. It seems he has been accused in the past of falsifying records, accepting bribes and erm ...'

'Spit it out, I don't have time for this.' Rutherford crossed her arms.

'He's never been charged and the matters were dropped, but the police still flagged it on the system. The doctor had changed his last name to his wife's. Probably why we couldn't find anything sooner.'

DI Rutherford smiled. It was a solid lead, even if there were still things that needed to be worked on. 'Good job! Gather the intel together and hand it over to the fraud department. If Raven paid this doctor off, we could be one step closer to stopping his bail.'

'Will do, boss.'

DCI Hastings should be pleased with the news. Abigail finally had something worth sharing. She bet the press would be interested too.

# Chapter 70

Maggie hadn't even had the chance to put her coat down before she noticed Bethany waving her arms frantically at her.

'What is it?' She walked over to Bethany's desk and waited for her to calm down.

'Just had a call from downstairs. You've got a visitor.' She grinned. 'One of the field team was out last night and noticed a suspicious-looking male matching your description of the guy from Burley Woods.'

'Where was this?'

'Not far from Knowle Hill where you initially lost him. When the officer approached him, he made off again. But he tripped and they made the arrest. He's downstairs in an interview room.'

'What was he arrested for?'

'They found a wrap of heroin in his pocket.'

Maggie fist pumped the air. 'Let them know I'm on my way down.' This could be the break they needed.

Grabbing a pen and checking she had her notebook, Maggie headed to the custody suite. She found out which interview room the man was in and jogged the short distance to the door. She stopped outside and caught her breath, before knocking.

'Come in.' She was greeted with a smile from a young PC. 'I'll leave you to it.'

'Thanks. I'll catch up with you after I'm done.'

She waited until the PC left the room before she took a seat opposite the man. Maggie clicked on the digital recording device and reminded him he was under caution before introducing herself. 'Hi ...' looking down on the statement she found his name, 'Craig. I'm DC Jamieson. You may remember me?'

The man briefly glanced her way before he returned to staring at the wall and biting his nails. His clothes were wrinkled, his hair unkempt and a stale smell of sweat emanated from his body. Maggie noted his hands fidgeting and wondered if he was nervous or desperate for a fix.

She leaned forward and let the silence build.

'Don't know what you're talking about.' He shifted in his chair.

'How about I refresh your memory? Burley Woods? You were lurking around watching the police at a crime scene like an addict waiting for his dealer to arrive. When I approached and called out to speak to you, you ran off in the direction of Knowle Hill. Why did you run off?'

'Why the fuck do you think?' He snorted.

'Did you have drugs in your possession at that time too?'

'What do you want with me? The drugs were for personal use, so just charge me, bail me, whatever. I don't have time for this shit.'

'I'd like to ask you *why* you were hanging around the crime scene? Did you see anything prior to the police arriving? Do you make a habit of hanging around crime scenes?' Maggie was beginning to wonder if this could be the mysterious man Raven had mentioned. Though the name didn't fit, it was likely Raven gave a false name to throw them off the scent.

'Thought you coppers were supposed to be clever. Why do you think I would be hanging around there? And no, I don't go hanging around crime scenes. What do you take me for? Some kinda weirdo.'

'Yes, that is exactly what I take you for. Look. Can we just cut the bullshit here? The sooner you answer my questions, the sooner you'll be back out and can go and get that gear you so obviously need. If you want to play games, I'm more than happy to keep you locked in a cell until you're vomiting your guts up all over the walls.'

'Fuck sake. Yes. I go there to score drugs, OK? Like you said, an addict waiting for a score. Happy now? There's usually someone waiting to deal, but when I saw the police tape, I just wanted to take a look. I had a little bit of gear on me and didn't want to be caught, so I freaked out and ran off. I live right around the corner. That's why you couldn't find me. I was watching you look around from my window.'

'So, you hadn't been to the woods earlier, or heard anything that sounded suspicious in the early hours of the morning? '

'Nope. Can I go now?'

'Can you account for your whereabouts?'

'If you're asking me where I was, I'll need to check my diary.' He smirked.

'This is no laughing matter. You could be facing serious charges.'

'Christ. Take it easy. I do work you know. *Long* hours. And when I'm done, I go straight home. My girlfriend works in the evenings, so I have to look after the kids. You can check that all out. Now really, are we done here? I don't want to lose my job.'

Maggie sighed with frustration. He was just some loser in the wrong place at the wrong time. 'I'll speak to the other officer. He'll deal with the drugs matter. If you think of anything, give me a call.' She stood and looked directly at him. 'Next time an officer calls out and wants to speak with you, *don't* run off.' She left the room and shut the door behind her.

After letting the custody sergeant know she was finished, Maggie headed back up to her office. She was disappointed that had led nowhere, however she sent a quick email to social care. The man admitted to drug use and having caring responsibilities for his children. They could deal with that.

She had known the minute she walked into the interview room that it would probably be a waste of time, as he didn't look like he had enough sense to tie his laces, let alone chop up a body. She'd get Bethany to check out his movements.

Bethany looked up with eager eyes as Maggie arrived at the open-plan office. 'Any luck?'

'Total waste of time. Drugs, nothing more. But can you do me a favour and check out these details for me?' She passed over a piece of paper. 'Any CCTV in the area?'

'Nothing so far. I'll keep you posted. Nathan called. He

wants you to meet him at Stafford Probation this afternoon. Said he booked an appointment with Tony Preston – he's Bill Raven's current officer.'

'Thanks.' Maggie wrote a quick email to Sarah Hardy to get the heads-up on Tony Preston. Although Probation were generally helpful, she had come across a few arseholes and wanted as much forewarning as possible. Her phone dinged and Maggie read the immediate response from Sarah. It confirmed her worst fears: Mr Preston was a pompous arse. Not the best officer, he was arrogant and manipulative and often behind in updating his records.

Maggie rang Nathan. She didn't have time to waste and would rather not have to trek to Stafford Probation office if she could avoid it.

*'DS Wright speaking.'*

'Hey. How soon do you need me?'

*'Don't bother. Mr Preston has nothing new to offer; in fact, he doesn't seem to know much about his own case and his records are a mess. They've agreed to send over his most recent risk assessment though, so we may find something there, once it's been updated that is.'*

'Why isn't his manager all over him?'

*'That's what I'm going to find out.'*

Maggie was relieved. After learning about Dr Vraines and then the recent avenue being a non-starter, she had enough paperwork to fill out before the end of her day. She didn't envy Tony Preston. If Nathan got his way, the Probation Officer might not be holding that case, or any case, for much longer.

# Chapter 71

With the start of a new week, Maggie was hoping that they would have something soon to push the case forward. She'd arranged a meeting with Dr Blake at her lab. Waiting for the forensic evidence to come in dribs and drabs made her struggle to put the full picture together. If she could talk everything through with Fiona, the missing pieces may fall into place.

Fiona worked from Staffordshire's Police Headquarters in a specially designed lab that was recently funded by the police crime commissioner. The pathologist report had confirmed that the most recent victim had died from suffocation before her body was dismembered into what Fiona guessed were eight parts, even though only the head, both arms and lower part of the left leg had been recovered.

Unfortunately, animals had made a meal out of the victim's face, so they'd need to rely on other techniques to get a formal ID. New and old track marks on the arms also established that the latest victim was an intravenous drug user and was likely drugged in captivity.

'In terms of the weapon, can you talk me through your findings?'

'No problem. In dismemberment cases, it's common that circular saws or large kitchen knives are used.' Fiona pulled down a screen, fired up her laptop and opened the post mortem pictures so that she could show Maggie the points she was discussing as they went along. 'You can see with our unidentified female here that the limbs were individually wrapped first in plastic shopping bags before being wrapped in black bin bags and then secured with silver duct tape. All items that you can purchase at local grocery or DIY stores.' Fiona flicked to the next picture. 'The examination of dismembered limbs requires a whole different approach. I need to investigate any wounds, tissue, bones and cartilage to make sure forensic evidence isn't lost in transit.'

'Do you think some of it's been lost?' Maggie pressed her lips together.

'You can wipe that look of concern off your face. My team are vigilant and we've recorded and compiled the evidence without issue.'

Dr Blake continued. 'We need to consider how the victims of murder are generally dismembered. Contrary to popular belief, a person doesn't need medical knowledge to chop someone up. Sorry to be so blunt.'

Maggie listened intently.

'It's quite demanding though, both physically and psychologically, so you're probably looking at someone in reasonable physical shape. But also someone who doesn't have a problem undertaking gruesome tasks.' Fiona spoke as if she was talking about what she was going to buy for her dinner.

Dr Blake put three pictures on the whiteboard of all three

victims for comparison. 'Have a look at these. A body is commonly dismembered into six pieces. Sometimes skin, tissue and muscle can also be removed in segments, this is often as an attempt to remove tattoos or fingers, anything to hinder identification. None of this occurred with our victims.'

Maggie took out her notebook and started writing down the key points to refer to at a later time. Why does the killer want the women to be identified, when this clearly helps the police build a case against them?

While Maggie was in mid-scribble, Dr Blake carried on. 'An electric saw was used to dismember the first victim, Lorraine Rugman.'

Maggie rubbed her temples.

'You'll see that after the first murder, the killer honed their technique and changed their weapon. They moved to a more efficient instrument.' She clicked to the next picture. 'A pair of long-arm ratchet anvil loppers. These are able to cut through skin, tissue, muscle and some bone in a quick and effective manner. Commonly used for cutting large branches out of trees.'

'Really? I'll be watching the gardener more closely now.' Maggie tried to lighten the mood.

Fiona laughed. 'I definitely believe the killer has refined their skills, and loppers are easily purchased and fairly cheap.' She put another picture up on the screen. Dr Blake pointed to it. 'See there? The teeth of the blade snagged the flesh here and here. Small particles of concrete dust and dirt were found in the cuts, so from that, I concluded that Lorraine was probably killed on a concrete floor, something like an unfinished cellar for instance. You'll recall the flat where Raven had alleged he murdered the victims had wood floors with some carpeting. No wood or carpet fibres were embedded in the any of the parts recovered. If you find the location, we can compare the samples.'

'But we know Raven couldn't have killed these women, so that's not surprising. What if the killer moved the body elsewhere to dismember it?'

'That's a possibility. Dismembering a body produces significant contamination of the scene and possibly the offender. Body fluids may seep into carpets, through floorboards, and between tiles and blood splatter would be inevitable if the victims were alive at the point of death.'

'So, when we do find the kill site, forensics will be looking for all those things?'

'Yes, and more. Limbs may have been lifted and rested on a surface to enable ease when sawing and this can leave tool marks on a variety of surfaces, for instance on the edge of a bathtub. This is just my personal opinion, but I think the disposal sites were carefully chosen. They were specific. The killer wanted the parts to be found, the same way they wanted the victims to be identified.'

'I agree with you. There are still parts that remain missing, though, and we want to be able to put the families' minds at rest.'

'Animal activity may affect that. I'd suggest you also look in any nearby lakes or canals. The parts may have been weighed down and disposed of.'

'We'll do our best.' Maggie managed a weak smile.

'Well, in terms of the trace evidence, and the hands in all three of the victims, the fingernails were first examined for damage and then sampled for the offender's DNA. We lifted finger and palm prints and searched the database. Due to their lifestyle, two of the victims were found in the system for various offences relating to drug possession and prostitution and now we're just waiting to confirm the third. I'll be sure to send that over as soon as it comes in. I'm going to have to kick you out now as there is a fellow waiting for me.' She pointed towards the mortuary examination room.

'Sorry for delaying you and thanks so much for all of this. I'll speak to you soon.' Maggie put her notebook away and headed for the door.

'Without being rude, let's hope you don't have to ...'

# Chapter 72

On the short bus ride back to the office, Maggie reviewed her notes. Three dead women and other than the J-man and Adrian Harrison, the team didn't have anyone else in their sights. Well, there was Bill Raven, of course, but they needed the connection. When she arrived at the police station, everyone was focused on their screens. Maggie said a quick hello, sat down and got to work.

The phone on her desk rang. Maggie answered it and listened as the caller spoke in a low tone.

'I've just watched the news and saw something about the murders of those women.'

'OK. Before you go on, can I just get your name and details?' Maggie raised her pen to the pad of paper on her desk.

'No! I'll tell you what I know, but I don't want anything leading back to me. If that's not good enough, I'll just hang up now.' His voice was shaky.

'That's fine, sir. What is it that you want to tell me?'

'Sasha Thompson. She's always with Adrian. If you want to find him, ask around for her. He won't be far from her.'

'Do you know who I should be asking for this information?' The man provided her with a few names. Maggie scribbled the details down as fast as she could. She hoped she'd be able to read her writing afterwards. They had already known about Sasha and Maggie had interviewed her with a few others at the start of the original investigation. At the time, she had been dismissed as a person of interest; lately, after providing details showing she was in Manchester when Lorraine's remains had been discovered, she had been ruled out of having any involvement. When they tried to locate her again recently, it was assumed she had left the area, possibly with Adrian.

'And they ain't gone you know.'

'What do you mean?'

'The news says they had left Staffordshire. That's a load of bull. Apparently, they came into some money, probably drug money. Robbing bastards. They're definitely still about though, as a friend of mine scored some weed off Adrian the other day.'

'Can I ask why you've waited so long to come forward? Is there any chance you can come in and speak to me? I'd like to get more details off you in person if I could?'

'I didn't think anything I had to say was important, but once I saw that bullshit on the telly, well I had to say something. Adrian's a prick. He deserves to get hassled. As for coming in ... Fuck that. I've told you all I know.' The man hung up.

Maggie stared at the receiver before replacing it in the cradle.

She didn't want to get her hopes up, he could be trying to

get Adrian in trouble for some drug deal gone wrong, but the caller had been so sure. She didn't realize she had been smiling until Nathan's voice broke her from the thoughts.

'Are you going to tell me what's happening, or do I have to guess?'

'You're not going to believe this. I think we finally may have something.'

He looked at her, head tilted and waited for her response. 'Well?'

'Someone has come forward. They saw the most recent press conference and remembered Sasha Thompson was with Adrian Harrison around the time of Raven's arrest.'

'Yeah, I thought we already knew that.'

'If you let me finish.' She gave him a frosty look.

Nathan's face flushed and he apologized for interrupting. Maggie immediately regretted being so sharp and updated him on what the caller had said.

'I'm going to pass some of the names he gave on to Bethany to check, and I'll check some too. Then go out and speak to anyone who may be able to shed more light on their whereabouts.' A wide grin spread across Maggie's face.

'Excellent work. As much as I hate to admit it, maybe the press conferences were a good idea after all.'

Maggie wasn't sure she agreed with Nathan's sentiment, her ego was more than bruised after the media had verbally slaughtered her, but she knew this was a promising development and hoped it didn't lead them down the wrong path. She gathered her notes and headed to the incident room.

# Chapter 73

DI Rutherford stormed into the incident room waving the pathologist's report around. 'Open your ears, people – *this* is going to throw a spanner in the works and the shitstorm it produces will be legendary.'

The room fell silent. 'We have an ID on the victim found in Burley Woods and ...'

'Come on, guv.' Maggie stood.

'... it does *not* belong to the third victim that Raven had confessed to killing.' There was a collective sigh in the room. 'So that leaves us with two questions: where the hell is Zoe Bridle and how does Veronica Chapel fit into this pattern of murders? We need answers.' She turned to the board, scanning the evidence and suspects. 'Maggie, I take it this is not the news you were hoping for?'

'I'd be lying if I said I wasn't disappointed ... Where is Zoe Bridle? We'll need to trace her.'

'She's technically a misper and we don't have the resources to take on other people's work. We can ask to be kept in the loop though. Have we located the J-man or Adrian Harrison?' She looked around the room waiting for a response.

'Not yet, guv.' Bethany opened her notebook and flipped through the pages. 'Everything we do know is there on the board. When I double checked with the prison, they were adamant that Harrison had given the address that he shared with Raven as his last release address, and when officers went around to chat with him they were told he hasn't been seen for months. We now believe that no address checks were undertaken by the prison and after returning to the flat to collect his belongings, Harrison fled the area with the Thompson woman.'

'Ah, ma'am. I have ...'

Rutherford held up her hand. 'Hang on, Maggie. Months? So how long between the last sighting and Lorraine's murder?' DI Rutherford felt flustered.

'About three months. One person in the building said they saw him leave with a large duffel bag. I guess we can assume that's when he left? The witness couldn't give an exact date but it tallies with the time Harrison was released. The landlord says that a lot of property had been left behind though. The reliability of those in that building is questionable given their ... um ... background ...'

'Excuse me, ma'am but I have ...'

'Two seconds, Maggie. I'd just like to finish this conversation if I can.' She glared for a moment before returning to Bethany. 'Care to expand on that?'

'Most, if not all, the residents are substance misusers. It seems to be the place the council sends anyone who flags up as homeless.'

'But the landlord surely can be taken at his word?'

'Well, he never actually confirmed a date when Adrian left. He had heard that Harrison had been released from prison and said he went around to collect the rent owed. When he got no replies to his visits, he left a note saying he is giving 24 hours' notice and then would be entering the premises. When he got no response to the final warning, he went in. The place was vacant. The landlord claims he then chucked out everything that was left behind.'

'Meaning perhaps Harrison may well be who we should have been focusing on all along. I thought he had a rock-solid alibi when Raven confessed. How was that missed?' DI Rutherford looked at Maggie.

'This is what I was trying to tell you. Adrian did have an alibi and it wasn't missed. Seems he spent a lot more time with the Thompson woman who claimed she was with him, than at the flat he shared with Raven. Followed her around like a lost puppy, according to everyone. That was one of the reasons it seemed likely that Raven committed the offences in the flat. No disruptions if his flatmate was never around.' Maggie's expression hardened. 'But I just spoke to an anonymous caller who said that Adrian and Sasha are still in the area – they never left. We don't know if they still associate anymore but I think it's fair to say that this could also call into question the original statement given to the police.'

DI Rutherford circled Adrian's name on the whiteboard. 'We're moving Harrison from a person of interest status to our primary suspect. We need to locate him. Speak to anyone who knows him ... *again!* Find this Thompson woman too. If they're not together anymore, she may shed some new light on the investigation. Bethany, do a trace on what type of vehicle he drives and flag it with the ANPR, please. We're also going to have to revisit everything we had in terms of Bill Raven, except this time, home in on Harrison. Let's see what we can find out from Raven. Maggie, Nathan, push him harder but be subtle. He may see it in the news at a later date but maintain the façade that we want his help rather than we're interrogating him.'

DI Rutherford noticed a distant look on Maggie's face and knew she was miles away, combing back through the evidence. She'd worked long enough with Maggie to recognize her habits. She left her to it. She had more important things to do, like explain to the DCI why they needed to revisit the original case file once more and point the finger at someone who they were all adamant had nothing to do with the case. The review commission were going to have a field day with this.

DI Rutherford needed a strong cup of coffee before she picked up the phone and made the call. *Maybe an email would be better?* She knew she'd have to speak to DCI Hastings at some point and she'd rather take the verbal beating now.

There was a time when her boss was a lot less stressed about things. It wasn't even that he was getting pressure from the higher ups. He just didn't seem to have his heart in being a DCI anymore and would find any excuse to get a complaint against him. Something was definitely going on but she wouldn't be the one to bite. If he wanted a way out or a demotion, she refused to have that on her conscience.

She took a deep breath and prepared for the onslaught of expletives that she knew would be coming her way.

'Hastings, here.'

'Hello, sir – it's DI Abigail Rutherford. I just wanted to update you on the murder cases we're investigating.' She relayed the information to her boss and was surprised at how calm he was about the situation. There were a few swear words, but ultimately, he thanked her and left her to get on with it.

She was worried now. There must be something going on in the background that she wasn't aware of. She'd have to worry about that some another time because there was a killer out there, a solid suspect and time wasn't on their side.

# Chapter 74

Maggie hung up the phone; there was only one more number left to call from the information the anonymous man had given her. It was not looking good. She picked up the receiver and dialled.

'Yeah. Who's this?'

'Hi. My name is DC Maggie Jamieson from Stafford Police Station—'

'He ain't done shit, OK. What are you bothering me for?'

'The reason I'm calling is because I was told you may be able to tell me where I can find or how I can contact Sasha Thompson?'

'What do you want her for?' The woman hesitated before speaking again. 'I don't know where she is, OK?'

'Are you sure? I was told you definitely had her number.'

'I don't know who fed you that bullshit, but like I said, I have no clue so stop bothering me.' The woman hung up before Maggie could get anything more out of her.

'Fuck.' There was something in her voice that made Maggie pause. Bethany walked over.

'What's up?'

'Well no one has Sasha's contact details. None of the numbers we have are sharing anything with us. Do you think you can get any details on their addresses? Maybe if we paid them a visit ...'

'I can try. But if they're burners, it's unlikely we'll get anything of use. I might have some news though.' There was a spark in Bethany's eyes.

'Don't keep me hanging.'

'I was going through the CCTV from the prison. Raven's visitors to be exact. You know how he said his brother visited?' Bethany began walking back to her desk and motioned for Maggie to come over. Sitting down, she pulled up a screenshot from the prison.

'What am I looking at?' All Maggie could see was the back of a head and a hand, partially covered by a long sleeve.

Bethany pointed at the hand. 'Look there. See that tattoo?'

Maggie leaned in to get a closer look at the screen. 'Yeah. Does that mean something?'

Bethany reduced the picture and pulled up Adrian Harrison's details and scrolled down to where information on body markings are recorded. 'Take a look at this ...'

# Chapter 75

Maggie had woken up feeling very positive about the day ahead. She wondered how long that feeling would last. Before everyone had left work last night, DI Rutherford asked them all to be back for 8 a.m. She'd had a quick conversation with Kate when she had got home, and they both seemed to be on the same page regarding the possible suspect. Moving Adrian up from a person of interest to prime suspect status lit a fire in Maggie, but what pleased her more was that it should ensure that Raven wouldn't get bailed. It could even further implicate him in the crimes. Although she often hated the media for sensationalizing things, she had to admit that it might have paid off on this occasion.

She picked her phone up from the nightstand and looked at the time. *Shit.* A quick shower and coffee would wake her up, and the walk to the bus stop would too.

Thirty minutes later, she opened the door and zipped up her duffel coat as the cold air hit her face and goose bumps began to form. A car alarm went off in the distance as Maggie walked briskly to the bus stop. She had to be careful as the path was slippery from the frost. Rubbing her hands together, she was grateful she didn't have to wait too long. The bus got her to the train station with only minutes to spare.

When she arrived at Stafford station, she texted Nathan to see if he wanted a coffee from Starbucks. Within seconds, her mobile pinged and she opened the message:

***Hell yeah***

She'd get Bethany and DI Rutherford one too or else face the wrath of their evil stares. The darkness had subsided, and the sun was making an appearance. Maggie smiled as she strode to the police station. Exercise was having a positive impact on her physical and mental well-being.

When she arrived in the office, everyone was already there, and she started to hand out the coffees.

'What's this for?' DI Rutherford eyed her suspiciously.

'I think, thank you is the actual response you're looking for.' Maggie laughed.

DI Rutherford raised an eyebrow. 'So, we're just waiting for Dr Moloney then.'

'Oh shit. I forgot to get Kate one.' Maggie rubbed her forehead.

'That's OK,' Bethany called out. 'I'm not much of a coffee drinker, she can have mine.'

Kate arrived at the office. Maggie smiled and gave her a wave, holding out the Americano that Bethany had kindly offered up.

'Morning, everyone. Ah, thanks, Maggie. Exactly what I need.' There were a few laughs in the room, but Kate seemed none the wiser.

'Now that everyone is here, let's make our way to the incident room and run through things.' DI Rutherford walked out of the room and the rest of the team followed.

Taking their seats, they listened as DI Rutherford went over the details of Maggie's interview with Craig, the man from Burley Woods and the field teams' update on Steven's son, the witness at Blackwood Estate. Neither of these men were considered a person of interest anymore. Their names were crossed off the board.

'After some digging following a few false leads from that anonymous caller Maggie spoke to, Bethany has now located what we believe is Adrian Harrison's current address.' Maggie silently clapped to herself, and Bethany couldn't hide her embarrassment. She wasn't one for taking credit, even when it was due.

'We're now just waiting on the warrant, which should hopefully come through in the next hour or so. When that happens, I want Maggie and Nathan to execute it. Bethany, keep digging and see if you can work your magic and locate Sasha Thompson. With any luck, she may well be at his property too, but we can't take any chances. Kate – I'd like to personally thank you so far for the profiles you've provided. They've really focused the team on avenues that we might not have considered initially. I'd like for you to stay back here, and cross-reference any links to Bill Raven.'

Kate nodded.

'Do we know when Raven is next due to appear in court? I take it we'll be handing over whatever we uncover?' Maggie directed her question to DI Rutherford.

'Nathan is collating all the details and once we finalize the arrest of Harrison, it will be ready to go. If it has any relevance, the CPS and the courts will take the appropriate action.'

'Playing devil's advocate here, and I don't mean to be difficult, but why are you all so sure that it's Harrison who is the accomplice? The reason I ask is that from all the information I have read about him and shared with you all, he comes across as more of a follower than a leader. I'm not sure he'd be the main instigator.' Kate finished speaking and everyone turned to look at her.

'What do you mean? Your profile fits Harrison, doesn't it?' Maggie went through her notes and pulled out the information that Kate had previously sent the team.

'It does ... and it doesn't. I was going over things again last night and while I believe that Adrian Harrison has played some part in the murders, I'm not sure I'd have him down as my main suspect. In fact, the more I think about it, the woman is the stronger and more dominant of this duo. I'm beginning to wonder whether she's pulling the strings with instructions from Raven.' There was a look of confusion around the room.

'But Sasha never visited Raven in prison. We've established that Harrison did. Do you think he was the messenger between the two?' DI Rutherford frowned.

'Yes. I initially thought exactly as you all did. Harrison was the accomplice. But on closer examination, he doesn't seem to have the brains to pull this off. These murders were organized. They took planning. Look at Harrison's history: he sells drugs and gets caught, so he isn't very good at covering his tracks. He isn't arrogant, has a low IQ; there are just too many variables that don't add up. Have you spoken to Sasha yet?'

Maggie shook her head. 'She was spoken to when Lorraine was found, along with all of Lorraine's associates. But we didn't find anything at the time, so she was dismissed as a person of interest. We haven't been able to locate her since either.'

'I thought Raven owns a house. Didn't I read somewhere that his grandmother left him a property? Or did he sell it?' Kate queried.

'No, he definitely still has it, but field officers went around there initially and nothing unusual was reported. It's a small bungalow in Doxley. I also went around there. It didn't look lived in from what I could see through the windows. There are no immediate neighbours in the vicinity and those I did speak with, said they haven't noticed any unusual activity.' Maggie looked around the room to see if any of her colleagues had anything further to add.

Kate played with her hair for a moment, then tugged her ear. 'Do we know if he owns or lived in any other properties? One that perhaps has a cellar?'

'Other properties? We haven't come across any others. Why? What are you thinking?' Maggie noticed the smile on Kate's face and her heart began to race.

'I'm thinking you had better search past records. The house may be the key.'

# Chapter 76

As the briefing ended and they were just about to collect the warrant, a call came in and the team were informed that the body of a male had been found hanging in a flat. Someone wanting drugs had stumbled across the body and rather than sticking around, they called 999 and made themselves scarce. Maggie raced to the pool car and waited for Nathan. She hit the steering wheel repeatedly. *Damn! Damn! Damn!*

Maggie made sure she would be the one driving to the scene. She wanted to be there before too many other people attended. The building was a beacon on the dilapidated street, surrounded by prefab houses, patches of yellow grass strewn with broken bottles and animal excrement. The area was well known for drug and gang activity.

When they arrived, Maggie stood in the doorway and mentally processed the image before her. The door had been open. Grimy windows and peeling wallpaper showed just how much the landlord and tenant cared about the upkeep. Maggie could hear a faucet dripping and the neighbour's TV could be heard through the paper-thin walls.

The body dangled from a metal beam that must have been placed there to stabilize the walls and floor above. He'd been right under their noses all along. Although they had yet to make a formal ID, Maggie was sure she was staring at Adrian Harrison. They would need to find out how long he had been renting this property, from whom and why the landlord never contacted them when the appeals for information had gone out.

She looked at Nathan, who seemed transfixed on the body and gave him a nudge. 'What's going through that head of yours?'

'Looks like a clear-cut suicide to me.' He shrugged.

'Look around the room, Nathan. What else do you see?' She threw her hands in the air, surprised he wasn't seeing the obvious.

Maggie watched as Nathan's eyes took in the room. Then the moment of recognition. 'The couch has been moved. A struggle maybe? The magazines have been knocked off that side table too.'

The forensic pathologist arrived at that precise moment and Maggie stopped her before she reached the body. 'Hey Fiona. Look, we haven't been near the body but something about this doesn't feel right.'

Fiona looked around the room. 'Are you thinking murder? He'll tell us whether this is staged or not.' She pointed at the figure hanging.

The pathologist went to the body and began her examination. They helped her cut Harrison down and lay him on a sheet of plastic.

'Looks like you might be right, Maggie,' Fiona said. 'Look.'

They crouched down next to the body and waited for the pathologist to explain. Eyes wide open, Harrison stared blankly at the ceiling.

Fiona pointed at the victim's neck. 'Along with the rope marks, can you see the additional bruising? My guess is, someone tried to strangle him first and then finished him off by hanging him. There seems to be some bruising on the face, might have been a punch?'

'Pretty sloppy for this killer then, wouldn't you say?' Maggie looked at the discolouration.

'The victim may have been in a fight previously, we don't know. We'll have to wait for the time of death.'

'Thanks, Fiona.' Maggie left her to continue with processing the rest of the scene. 'You heard her, boss. Not a suicide. Do you think the killer was interrupted?'

'You know I hate when you call me that. Could be the witness that found him scared off our killer. We'd better round up the troops.'

She radioed back to the office and gave them an update. Preliminary checks would be undertaken while Maggie and Nathan finished up at the scene.

Maggie couldn't believe this. Their prime suspect was dead. Was it because of what he did or what he knows?

# Chapter 77

DI Rutherford paced her office. At the rate she was going, she wouldn't have any carpet left by the end of the day. The pathologist had confirmed Adrian Harrison had been drugged and strangled prior to being strung up in his flat. A near fatal dose of heroin had been administered, more than likely to make the kill easier for the murderer.

Forensics from the empty cargo bin had also come in and showed the towel was covered in pigs' blood. The other blood droplets found were also animal. Raven had led them on a wild goose chase. No drug paraphernalia was found in the container and when the landlord of Harrison's old flat was pushed, he advised that he had received a threatening letter from an unknown source to warn him not to cooperate with the police. There was no J-man after all.

The team would be disappointed. They had been hoping to wrap up the ongoing investigation, as everything had been pointing to Harrison as their killer. The question of whether or not Bill Raven was involved in any of the murders was still open to debate, although given the new information, it was looking more and more likely. DI Rutherford wasn't looking forward to breaking the news to the team and still trying to maintain their morale. She reached down and picked up the glass of water from her table. Her mouth was dry. The cold water against the back of her throat made her body tremble. Gathering the details from pathology, she left her office and headed out into the open-plan section.

The room was quiet; she almost didn't want to interrupt her team. They were in the midst of putting all their findings on the police system and filling in the necessary paperwork. She cleared her throat. 'Can I have everyone's attention for a moment, please?' Chairs turned in her direction. 'I've had the report back from pathology.' She could see the gleam of excitement in their eyes and it nearly broke her to have to carry on. 'I'm afraid it's not the news we've been expecting.'

'What do you mean, ma'am?' Nathan spoke the words that others couldn't.

'Well, it's now been officially confirmed. Adrian Harrison was murdered and then hung to make it look like suicide. It also seems Mr Raven had fed us bogus information about the freight cargo bins – there is no J-man. I'll send around the full details of the report, so you can all read the specifics for yourself, but that means the investigation is still open.' The room erupted in a wave of curses. 'OK. OK. Quiet down. We can't let our emotions get the best of us. We still have a killer out there who wanted us to believe that Adrian Harrison was our man. Now that we know that's not the case, we need to trace his last movements, talk to his neighbours and find out who else has been inside that flat.'

Bethany interrupted. 'I'll start interrogating the CCTV of

the surrounding area, ma'am. Track down people and dig up anything else that may be relevant.'

'Excellent. Report any findings to Nathan. Maggie, will you go out with a few of the field officers? You know this case inside out. DCI Hastings is going to want a complete update as of yesterday, so can we get this done as soon as? We need to be one hundred per cent sure we have everything.'

'On it, ma'am. What about Sasha Thompson? Do we have anything yet?' Maggie waited for further instruction.

DI Rutherford looked around the room. 'Bethany is working on locating Sasha after that phone call. She has to be our prime suspect after what Kate said and now that everyone else is falling off the list. Bethany will let you know when she has a location or some information to follow up on. Nathan, I want you to work with the COMMS Officer and release a brief update to the press. Do not link anything to the other murder cases and don't answer any questions. Am I clear?'

'Crystal. I'll read over this report and then draft something.'

'I'll be placating Hastings and any of the other senior officers who'll want more of an explanation than we have here. Everyone knows what they need to be doing.' There was a resounding *yes* from the room and DI Rutherford thanked them all for their time. She knew that they'd just had their bubble burst and she wasn't looking forward to the bollocking from the DCI that awaited her.

Returning to her office, she sat down and rubbed her temples. She could feel a migraine setting in and had to fight it off. Her team needed her, and she wasn't about to drop the ball by giving in.

# Chapter 78

Maggie couldn't hide her feelings about Adrian's death or the news about the J-man and the cargo bin. She kicked the side of her desk and then instantly regretted it as a sharp pain travelled from her big toe, right up to her hip. *Damn.* Her desk had more than enough dents in it now after this case.

She shut down her computer and began to gather what she'd need before she headed downstairs to grab a few of the field officers and go over to Adrian Harrison's property. It might give her a better picture of the situation.

'Can you let Nathan know I'm off now.' She waved to Bethany as she left the office.

Maggie took the stairs two by two and nearly tripped over when she reached the bottom.

She stood for a moment and straightened her shirt before opening the door that led to the main floor field team office. She scoured the room to see who might be free and immediately spotted PC Jeff Oakes and a PCSO she didn't recognize. She knew PC Oakes from before she joined the murder team and he always had a keen eye for detail. She hoped he would be free.

'Jeff!' She waved. 'Any chance you and another body are free to accompany me to a crime scene? I need to interview some of the tenants and have a look around the flat again.'

'Hey!' He had a warm smile and appeared genuinely pleased to see her. 'Sure. Let me just finish up here and Brian can join us too.' Maggie acknowledged the PCSO and thanked Jeff. Looking out the window she ran through the information they had so far in her head.

'All set. Are we taking the pool car?' Jeff signalled to the PSCO to follow.

'If there is one, that'd be great.'

'Not a problem, Brian can sign it out and meet us out back.'

Maggie nodded and accompanied Jeff to the back parking lot.

Just under a half hour later and they had arrived at the scene. The area was rundown and in need of some attention, if the local council could ever be bothered. The residents wouldn't be happy to see more police presence in the area. This was a high crime area, mainly because most of the people placed here were on Probation, just released from prison or involved in some sort of criminal activity. Maggie caught a few people staring at them from the windows and nudged Jeff. 'Do you want to start on the third floor and I'll take Harrison's floor? Brian can speak to residents on the first floor. Just remember to write down anything and everything, even if it seems insignificant. I know I don't need to say that, but my gut tells me there is something here that we have missed, and I don't want to be caught out at a later time.'

Both men nodded, and Maggie led the way into the building. The floor was sticky. Her shoes squished underfoot. Maggie jogged up the stairwell to the second floor and as she made her way to the entry door, she noticed drug paraphernalia in the corner on the landing. She shook her head and took extra care. Her first port of call would be Adrian's flat.

Entering his flat, there was a pungent odour that burned her nostrils. The smell of death coupled with garbage and putrid water, if she had to guess. The room before her was a mess. She took out the blue protective gloves she had stuffed in her pocket before leaving the station. If she did happen upon anything missed, she didn't want it to be compromised.

The flat consisted of three small rooms and a bathroom – the living area, the kitchen and a double bedroom. The floor creaked as Maggie made her way to the bedroom. Clothes covered the manky carpet and other than a mattress on the floor and a broken wardrobe, there wasn't much to be seen. She prised the wardrobe door open and found nothing but more dirty clothes. Next stop was the bathroom. When she looked in the mirrored cabinet hung loosely on the wall, there were a few empty prescription pill bottles which she suspected were stolen, given none of the names matched Adrian's. Next she went into the kitchen. Opening the drawers, she found some cutlery, some take-out menus and a junk drawer filled with screws, old needles and other knick-knacks. She left that final drawer as it was; she didn't want to risk getting jabbed with a dirty needle. Those should have been disposed of when the property was searched.

In the living room, her eye was drawn to a wooden coffee

table that had two drawers, and although the fingerprint dust confirmed it had already been checked, she wouldn't feel right until she looked over it herself. It looked like Adrian had a lot of unpaid bills. Leafing through each one, she noted a few had stuck together. When she carefully prised them apart, she found what looked like a mobile number written down, although at first glance it just looked like a random grouping of numbers. Easily missed. She reached into her pocket and pulled out her mobile phone to take a picture. She'd ask Bethany to find out who the number belonged to when she got back to the station. She placed the envelope in an evidence bag, sealing it and placing it in her bag. Chain of evidence is important; she wouldn't risk anything being thrown out on a technicality. Maggie straightened up, hands on hips and looked around the room.

In her head, she pictured Adrian and the killer sitting on the couch before her. Maybe having a conversation; she was confident that he knew his killer. She wondered if he had willingly taken the heroin without realizing the strength or if it had been forced into him. The pathologist may be able to tell from the puncture wound. She made a note to ask Dr Blake when she returned to the office. If Adrian had been under the influence, his head probably hung over the back of the couch. The killer could then come up behind him and strangle him before tying the noose around his neck. She looked up at the beam that divided the living room from the kitchen area. Would it have been easy for the killer to throw the rope over the bar and pull Adrian up into the hanging position? With his small, thin frame, it probably wouldn't have taken much effort.

There was no chair nearby. *Big mistake.* The killer had not thought about this – they must have been in a rush. Looking at the floor, Maggie inspected the scratch marks from the couch. This is how the killer got Adrian in position. Pushing the couch with him still on it to just below the beam.

Maggie had seen enough. She spent a further hour speaking to the residents on the second floor, but got nothing of interest. The killer underestimated the police if they thought this would be ruled a suicide. Or maybe the killer wanted them to know. Maybe the killer was leading them into a trap.

# Chapter 79

Maggie caught a lift back to the office with her colleagues. They stopped to get some treats first. She was gasping for a coffee and against her better judgement headed to the communal kitchen and made the rest of the team one too. She tried to balance the tray of drinks and make it back to the office before they all spilled out. This was the reason she never volunteered to make the hot drinks; more liquid ended up on the tray than was in the cup by the time she had arrived at the destination. But the team had been working flat out and she knew they would appreciate the gesture.

'Hot drinks! I stopped by Greggs on the way back so there are some cakes too. Help yourselves.' Within seconds she was surrounded by her colleagues who were grabbing at the cakes and drinks like vultures. She picked up her own mug, a blueberry muffin and headed back to her workspace. Placing the drink on a coaster, she stared at her screen. There was a flash of someone heading in her direction. Looking up, she saw DI Rutherford holding a piece of paper.

'I just received this message. I think you'll want to handle this. A witness has come forward about our appeals for anyone who may remember something from two years ago. It may be nothing, but I figured you'd want to deal with it personally.' She dropped the number on Maggie's desk and walked away before Maggie had the chance to respond.

She opened the folded piece of paper and looked at the details. She didn't recognize the name, but that didn't mean anything. She typed the name in the system but found nothing.

Maggie picked up the phone and dialled the number. She was just about to hang up after the fifth ring when a female answered.

'Hello?'

'Hi. Is this Ellen O'Mara?'

'Uh – yes. Who's this please?'

'My name is DC Maggie Jamieson from the Major and Organised Crime Department. I understand you might have some information for us after seeing our appeal on the news. Is that right?'

'Oh, hello.' She sounded surprised. 'I didn't think anyone would get back to me so quickly and, to be honest, I'm not sure what I have will be of any use.'

'Well, I'd be happy to meet with you and take down what information you do have. Do you have a day you are free? I can come to your house or you can come here, to the station?'

'Oh, I'll come to you. Please don't come to my house. Just tell me a time and date, and I'll be there.'

'OK. How about tomorrow morning? Would 10 a.m. be good for you?'

'That's fine. I'll see you then.' Before Maggie had a chance to thank her, Ellen had hung up. She shrugged and recorded the appointment in her diary. They needed something solid in this case and she hoped that whatever Ellen had to tell her would be just the thing they were looking for.

# Chapter 80

When Maggie arrived at the office the next morning she couldn't keep still. The clock was ticking with Raven's next court appearance in a week or two, and he could be granted bail pending further investigations. She couldn't let that happen. She clenched her fists as she paced the office hall.

'You need to calm down. Pacing and cursing to yourself isn't going to help the situation,' Nathan said. She knew he meant well, but she needed him to leave her alone.

She ignored him and kept pacing.

'Well you have an hour before Ellen O'Mara comes in. Grab a drink – I'll have a coffee, and pop into my office. Let's run through what you'll be discussing.'

Five minutes later, two coffees on the table in front of them, they both sat in Nathan's office.

'What do we know about this Ellen O'Mara?' he asked.

'Nothing at the moment. Preliminary checks in the system have drawn a blank. Ellen O'Mara is squeaky clean.'

'Did she move in the same circles as the victims two years ago?'

'I'd guess so. But I'm going into the interview blind. Christ, we need to end this. If another woman dies ...' Maggie smacked her fists on the desk.

'Hey, we all feel the same. Let's focus. Why do you think this witness was adamant about coming to the station, rather than meeting at her house?'

'Maybe she's trying to hide her past from someone?' Maggie tapped her finger on Nathan's desk but stopped when she saw the look of annoyance on his face. 'Sorry.'

He laughed. 'It's fine, really. Just haven't slept much with the case hanging over us. I'm sure you've been the same.'

Nathan's internal phone rang. Miss O'Mara had arrived.

Nathan hung up the phone and looked at Maggie. 'You ready? She's here and the enquiry desk says she seems a bit anxious, so it's probably a good idea to get started.'

Leaving her mug on his desk, she waved a thanks and picked up her notebook and a pen. She ran downstairs and checked which interview rooms were free before she collected the witness.

Finding Interview Room Three was available, Maggie opened the door that led to the reception area and called out 'Ellen O'Mara ...'

A small, thin woman in her forties stood and nodded at Maggie.

'Would you like to come through, please?' She led Ellen into the interview room and pointed at the seat across from her.

'Hi, Miss O'Mara. I'm DC Maggie Jamieson. We spoke on the phone yesterday.' She extended her hand and Ellen shook it. 'Would you like a cup of water before we begin?'

She nodded. Maggie filled two cups from the water cooler.

'Do you mind if I record the conversation? I don't want to get anything wrong.' Miss O'Mara nodded again, and Maggie switched on the digital recording device. 'You mentioned that you may have some information for us. Can I just ask why you came forward now?'

'I'm not sure I can really tell you anything, but after seeing the police appeals on TV and knowing that those missing women have families who'll want closure, well the guilt was eating away at me. If anyone else dies because I kept my mouth shut ... well I couldn't live with myself. I just thought I'd say what I could remember. Clear my conscious after all these years. I've left my past behind me. I've been clean for about sixteen months now and I suppose I just wanted to forget that time in my life. But I do remember a big warehouse party; I'm pretty sure that Yvonne and Lorraine were there. I don't know if there are any others, but it is too much of a coincidence.'

'Hang on. A warehouse party? When was this?'

'Sorry, I can't give you an exact date. I was using heavily back then. But it was about two years ago. I'm pretty sure it wasn't long after that party that Bill Raven confessed to killing those women ... one of them being me.'

Maggie's heart jumped in her chest. 'Sorry? Did you say that Mr Raven confessed to killing you?'

'Yes. Ellen O'Mara is my real name, but back when I was using, I was known as Zoe Bridle.'

*Holy shit!*

Maggie didn't want to scare Ellen and she remained poised

as she continued the line of questioning. 'OK. Can you tell me about this party then?'

'It was really strange. Free drugs, booze. People were having sex, probably for money but I don't know that for sure. Taxis were paid for. Like I said, it was really strange. I remember chatting to Lorraine. I remember her saying that Adrian Harrison had organized the party. Either he or Bill Raven had come into some money. I can't remember which one. I got off my face and then went home. A few days later the story about the murders broke.'

'Can you remember anything else about the party?'

'There was a woman there. I don't know her name, but she was kind of ... hmm, I'm not sure how to explain it. It was like she was watching people and making note of things. She didn't stray far from Adrian or Bill the whole time. But she creeped the hell out of me.'

'Can you describe her to me?'

'Average height. She looked like she worked out though – short, dark hair. I guess you could say she was a stocky build. Not much make-up. Sorry, that probably doesn't help much'

'No. That's great. Could she have been a ... um ... friend of Adrian Harrison?'

'If she was, she didn't pay him much attention. She mainly spoke with Bill. I don't think she was drinking or partaking in any of the ... erm, other activities either.'

'What makes you say that?'

'She never had a drink in her hand, and she basically stayed in the same spot most of the night.'

'And you don't recall her name?'

'No, I'm really sorry. She seemed to know a few other people. I could give you their names, but I have no idea where they are now, and I honestly don't want to know. If you could keep my name out of it, that would be great.'

Maggie passed across a piece of paper and a pen. 'If you could just write the names there, we can try to trace them ourselves. Can I ask you just one more thing, Miss O'Mara?'

'Of course.' Ellen shifted in her seat.

'When you first heard your name on the news, or rather Zoe Bridle's name, why didn't you come forward?'

'I was hoping you wouldn't ask that.' Ellen's face flushed. 'I was in a bad place then, but I wanted to sort myself out. When Bill Raven said he had killed me, I thought it was my chance to start again. I went back to using my real name, went away to rehab and changed my life. As far as I was concerned, Zoe Bridle did die back then. But then the guilt started eating away at me. I knew I was hurting my family, so I returned and swore them to secrecy. Threatened that I'd disappear if they said anything. That wasn't fair on them. I know it's awful, but I have a good life now.'

'I understand, but I can't make any promises. If the information you have provided leads to an arrest, you may be called to court. Thank you so much for your time. If you do think of anything else, here is my direct number. Please call me, OK?'

Ellen took the card from Maggie's hand and smiled. 'OK.'

Once Ellen had been escorted out, Maggie returned to the office with a spring in her step. The team were shocked when she relayed the news that Ellen O'Mara was Zoe Bridle. Then

Bethany dropped the bombshell that Dr Vraines had been arrested for fraud.

Brick by brick, Raven's wall was crumbling.

# Chapter 81

DI Rutherford had been on call over the weekend and had had to deal with a few alcohol related assaults, leaving her shattered. She still hadn't caught up on her sleep. It was still dark when she had left her home this morning, and from the way her knee ached she sensed there would be rain soon.

At her desk, Abigail immediately started up her computer knowing the team had a big day ahead of them. They had their answers in relation to who the murderer was, and it looked like Maggie was correct – Raven *was* working with someone.

She heard a noise in the open-plan office. Looking up and through her door, she was not surprised to see Maggie at her desk.

After Bethany had traced the names that Ellen had given to Maggie, the team learned that Sasha Thompson was in charge at the warehouse party. From what they could gather, the party had been arranged to choose the victims and drugs were used to control them in captivity. She knew that there were some details that they would not be able to fill in until they had their suspect in custody. Abigail invited Dr Moloney to attend today's briefing and hoped that with all the information the team now had, she may be able to tie up some loose ends too.

Looking at the time, she gathered her notes and headed to the conference room. Abigail felt confident that today would be a major turning point in the case and that an arrest was imminent.

There was a buzz in the room and DI Rutherford greeted her team.

'We have something more!' Maggie shot up out of her chair before Abigail could say anything else.

'It must be something big, judging by your reaction. Carry on then.' She stepped aside and let Maggie take the floor.

'Remember when Kate asked if Raven owned any other properties?' The group nodded. 'Well Bethany harassed social care and finally got us some details from their archived files. We got the address for Raven's childhood home. Turns out it must have held some special memories for him because he worked very hard to buy it back from the couple who bought it off his grandmother. He used his mother's maiden name, an alias he had used in the past. That's why nothing flagged up before. He must have used the money his grandmother left him to purchase it, and have a guess where it's located ...' Maggie went over to the evidence board where they had the geographical profiling map posted. She smacked the big circle in the centre. 'Crinlock Chase! The anchor point we identified.'

# Chapter 82

## FRANCINE

Her head hurt, and she woke up feeling groggy. That last hit of gear made her heart race and her breathing came in short, sharp bursts.

She thought – no, wished – it was the end for her. If only her captor had misjudged the amount of gear and accidently overdosed her. No such luck.

There was that smell again. Cologne or one of those deodorant sprays. So strong it burned her nostrils through the cloth bag that covered her head. She coughed but her mouth was still covered with tape.

She wasn't alone.

Without warning, the bag was removed from her head. She could tell it was daytime because of the light that was seeping through the corner of the tape that covered her eyes.

Her captor tore the tape from her ears roughly, catching her hair – she stifled a scream. Next, the tape was being removed from her eyes.

*Oh my god. This is it.*

The tape clung to the side of her head. She had to blink twice, the light was so bright. And then she saw ...

*You?*

*YOU!*

Chaos erupted above as Francine heard muffled shouts and a loud bang.

*What the fuck was happening?*

*Oh Christ!*

*What the fuck was happening?*

# Chapter 83

DI Rutherford had pulled some strings and eventually the team had got their warrant for Raven's childhood property.

Maggie was going to ride with Nathan and the remainder of the field officers were going to meet them there. Maggie reached under her desk for her trainers, as they would be more comfortable if she had to give chase.

Pulling on her stab vest, she checked the pouches to make sure she had her baton, personal radio, PAVA spray – an incapacitant similar to pepper spray – cuffs and Taser. She wasn't taking any chances. 'We ready, Nathan?'

'Two secs. If you head down and get the car sorted, I'll be with you shortly.'

Maggie made her way down to the enquiry desk and signed out the car. Nathan made a mistake by asking her to do it; with the keys in her hand, she would be the one driving. She smiled to herself and got behind the wheel, adjusting the seat and mirrors while she waited for Nathan. He arrived within ten minutes and before he had even buckled himself in, she was off.

'Where's the fire?' he joked.

'Well if Sasha *is* there, I want to be the one to arrest her.'

Nathan shrugged. 'I don't care who does it. I just want to get her into custody and hope to God we don't find another woman dead.'

Maggie took that as a cue to speed up. She laughed to herself as she noticed him reach out and grab the dashboard.

'Just get us there in one piece.' He scowled.

'I'll do my best ... boss.'

The drive took a little over forty minutes and a few other officers were already there. They had waited as instructed for Maggie and Nathan to arrive. Nathan gathered them together and explained the plan.

'Maggie and I will go in the front with you and you.' He pointed at the relevant officers. 'You two go around the back and make sure no one gets out that way. Take either side of the property and keep a look out. We all clear?'

They nodded.

The grass was overgrown and the team had to make their own path to the doorway. Cobwebs hung like curtains from the windows and the house was covered in ivy.

Maggie felt the adrenaline rush through her. She followed Nathan to the front door. He knocked: three hard, forceful knocks. 'Police, open the door,' he shouted. They waited for a couple of minutes before Nathan gave the nod for the battering ram. Maggie took a step back to clear the way for the officer. It was a sturdy door and took a few goes before they heard a crack and the lock broke.

Two officers made their way upstairs while Maggie and Nathan searched the ground floor. The living room was clear, as was the dining room and kitchen. Maggie noticed a familiar smell, but she couldn't place it until she spotted the can of Lynx on the kitchen counter.

She looked around the room for any other tell-tale signs of someone being in the property, but there was nothing. Maggie looked out back, through the kitchen window. There was no shed or anything else that would potentially hold a person, but there was a significant area of land beyond the garden fence. The ground looked uneven, but it was too far away to see anything more. Something niggled at Maggie but she couldn't figure out what ... or why.

Kate had told them to look for a cellar. Maggie searched the kitchen floor, hoping to find a hatch of some sort, but there was nothing. She looked in the living room. Tapped the walls, in case there was an entryway easily missed if you didn't know what you were looking for. Nothing.

She returned to the hallway; this would be where you would expect to find a cellar entrance. She scanned the area and her eyes stopped short at the bookshelf against the wall. It looked odd, and as she got closer, she could feel a draught.

'Nathan ...' she whispered, 'come here.'

When Nathan was beside her, she pointed to the bookshelf. 'Can you feel that?'

Nathan moved closer to the shelf. 'Feel what?'

'The draught. I think this is a door.' They both looked at the shelf more closely, and Maggie moved a few books aside. 'Shit. There's a handle!'

'Nice spot. I'll open it on three. One, two ... three ...' Nathan pulled the handle down and pulled the bookcase to the side.

The smell hit them like a wall and left them gasping for breath. Bleach, metal and something more pungent. The stairs were battered; there was a single bulb above them. Maggie felt alongside the wall for a switch and when she felt it beneath her fingers, she flicked it on and prepared for the worst.

# Chapter 84

Maggie waited as Nathan radioed the two other officers who were in the house. They needed to be prepared for whatever waited for them at the bottom of the stairs. When the pair arrived, Maggie took a deep breath and followed Nathan down the stairwell. The steps were old and every now and then one would creak. Maggie took out her flashlight, even with the light on, the room was dim and damp. That smell ...

When they reached the bottom, they were met with a scared, bound and gagged female. She looked emaciated. Her eyes were wide and there was a piece of silver gaffer tape hanging from the side of her head. It looked like she was trying to say something as her eyes darted to the back of the room and then back to them.

'I'll call it in.' Maggie used her radio and called for an ambulance. The other two officers headed to the back of the cellar where there was a door. She looked around and noticed the windows were covered with dirty blankets, keeping any source of light to a minimum. Maggie quickly touched base with DI Rutherford while Nathan began to untie the female on the bed. Just when he was about to remove the tape from her mouth, something ... or someone darted out from the shadows. Maggie heard two thumps as the officers fell to the ground. Before Maggie could get to them, she heard Nathan scream in pain.

'Maggie, they have a knife. Look out!' Nathan fell to the floor.

As the shape came towards her, Maggie attempted to radio for backup while taking out her PAVA spray. She aimed it at the person coming towards her. It was a woman.

'Drop the knife or I'll will spray you.'

The figure continued towards her with a strange look in her eyes. Maggie emptied the can into her face and heard a wail of pain. Despite being sprayed in the face, the woman rammed into Maggie, knocking the wind out of her. Maggie used the stair behind her to push herself up, ducking out of the way as the woman waved the knife around. Maggie grabbed her wrist and pushed it back. The knife dropped to the floor and Maggie kicked it against the wall. The woman tackled Maggie to the floor and got in a punch before Maggie rolled over and grabbed an arm, then twisted it behind her back. Resisting the urge to smack her face into the concrete floor, Maggie grabbed the other arm, placed the cuffs on the woman and pushed her flat to the ground.

'Sasha – I'm arresting you on suspicion of murder, kidnapping and assaulting a PC. You have the right to remain silent but anything you do say can be used against you ...' Maggie continued to explain the details of the arrest to Sasha.

Two field officers appeared before Maggie. 'Take her away,

and make sure you tell the ambulance that we have a female who needs immediate medical attention, two officers who sustained blunt force trauma to the head as well as an officer with a stab wound.' They nodded and pulled Sasha up – surprisingly, she didn't struggle.

After checking that the other two police officers were OK, Maggie walked over to Nathan and bent down. 'Are you OK?'

'It's only a graze. This is Francine Xander. She says she's not sure how long she's been here, but she is definitely dehydrated. She's drifting in and out of consciousness.'

'Look here.' Maggie pointed to the floor where a large plastic sheet lay. 'It looks like we were just in time.'

Maggie was desperate to open some windows. The stench of bodily fluids mixed with infected wounds stuck in her nose. She noticed a bedpan, a plate with a half-eaten, mouldy sandwich on the floor and an empty bottle of water. Sasha was feeding them the bare minimum to carry out her evil plan.

Maggie stood by Nathan. Forensics were on their way and the ambulance would be here any minute. 'Can you walk, Nathan?' He nodded. 'Why don't you go up and get some fresh air? You can wait for the ambulance and I'll stay here with Francine and those two.'

Nathan stood up and limped his way slowly up the stairs.

'Hey sweetheart. You're safe now. Is there anyone you want me to contact?'

The woman shook her head. She was shaking.

'I'm thirsty.' Francine struggled to sit up and winced with each movement she made.

Maggie looked around and noticed a bathroom in the far corner where Sasha, or someone, must have dumped the contents of the bedpans when they were full. There were three other camp beds but she didn't go over to them as she didn't want to risk contaminating the crime scene. She radioed to a colleague upstairs and asked him to find some water and bring it down. Within a few minutes the water was there, and Maggie held the glass while Francine gulped it down. When the ambulance arrived, Maggie held Francine's hand while the paramedics did a quick check and placed her on the gurney. She followed them up the stairs and watched while they positioned Francine in the ambulance. Nathan went with her, so he could get himself checked out. The other two officers were taken to the hospital by a colleague.

When forensics arrived, Maggie spoke briefly to the duty SIO and then left them to it. DI Rutherford had called Maggie back to the station and she was looking forward to interviewing Sasha.

Parking the pool car outside the station, she raced inside and dropped the keys off at the enquiry desk before sprinting up the stairs.

She popped in to see DI Rutherford who was on the phone. The DI held a finger up. Maggie stood by. Once the guv hung up the phone, a smile crossed her face briefly. 'Well, I heard you had an eventful time at Raven's house. Bloody lucky that social care gave us the address of his childhood home.'

'I know. If Claire hadn't got hold of those archives when she did, it would have been Francine's body parts we found next. Sasha was prepping for it before we arrived. The poor woman was tied to a bed. Nathan was injured while he was helping her, and the two field officers may have a headache for a few days. Luckily, it seems Sasha only grazed his leg with the knife.'

'I know. I just spoke to him on the phone. It looks like Francine was drugged. She was covered in bedsores and bruises. As well as being dehydrated and definitely underweight, the hospital seems to think with medical attention she'll be OK physically. You reached her just in the nick of time. God knows what psychological scars she will carry with her though.' DI Rutherford shook her head.

'When can I interview Sasha?'

'She started kicking off when she arrived here. Screaming she had been blinded and attacked without reason. She's in a cell now, waiting for the doctor. It'll probably be tomorrow before you can interview either her or Francine. It's late. You may as well get yourself home as it is going to be a very busy day tomorrow.'

Maggie turned and was on her way out the door when the DI called her back.

'Good job, Maggie.'

'Thanks. I'll see you in the morning.'

# Chapter 85

Maggie arrived early to prepare herself for the interview with Sasha Thompson. She didn't bother going to her desk first; instead, she headed straight for the incident room.

Maggie looked at all the information they had collected while she waited for the rest of the team to arrive. A late-night email from DI Rutherford had informed them that the initial forensic report was back after Dr Blake's team, despite the staff shortages, worked around the clock. There were also some additional details to share with them. Maggie hoped that this would be enough for the CPS to proceed with the case against Sasha and keep Bill Raven behind bars.

Maggie only wished they'd had the archive details from social care sooner. She should have realized that the bungalow his grandmother left him had only been bought ten years ago. She could have kicked herself for not pushing the matter. On reflection, Raven had given the illusion that he was residing permanently in the flat and no one bothered to check that Raven's grandmother had been in a care home in the last few months before she died. Had they done so, they may have looked deeper into her property and realized that she had owned another home before she downsized. There was no evidence to suggest that the Doxley residence had any links to the murders. She and the team would have to deal with the consequences of this oversight once the case was closed.

She leaned in and scrutinized the snapshots of the garden on the evidence board. When she had been at the property, she recalled looking out the back and an odd feeling coming over her. Initially she had put that down to the adrenaline and fear that had been racing through her veins the moment before they discovered the secret door. Now that she looked more intently at the pictures, just beyond the fence, there seemed to be bare patches that looked completely out of place. The grass surrounding had grown long and wild.

'What are you looking at?' Nathan had come into the room without her even realizing it.

She pointed at the photograph of the back garden. 'Look at those patches of bare earth. Isn't that weird?'

Nathan leaned forward, but before he could reply DI Rutherford and the rest of the team entered the room. DI Rutherford motioned for them both to sit.

'Right, folks. Let's not waste any time here. Forensics are back and there's a definite link with Sasha Thompson and the property. Not only were her fingerprints all over the house and the knife, but hair strands were discovered on the blanket that covered Francine Xander. A partial print was also found on a circular saw located in a storage bin in the cellar. Finally, more prints were on the plastic sheeting which had been laid out on the floor. We can assume that was going to be used to wrap Francine. What appears to be the same brand of plastic sheeting was used to dispose of Lorraine Rugman's, Yvonne Greene's, and Veronica Chapel's body parts. So as far as I am concerned, we have Sasha for those crimes.'

'Christ. She obviously didn't think she would be caught if she left that much forensic evidence around.' Maggie shook her head.

'The forensic report does say that it looks like other things in the property had been wiped down, so I suspect she just hadn't got around to doing it. More than likely she would have been waiting until after she got rid of Francine's body.' DI Rutherford took a sip of her coffee. 'They also found cement bags that had Adrian Harrison's partial fingerprints on them. These were uncovered out back, leaning up against the house with a cement mixer and covered over in a black plastic sheeting. Based on this, we've been given the go-ahead for the divers to go out to some of the crime scenes to trawl the canals and any surrounding rivers or waterways. It may be that the remaining body parts were encased in concrete and disposed of in the rivers or canals.'

Bethany interrupted. 'I've looked at the CCTV for surrounding DIY stores and, on two occasions, Sasha had been seen in the shops thirty miles from the house purchasing plastic sheeting, heavy-duty bin bags, cement, gaffer tape and a large garden lopper. Interestingly, Sasha had been driving a white van which was not registered to her. We missed it because we were looking for a male and focusing on the wrong area.'

'Christ.' Maggie muttered.

'We have a lot of evidence to link Sasha to the murders

and we can assume that Adrian was at least involved in concealing the bodies. It seems that the witness who provided us with Sasha's whereabouts had warned her beforehand, which is how she knew we were on to her and probably the reason she killed Harrison. Tying up loose ends and trying to frame him for the murders.' The DI rubbed her forehead.

'So now we know the role Sasha and, perhaps, Adrian played, how can we tie this to Bill Raven?' Maggie wasn't going to let the connection go.

'Hopefully, some of the answers to that will be forthcoming in your interview with Sasha. Let's be clever and make her think that if she gives up Raven, she'll have mitigating circumstances and the court might consider reducing her sentence. What I can tell you is that when Francine was spoken to at the hospital this morning, she told us about meeting Raven at a house party just prior to waking up in the cellar. She claims that she went back to a flat with him and he provided her with more drugs. She also remembers having a drink but that's when everything went blank. The next thing she remembers is waking up blindfolded and tied to the bed.'

Maggie rubbed her temples. 'So, do we know an approximate date for this? I mean, could it be that all the women were chosen at this party, kidnapped and held hostage?'

Nathan jumped in. 'That's a possibility. What we don't know is why Raven then confessed. What was the plan?'

'Dr Moloney had previously mentioned in her profile notoriety and grandiose beliefs. I wonder if Raven actually believed he was committing the perfect crime. Perhaps he was living out a fantasy of killing his mother? Some of these women had children who were taken into care because of their lifestyle choices. He must have planned this all with Sasha. He would confess, get all the attention he desired and then when the body parts started showing up, his solicitors would have enough to launch an appeal. He'd go free, get compensated financially, huge media attention and continue the killing *with* Sasha. Could that have been it?' Maggie looked around the room.

'Well, there's one way to find out. You'll be interviewing Sasha in about half an hour, so get your thoughts together, talk it over with Nathan and make sure you get a confession.'

'No pressure then, guv.' Maggie smiled.

'Oh, and Maggie, one more thing. The DNA tests also showed a familial link.'

'What the fuck?'

'Sasha Thompson is Bill Raven's sister.'

# Chapter 86

After the bombshell that DI Rutherford had just dropped, Maggie's head was spinning. The motive was still unclear, especially in relation to Sasha. And now that they knew Sasha was Raven's biological sister, it was even more confusing.

*Does Raven know that Sasha is his sister? Was she a new pawn in this game of chess they were playing?*

Dr Kate Moloney suggested that their childhood and substance misuse was what drew them together. Perhaps they both had a shared interest in harming individuals who they felt were just as worthless as those who were meant to protect them. Kate advised that when Maggie and Nathan interviewed Sasha, they didn't try and empathize with her. It was clear that Sasha was intelligent and cunning and wouldn't appreciate the police trying to get her onside. Kate conjectured that her loyalties lay with Raven. But if they could convince Sasha that Raven didn't share that same loyalty, they might be able to get her to turn on him.

'Are you set?' DI Rutherford looked at Maggie. Her face gave little away, but Maggie suspected she was concerned about the implications should Sasha decide to go 'no comment' in interview.

'I heard from the custody sergeant this morning on my way in that Sasha has not been the easiest prisoner overnight. She'll be tired and although I've no doubt she's clever, her defences may be down. The duty solicitor is in with her now.'

'How do you know that?' DI Rutherford frowned.

'I asked to be kept informed and a text came through a little over half an hour ago. They'll call up when Sasha is ready to be interviewed.'

As if on cue, the phone in the incident room rang and Bethany answered.

'OK, folks. Let's do this!' Rutherford thanked them all and made her way back to her office.

'I'm just going to grab the file and we can go down together.' Nathan stood and walked to his office. Maggie finished the remainder of her coffee and threw the cup in the recycle bin. She waited for Nathan in the corridor.

Her stomach rumbled, reminding her that in her haste she had forgotten to eat something this morning. She would need to make sure she had plenty of water to hand or risk becoming dizzy while in the interview room. There was no way she was going to mess this up. After the whole fiasco with Raven, Maggie felt as if she had something to prove to the team. Deep down, she knew her colleagues didn't feel the same way, but she couldn't help the self-doubt at times.

Ten minutes later, Nathan headed down the hall towards her. 'How are you feeling?'

'My nerves are shot, and my head is pounding, but I know we have at least one part of the puzzle down in the cells.'

His face twisted in a cheeky grin. 'Seriously though, if anyone can break Sasha, it'll be you.'

# Chapter 87

Maggie massaged her head to avoid the headache she felt creeping up on her. It was stress-related, and she needed to be on point. She shook her legs out and before they headed to the interview room, she walked to the kitchenette, grabbing a glass from the cupboard. She filled the glass and returned to her desk, placing it down while she rummaged through her bag for some ibuprofen.

'Are you looking for these?' Nathan held out some tablets, with two missing.

'Ah. You have a headache too?'

'Not yet, but definitely feels like it is not far off. Is it show time?'

'Nearly, but the nerves have kicked in.'

'Hey, don't doubt yourself. We'll get them. Both of them, OK?'

'I wish I had your confidence. Let's just get this over with.' Maggie picked up her notes and smiled at Nathan. He had proven to be not only a great friend but a good boss. She hoped he decided to apply for a permanent DS post, as he definitely was made for the job.

'Why are you looking at me like that?' His head cocked slightly to the left as he spoke.

'In case I forget to tell you, thanks for everything you've done for me with this case. Your support has meant a lot.'

'Christ, Maggie. Are you going soft on me?'

'Ha!' She couldn't help but laugh. 'It will be the last compliment I pay you for a while, so you'd better remember it.'

The tension in the room was broken and Maggie felt much better about the task ahead. Nathan led the way down to the custody suite. The desk sergeant informed that Interview Room Three was ready for them. The room was empty. Sasha was still speaking with her solicitor next door, so Maggie and Nathan got settled and briefly discussed the main points they would raise when Sasha arrived. Maggie laid the crime scene photos out on the desk, facing where Sasha would be sitting. They wanted to see her reaction when she sat down. As Maggie placed the last photo of Francine, the only surviving victim, on the table, Sasha and her solicitor walked in.

The accused fingered the desk as she walked around and sat down opposite Nathan. She flashed him a smile, which made Maggie feel sick. She noticed the change in Sasha's appearance immediately. Her muscles were evident through the T-shirt and leggings she wore. Gone was the haunted look of a drug addict, and Maggie guessed the bruise she had been sporting was probably self-inflicted.

'We're not going to beat around the bush. My colleague, DS Wright, has just explained the charges and cautioned you, and you see all the evidence before you. Would it surprise you to know that forensics links you to the scene? What do you have to say for yourself?'

Sasha leaned across the desk and stared Maggie in the eye. 'DC Jamieson. It's lovely to meet you again. Were you expecting me to come in and confess, beg for mercy and maybe shed a few fucking tears?' Sasha mimicked crying, rubbing her hands across her eyes. 'Well you can fuck-right-off. I don't know anything about any of this shit.' She leaned back in her chair and crossed her arms.

'Are we seriously going to play that game?' Maggie opened the folder before her and took out the report from forensics. She was curious why Sasha's solicitor hadn't spoken since entering the room, but she guessed that they'd learn soon enough. 'What I have here is a forensic report. The report highlights a few things that you might find interesting. Let's start with the obvious. You've been charged with GBH – that's grievous bodily harm with intent after stabbing my colleague here in the leg, along with AOABH – Assault Occasioning Actual Bodily Harm – on the two officers you knocked out. Not only was I witness to it all, but your fingerprints are on the knife. Would you care to explain?'

Sasha's solicitor was about to speak, when she raised her hand to hush him. 'Your colleagues frightened me, I was defending myself. You all barged into a property that I had just started to stay in, and I'd only just discovered that poor woman down there. I got the knife to cut her loose when I heard you all. You didn't identify yourself as police. I thought you were hurting that woman and I attacked *him* to stop anything bad happening. The other two officers were coming at me; I hit them to escape.' Sasha smiled like a Cheshire cat and Maggie noticed even her own solicitor rolled his eyes.

'Well that is some story. The only problem is, Francine Xander has identified *you* as the person who imprisoned her. Do you want to try that answer again?'

'Clearly she's confused. I mean, fuck sake, what an ordeal she has been through. To be locked away like that. She must have me mistaken for someone else.'

'How do you explain your DNA in the cellar, on the blanket that was covering the victim, on the weapons in the room that had been used to dismember Lorraine Rugman, Yvonne Greene, Veronica Chapel and—'

Sasha started coughing uncontrollably.

'We're going to have to take a break now, officers. Can't you see my client needs medical attention?'

Nathan left the interview room to get the duty doctor. Another delay tactic. Maggie ended the interview and glared at Sasha as she continued with her coughing fit.

'Could you leave me to speak with my client, please. This is all too much for her to take in.'

'Fine,' Maggie grumbled. 'But we're not delaying this interview. Once the doctor confirms she is OK, and let's be frank, we all know she *is* OK, we'll be back, and this interview will proceed exactly where we left off.'

# Chapter 88

Sasha's dramatics didn't last long, and after screaming at the doctor, she was deemed fit to continue. Maggie was determined to keep the pressure on but made sure she didn't give Sasha any excuse to back out of the questions.

'So, whose vehicle did you use to dump the bodies?' Maggie tilted her head in expectation.

'I've no idea what you're fucking talking about.' There was no emotion behind Sasha's eyes.

Maggie leaned in closer and maintained eye contact. 'Ah, that's right. You're not actually clever enough to have pulled this off on your own. This took planning. It was calculated ...' Maggie leaned back in her chair and nearly missed the twitch of annoyance that displayed on Sasha's upper lip.

'Oh, I'm clever enough ... off-i-cer.' Sasha shrugged. 'We almost done here? I'm tired.' She stretched her arms above her head and yawned. Personality wise, Maggie could now see a lot of Raven in Sasha. She wouldn't let her get under her skin though.

Maggie could see that they were getting nowhere. They needed to up the ante, and with the current charges, she wasn't going to be released on bail any time or soon. How could they catch her out in her own lies? Maggie tapped her finger on the table.

She looked over at Nathan with wide eyes and hoped he would follow her meaning. 'Why don't we take a fifteen-minute break now?' She looked at her watch. 'I'm expecting a call from your boyfriend shortly. This is an ideal time to stop.' Maggie noted the twitch again on Sasha's face. She gathered her notes and stood. 'DS Wright and I will be back shortly. Maybe you want to rethink your plans on cooperating with us. We'd hate for your boyfriend to get in there first.'

She held the door for Nathan, and as soon as he heard the click to confirm the door was closed, he raised his eyebrows and opened his mouth to speak but then seemed to change his mind. He turned on his heels and gestured for Maggie to follow him. She noticed him looking in the windows of the interview rooms and once he found a free one, he motioned her inside.

'Do you mind telling me what was that all about?'

Maggie couldn't help grinning as she relayed her thoughts to Nathan. For once he gave nothing away in what he was thinking. He just nodded as she spoke.

'We just need her to bite and we'll have both her and Raven ready to serve up to the CPS on a plate!'

# Chapter 89

'After you.' Nathan pointed at the door and followed Maggie back to the interview room. They peered through the plexiglass window and knocked on the door. Whatever heated conversation Sasha was having with her solicitor ended abruptly and he waved at them to enter.

'Do you need a few more minutes? It looks like we're interrupting.' Maggie directed her question to the solicitor, but it was Sasha who answered.

'Ask your questions before I start throwing around the no comments.'

Maggie reminded Sasha she was still under caution and that the interview was being recorded. After noting who was in the room and the time, she began her questioning.

'I've just had an interesting conversation—'

'I find that hard to believe. It's not as if Bill has a mobile and can just ring you as he pleases. Where did you get the ridiculous notion that he's my boyfriend?'

'Did I mention Bill Raven? Perhaps you just want to get it all off your chest, before someone else points the finger at you?'

Sasha held her hands up, mocking defeat.

'OK, detectives. I'll be honest with you. Adrian Harrison was responsible for everything. Why do you think he killed himself? I didn't connect the dots myself until it was too late.' Sasha leaned back in the chair and crossed her arms.

'I'm glad you brought that up, Sasha,' Nathan chimed in. 'I'd like to point out that we know Mr Harrison didn't kill himself. You see, someone either coerced him into taking heroin or injected him against his will.' Nathan pulled out the crime scene photos of Harrison's flat and laid them in front of Sasha and her solicitor. 'You see here.' He tapped on the photo which showed Harrison hanging; Maggie could almost see a sparkle in Sasha's eye. Like she was proud. 'There's no chair. Nothing that he could have stood on to hang himself with and then kick away. Rookie mistake in my opinion. Do you have anything to say about that?'

'Why would I have anything to say?' Even though Sasha looked like she wasn't bothered, the twitch on her upper lip once again gave her away.

'But that wasn't all we found.' Nathan pulled out some papers.

Maggie smiled; she knew what Nathan was about to say. The smirk on Sasha's face would be well and truly wiped off.

'We also found DNA evidence. Skin cells, to be precise. Someone made a huge mistake with the rope that was used to hang Mr Harrison.' He pushed the paperwork her way.

'But that's im—' Sasha stopped mid-sentence, obviously realizing that if she carried on, she would be admitting her role in Adrian's murder. She turned to her solicitor, who just shrugged his shoulders.

'Please continue, we're dying to hear your explanation. For someone who claims to be so clever, you really dropped the ball on this one. Maybe your solicitor has something he wants to add?'

'Fuck you both. No comment.'

'We're going down that route now, are we? OK, Sasha. Well I can tell you that it was *your* DNA we found on the rope. Perhaps you forgot to put your gloves on at some point, and we know you did use gloves because there was no other DNA present in the flat. Or maybe you were disturbed, had to rush before someone came to get their next fix off Harrison? So, like I said, rookie error. Your *brother* won't be impressed when he hears this.' Nathan sat back and waited.

The colour drained from Sasha's face.

The rest of the interview carried on with 'no comments' and with Sasha growing increasingly pale and despondent. They set their theory out to Sasha and her solicitor: that Raven and Sasha had planned this out from before Raven had been convicted. The perfect crime. Raven needed to get clean for it to work, so he confessed to abducting and murdering three women, only he knew that one woman would be found alive – Zoe Bridle; although it backfired a little on him as he probably had hoped the police would have found her sooner. Raven should have been released, if their plan had been foolproof, but that failed because Sasha was rushed when killing their fall guy, Adrian Harrison. Zoe also tied Sasha and Raven to the abducted women – her getting clean was not factored into the plan. The pair were not as clever as they had thought. With Sasha not talking, it was put to her that this all boiled down to their anger against their own mother. A drug user, who treated her kids like garbage. The victims shared a similar background and some had kids taken into care. It all made sense in hindsight.

Maggie was going to take a lot of pleasure in pointing this out to Raven. The trouble was they always thought they were smarter than they actually were and that was their downfall.

'Sasha Thompson, we're charging you with the murder of Lorraine Rugman, Yvonne Greene, Veronica Chapel and Adrian Harrison. You're also charged with the abduction/kidnapping of Francine Xander, assaulting two police officers and the attempted murder of DS Nathan Wright. Do you have anything further to say?'

'Yeah, I fucking well do. You might want to *dig* a little deeper. I ain't taking the full blame for all this. I had no choice.'

'Hang on, what do you mean by that?' Maggie slammed her hands on the table.

'Figure it out yourselves, bitch. No-fucking-comment.'

# Chapter 90

After the interview with Sasha, Maggie raced back upstairs, leaving Nathan to deal with the solicitor and finalizing the charges with the custody sergeant. Something Sasha had said had stuck in her head and she needed to check it out.

In the incident room, she immediately went to the crime scene photos of Bill Raven's house. She stared at the picture of the strange bare patches of earth in Raven's garden.

*Dig deeper.*

'The back garden. We need to dig up the back garden!' She knew there was no one else in the room, but saying it out loud, reinforced the importance of this. Maggie walked straight into DI Rutherford's office.

DI Rutherford raised her eyebrow at Maggie.

'Sorry, ma'am. We've just interviewed Sasha. She didn't outright confess but we have enough to charge her. The CPS will most likely push for remand and then it's up to them to build their case.'

'OK, and this couldn't wait because?'

'Sasha hinted that there was something in Raven's back garden. Before the interview I was looking at the crime scene photos and just beyond the back garden there were weird bare patches of grass. Most of the grass was long and wild, but there were these odd, dead patches.'

'You think we need to dig up the garden? Is it owned by Raven?'

'I'll have Bethany check it out, but yes. I think this will be the final piece of the puzzle.'

Maggie watched DI Rutherford pick up the phone. 'Leave it with me. Let's close this case.' Maggie thanked her boss and returned to the open-plan area.

Seeing Bethany typing away, she interrupted her.

'Could you check who owns the property behind Bill Raven's place? I've a hunch and DI Rutherford wants the landowner confirmed before we go any further.'

Bethany looked up. 'Give me half an hour and I'll sort it.'

Maggie went back to her desk and turned on her computer. She opened the file on Raven, hoping something would stand out. But nothing did.

Maggie looked at Raven's Social Services details. Claire Knight had collated some information and put it together in a simple report for her. Although Maggie had read the file a hundred times, something was drawing her to it again. While she waited for Bethany to come back to her, she clicked opened the report and began reading. That was when she saw it.

*I've got you now, you bastard.*

Staring right at her the whole time: she looked at the information that Raven's social worker had noted in the file and smiled.

*After my last visit with Mrs Raven, Billy's grandmother, some concerning information was brought to my attention by a farmer who resided in the area. Local animals were going missing and neighbours suspected that 'the weird kid' had been harming the pets and farm animals. When I questioned them further, they had mentioned that they sometimes saw Billy in the field beyond his grandmother's house. Sitting and talking to mounds in the grass.*

The information was dated in the late Eighties. And when Maggie scanned the rest of the documents, it didn't look like anything had been passed on or acted upon. If her hunch was right, there may be a formal investigation into why it had not been investigated further at the time.

Maggie stared out of the window beside her desk. Although the sun was shining, she felt cold dread run down her spine. She was about to read on, but Bethany's voice brought her back into the room.

'The area you asked me to look at does belong to Raven. Quite a large portion of it actually.' Bethany handed some papers over to Maggie, and she looked in amazement. It was vast. And if she was right, Maggie could be looking at a mass graveyard.

She thanked Bethany and took the papers to DI Rutherford. Nathan was with the DI and they both gestured for Maggie to come in.

'Do you want to explain why you rushed off and left me to deal with everything down there?' She couldn't tell if Nathan was joking or serious. She didn't have time to find out. Maggie showed them both the information that Bethany had found and also told them about the Social Services records.

'Damn. This isn't looking good. I'll speak to the DCI and you pair start writing up everything so far, while it is fresh in your mind. Dot every "i" and cross every "t". We're not going to lose this case on a technicality.'

Maggie left her office with Nathan hot on her heels. 'We might finally have him.' She couldn't help the smile that formed on her face. 'He's a cold-blooded killer, a danger. And we're so close to ending this now.' Her hands shook as the enormity of the situation flooded through her. 'He can never be let out. I suspect there'll be more than just animal bones buried in that land. Animal killings would've just been the start.'

Just as Maggie was about to sit down, DI Rutherford popped her head through the door. 'Listen up. Arrangements have been made to dig up the land behind Raven's property. Finish up what you're doing and go home. It's an early start tomorrow: 7 a.m. sharp. And you're both expected to be there.'

# Chapter 91

Maggie yawned as she got in the passenger side of Nathan's car. Her brain had been in overdrive last night and she was exhausted.

'Didn't get much sleep either?' She looked at Nathan as he yawned and put the car in gear.

'Nope. I hope you're right about this. I could've used a few more hours in bed.'

The drive to Raven's property was uneventful. Each of them focused on the task ahead. At this time in the morning, traffic was light, and they made their way down the lanes without much issue. Nathan pulled into the property and found a free spot among all the other vehicles. After signing in, they followed the excavator out to the back of the property. In his hand, he held an aerial snapshot of the land and there were red crosses where they were meant to dig. Maggie and Nathan waited behind the low fence as the digging commenced.

After an hour they heard a shout from someone. Bones had been found. Dr Fiona Blake had arrived earlier, ready to confirm Maggie's worst suspicion. The waiting was killing her, and she stared out at Fiona, watching her work. There it was – the thumbs up. They had found bones. She turned and looked at Nathan – unsure whether or not to smile as it didn't feel right. A forensic anthropologist would need to confirm the findings as human.

'You were right. Why so glum?'

'Because we now have more victims. More families to tell. As good as it feels, at times like this, a small part of me was hoping I had been wrong.'

Nathan squeezed her shoulder. 'I totally get that, but for now, let's focus on bringing some closure to the families. The investigation will be dealt with by the cold case team working with Missing Persons no doubt, so at least we can put the matter to rest.'

All in all, the forensic anthropologist had verified that four bodies had been found along with various animal bones. This was Raven's killing field. Maggie sighed. It took just over a week to confirm the identity of the victims through dental and missing person records. They had been teen runaways, known to Social Services but lost in the system and forgotten about. It made for depressing reading. An enquiry into the practises of Social Services at the time would be opened. Claire Knight had told Maggie that the social worker who had initially raised suspicions had died eight years before. She didn't know what would happen, but that was for their agency to deal with.

As selfish as it seemed, all Maggie cared about now was ensuring that Raven would be convicted of these murders. Based on all the evidence, it seemed it would be an open and shut case. It looked like the younger Raven had not been too knowledgeable on DNA evidence; he buried his trophies in a memory box with the bodies and although it had deteriorated over time, his DNA was all over the items found. Posters of missing animals in the area. Children's things: a friendship bracelet, a cheap silver ring, locks of hair. It saddened Maggie when she looked at these tokens that had once been precious to these young girls. They would hand it over to the prosecution team dealing with Raven's appeal. She had made plans to visit Raven and couldn't wait to see the look on his face when she told him it was over, and he would never get out of prison.

That night was the first night Maggie slept well.

# Chapter 92

ONE WEEK LATER

Nerves and excitement had Maggie buzzing as she pulled into the prison parking lot. It had rained heavily the night before, and she cursed as she stepped out of her car and into a giant puddle. The water drenched her feet, but even that was not going to dampen the mood she was in. She practically ran to the door and, once inside, waited patiently in the line with the other legal visitors.

When she was finally escorted into the room, Maggie sat down and waited for Raven to be brought in. She saw him and a smile broke out on her face. When he entered the room he initially just stood, staring, but Maggie was not going to let him intimidate her. No longer would Bill Raven invade her thoughts.

'Are you going to take a seat?' She cocked her head to the right and pointed at the chair opposite her.

'I'm curious, DC Jamieson. What reason would you have to visit me now?' He pulled the chair back and sat down.

'I wanted to see the look on your face when I told you that

it's over now. You won't see the light of day. We found the bones of your first victims. We found your memory box and journal. And we know you are at least partially responsible for the killings attributed to The Chopper – maybe not directly, but you were most certainly involved. You see, your *sister* gave us a tip. She doesn't like you very much, does she? Do you have anything you want to say?'

'Well DC Jamieson, aren't you a clever girl?' Maggie cringed at his condescending tone. 'It took you long enough to figure it all out, didn't it? Are you proud of yourself? I hope this doesn't mean that this will be the last I see of you. I've grown rather fond of you.'

'You'll never get parole. Along with the conspiracy to murder charges, you'll also be charged with four further counts of murder and there's no way for you to weasel your way out of it.'

'I have no desire to deny anything at this stage. You see, I have quite a following now, DC Jamieson. I don't have to be in the community to do what I love doing. I may not get the same thrills, but I'm sure I can improvise. And as for my ... sister,' there was venom in his voice, 'she'll get what's coming to her.'

Maggie shuddered. She knew he wasn't bluffing. 'I'll do my best to make sure that you don't have any of those opportunities, Mr Raven. I don't know how, but you can trust me when I say, you'll never get the chance to harm another individual if I have anything to do with it.'

'If you say so. We'll just have to agree to disagree at this time, won't we? Before I go though, did you ever find your cat?' When Maggie didn't answer, Raven stood up with a smile. He turned to go, leaving Maggie's brain racing.

'Wait! What do you mean?'

Raven refused to answer and stood waiting for the guard to take him back to his cell.

'What did you do to my cat? How do you know about that? Answer me!'

He looked her directly in the eyes. 'Never underestimate me, DC Jamieson. You may think you know it all – but trust me, this was only the beginning.'

The guard arrived and led Bill Raven back to his cell.

Maggie sat in the room alone for a moment while she gathered her thoughts. How the hell did Bill Raven do that? Messing with her mind, when she thought it was all over.

She shook the thoughts out of her mind. He was trying to get under her skin. She clenched her fists. Maggie left the prison and headed home; she needed rest and she'd speak to Nathan in the morning.

The drive home let her think back to when Scrappy went missing. It had been so long, she just assumed he was dead and if what Raven was saying was true, he probably was. The cars whizzed by her as she drove on auto pilot.

Pulling up outside her house, she grabbed her things from the passenger seat and went inside. Her brother was still sleeping. As she entered the hall, she could hear him snoring. Dropping the keys on the side table, she removed her shoes and hung up her coat. A glass of wine would be perfect to unwind and help her forget the cold look in Raven's eyes.

Maggie placed her bag on the floor beside the couch and walked into the kitchen. She had to stifle a scream when she saw Scrappy in his cat basket. He was asleep. As if he never left.

She whispered. 'Scrappy? Hey boy, where have you been?' She tiptoed over and knelt on the floor in front of him. He raised his head and half opened his eyes. He looked like he had been drugged and there was something attached to his collar. Maggie gave him a gentle pet on the head to reassure him that everything would be OK, and she removed the note from his collar. Opening it carefully she was not prepared for what was written on the note:

*I TOLD YOU*

Maggie gave Scrappy one more gentle pet and went upstairs to her brother's room. Knocking on his door she asked, 'Andy. Are you awake?'

A low grumble before she heard him say, 'Yeah, erm ... what time is it?'

'Can I come in? It's just after five.'

'Sure. I need to get up soon anyway.'

She pushed open the door as her brother sat up in his bed.

'Did you know Scrappy was back?'

'Oh yeah. I was going to text you, but things just got on top of me and I forgot. He came back earlier. Was a little wobbly on his feet. You might want to take him to the vet. I wasn't sure what to do; he seemed OK, so I let him sleep.'

'Did you notice anything else when he came in?'

'Uh, no. Why? What's wrong?'

'He had something around his neck.'

'Oh yeah. Sorry. I left you a note. I told you he'd make his way back.'

Maggie collapsed on his bed. Pulling him close she gave him a big hug. 'Thank God for that. Sorry. I didn't recognize your handwriting.'

'OK now you're being weird. I didn't know if I would be home when you got back so thought I would leave a little note around his neck. I left my phone in the car and couldn't be arsed to get it. Is everything OK?'

Maggie laughed. 'Yeah, though I wish you would've just left the note on the counter. It freaked me out a bit after a conversation I had earlier.'

'Oh. Sorry 'bout that. Next time, I'll be sure to leave it in a better place.'

She smiled and left her brother to get ready for his shift. She went back into the kitchen and Scrappy seemed to be coming around. She'd call the vet and make sure that nothing untoward was going on. Perhaps Raven was just winding her up.

# Chapter 93

Raven lay back on his bed. Staring up at the ceiling. He rubbed his leg.

*My sister, eh?* Sasha would be taken care of. Foolish girl. His parents must have had her after he and his brother left. The age matches that. Was she going to try and exact some sort of revenge? No one betrays him. *And to think, I nearly shagged her.*

Closing his eyes, he smiled as he played back the interview with DC Maggie Jamieson in his head.

His trophies.

He could see it all in his mind. Just like it was yesterday. Holding the lifeless bodies in his arms. Stroking them. His heart raced.

Sitting in the field, talking to his buried treasures. All of them.

Collecting the missing animal posters and folding them neatly. Placing them in his memory box so he could relive the experience at a later time.

The excitement overwhelmed him.

He came.

Wiping his hand with a tissue he smiled again.
As for mummy-dearest, I have plans for her. One day.
*Thanks for the memories, DC Jamieson.*

# Chapter 94

'You did it, Maggie, and you were right all along. I'm sorry we ever doubted you.' She couldn't say for sure, but Maggie thought her boss almost looked embarrassed.

'To be fair, it wasn't just me. It was all of us. But thanks for giving me the leeway, even when you didn't want to. Kate really pulled things together for us. I'm just angry that people still died before we had all the solid evidence we needed.'

Despite the fact that Raven's appeal was thrown out of court and there was no chance he would be released, Maggie didn't feel like celebrating. She couldn't help but wonder if she had pushed harder, demanded the higher ups took her more seriously, maybe Raven's sister could have been brought to justice sooner. She wasn't surprised to learn that Sasha had been found dead of a heroin overdose in her cell. They had requested that Sasha be put in the Vulnerable Persons Unit for her own protection, but she refused. Although it couldn't be proven, Raven clearly did have reach and influence beyond his prison cell.

Maggie had been bombarded by the media on a daily basis since Raven's further arrest but refused to speak with them.

All interviews would go through police Comms and they'd give the official line. She could just imagine how embarrassing that would be. Although nobody knew how active a role Adrian Harrison or Raven's sister played at the time of the original conviction, and with Harrison and Sasha dead, it would only be Raven who faced the consequences.

It was almost a fluke that the team, well Bethany and her eagle eye, had discovered that Raven's estranged brother had never visited him in custody and that it was in fact Adrian Harrison posing as his brother. The police suspected that it was at these visits that Adrian and Raven worked the plan to get Raven out. Sasha was claiming that Raven had threatened her to go along with everything or he would have her killed, but Maggie was sure there was more to the story. Maggie had no doubt that Bill Raven would be holding that information close until he felt it may be of some benefit. Perhaps a bargaining tool for something he wanted in prison.

She only hoped that the victims' families' anger would subside, though she couldn't blame them. The courts had nearly released the man who conspired to murder their loved ones, and who had murdered young women in the past. The media lapped it up with their sensational headlines.

'You can't beat yourself up about this, Maggie. You worked hard to ensure that we kept Raven in our sights, even when we didn't want to. The CCRC still noted their own concerns about how the initial investigation was handled. There will be criticisms and learning points to take away but, ultimately, no blemish on your record. That's a positive and I think we can all take something away from this. Things could have ended up very differently if you had not persevered.'

'That's very kind of you to say, ma'am, and I do appreciate it. I really can't take all the credit – Dr Moloney was key in all this.'

'Yes, Dr Moloney and you work well together. I was speaking to DCI Hastings about the possibility of funding for a consultant on our team.'

Maggie couldn't hide her excitement. 'And?'

'Well, let's just say that he wasn't against the idea and the PCC has asked me to put together a proposal. I'll need your help if you're up for it? Dr Moloney's secondment in the DAHU is coming to an end soon, so I'll speak to her. See if she is up for some profiling work on a consultancy basis with us for a bit.'

'Yes, ma'am.' Maggie smiled.

'I've seen what she can do, and I'm more than impressed. But let's not get ahead of ourselves just yet. I meant to ask: has anything come about with those threats she'd been receiving?'

Maggie's face twisted. 'Not yet, ma'am. Everything has been logged and Kate is keeping the police informed, but I don't think they believe it's a feasible threat at this time. The tests on the box came back showing it was coloured water, not blood, and pieces of dried pork rather than human skin.' Kate had become increasingly reserved since it all started, but it wasn't for her to point that out. If Kate wanted to talk about it, she would, and she hadn't.

'Is everything OK, Maggie?'

'What do you mean?'

'Look, I'm not going to push you, but if there's something that I should know, I trust you'll tell me about it.'

'Of course. There's nothing, well nothing in terms of me. But if I do feel it's relevant and my place to say something, I will.'

'Shall we head back out to the team and update them on everything?'

'Sounds like a plan, and boss ...'

'Yes.'

'Thanks again.'

DI Rutherford's lip curled, and Maggie almost saw a smile crack on an otherwise stern face. She followed her boss out and was pleasantly surprised when her colleagues cheered.

Nathan called out to her, his breath shaking.

'What is it?' Her heart drummed.

'You're not going to like this one bit.'

'Spit it out, Nathan. You're beginning to ruin my mood.'

'Just had a call come in. Police are on the scene. Body of a female has been found. Initial description sounds just like your friend Dr Moloney. I'm so sorry, Maggie ...'

THE END

Acknowledgements

Once again, there are just so many people to thank, so I have to apologize if I am too vague or if I miss anyone out – it is not intentional. Just know that you're all amazing!

I'd like to thank my family and friends both near and far, for the tremendous support they have given me from the moment they learned I was interested in writing and for cheering me on when *Dead Inside* was published.

A massive thanks to Finn Cotton, editor extraordinaire for his patience, guidance and belief in me as a writer and to the whole Killer Reads/One More Chapter team who have been fantastic since this crazy journey began.

Special thanks to my beta readers. You blew me away again with your generous praise and feedback. Thank you to everyone who has allowed me to use their names! And for the *most* part, their characters are nothing like them in real life ... ha ha!

A heartfelt *thank you* to all the authors who have been so incredibly supportive, you have no idea how much it means to me – particularly Angela Marsons, Martina Cole, Nic Parker, Graham Smith, Mel Comley, Emma Kennedy, Mel Sherratt,

Ian Rankin, Robert Bryndza, MW Craven, Howard Linskey, Michael J. Malone, Lisa Regan, Chris Merrit, KL Slater, Rona Halsall, Craig Robertson, Gordon Brown and Caroline Mitchell – a thousand #thankyous would never be enough. Apologies if I missed anyone out.

To the crime writing community – do you know how SUPERB you are? Seriously! I wish I could name each and every one of you – your kind words, encouragement, inspiration and overwhelming support continues to amaze me. Don't ever change.

To my amazing blogger friends, I want to name you all, but I can't – so if you are reading this and thinking 'is she talking about me?' the answer is – *Hell yeah, I am*! Love you all. Special mention to the original #blogsquad, as well as Kim Nash, Anne Cater, Rachel Gilbey, and JB Johnston for always letting me be me. You all make me smile each and every day!

A massive thanks to the Bookouture team (both the authors and my colleagues) for all the amazing advice and support!

Of course, I will always mention Tamworth Probation/Tamworth IOM; Stafford IOM; and all my remarkable ex-colleagues within the Police and Probation Service – both the public and private sectors. Your dedication and professionalism astound me – I may have been 'paroled' after 18 years of service, but I think about your truly fantastic work all the time – and all the stories I now have to tell! Many thanks to the real DS Jim Hooper and his fabulous wife Rachel for answering any questions I had.

Finally, a massive thanks to all the readers. There are just no words to convey how much your support and reviews have meant to me. You make me believe I can keep on doing this and give me a reason to write.

# *A Note from Noelle*

I said this in my debut novel, *Dead Inside*, but it is worth noting once again. The book is set in Staffordshire; however, I have used some literary licence by making up names of towns/places to fit with the story.

Having been a Senior/Probation Officer for 18 years, I left in 2017. There are some references to the changes that were implemented in 2015, but I went all nostalgic and some of the work/terms refer to a time when Probation was all one service – though it seems I may have been psychic as the service is coming together under the public banner once again. Regardless, it made things a lot less complicated. Any errors to police procedure/probation or any other agency mentioned within the story are purely my own or intentional to move the story forward.